Trussed as tightly as the pack still on his back, Sander found himself pulled aloft. It appeared that his captors were creatures who considered trees their natural roadways. He was tense with foreboding as they swung him across wide expanses, sure that sooner or later he must crash helplessly to the ground beneath. At last he closed his eyes tightly, determined to hoard his strength for any effort he could make at the end of a nightmare journey.

There came a final downward swing, which ended in a vicious jerk, sending pain red and hot through his head. Then Sander lay flat on the ground in an open place, the sun beaming harshly into his eyes.

When he turned his head as far as he could and cautiously opened his eyes again, it was just in time to see the last of the hairy men swing upward into the trees again on the other side of the clearing.

Had they left a guard? If not, was there any way to escape?

No Night
Without Stars

A NOVEL BY

Andre Norton

FAWCETT CREST • NEW YORK

NO NIGHT WITHOUT STARS

THIS BOOK CONTAINS THE COMPLETE TEXT OF
THE ORIGINAL HARDCOVER EDITION.

Published by Fawcett Crest Books, a unit of CBS Publications,
the Consumer Publishing Division of CBS Inc.,
by arrangement with Atheneum Publishers.

ISBN: 0-449-23264-6

Printed in the United States of America

15   14   13   12   11   10   9   8   7   6

The thick plume of the greasy-looking black smoke rising from beyond the ridge was warning enough. Sander slipped off Rhin, crept up-slope, his mount padding behind him with the same caution. They had seen no campsite for days, and the provision bag, still knotted to the pad strapped about Rhin, was empty. Hunger was a discomfort within Sander. This land had been singularly empty of game for the past twenty-four hours. And a handful or two of grain, pulled, barely ripe, out of a straggle of stalks, was far from filling.

Five days ago Sander had passed the boundaries of the territory known to Jak's Mob. When he had ridden out of the ring of tents, blackly bitter at his treatment, he had swung due east, heading for the legendary sea. Then it had seemed possible that he could achieve his purpose— to find the ancient secrets whereby he could better forge the metal brought by Traders, so that, upon his return, he could confront Ibbets and the others and force from them an acknowledgment that he was not an apprentice of little worth, but a smith of the Old Learning. This long trek through a wilderness he did not know had taught him caution, though it had not yet dampened the inner core of his rebellion against Ibbet's belittling decision.

Now he wedged his shoulders between two rocks, pulling his hood well down over his face so that its gray color would blend well with the stones about. Though he was no hunter by training, each member of the Mob was lessoned from childhood in the elements of hiding-out when confronted by the unusual, until he could make very sure there was no danger ahead.

Below lay a wide valley down which a river angled. And where that opened into a much larger bowl of water (of which he could see only one shoreline, the one into which the river cut), there stood a collection of buildings, a small village. Those log-walled shelters appeared to be permanent, not like the hide tents of the Mob that were easily moved from one place to another. However, small sullen tongues of fire now showed here and there, threatening complete destruction of the buildings.

Sander sighted even from this distance what could only be a huddle of bodies lying along the river bank. There had been a raid, he deduced. Maybe the dreaded Sea Sharks of the south had struck. He doubted if there was any life left in that collection of huts.

The fire burned slowly, mainly along the river bank and the shoreline of the large body of water beyond. There were a few buildings seemingly still untouched. They would have been looted, of course. Still, there was a chance that not all of the provisions collected by those settled here had been carried away. And this was harvest season. His own people (or those whom he had believed to be his close kin—he grimaced at that thought) had been engaged in late season hunts and the drying of meat when he had ridden out.

Though the nomadic Mobs roamed the wide inner lands, Sander had heard enough tales from the Traders to know that elsewhere men lived differently. In some places clans had settled permanently upon the land, planting

6

and tending food which they grew. Here, in this near-destroyed settlement, they must also have fished. His stomach growled and he shifted a little, surveying the scene of the raid carefully to make sure that if he did go down he was not running into active trouble.

Rhin whined deep in his throat, nudged Sander with his muzzle. His yellow-brown coat was already thickening with new winter growth. Now his jaws opened a little, his pointed tongue showed. His ears pricked as he watched the burning buildings with the same intense stare as Sander. But he betrayed no more than the common caution with which he approached all new situations.

His green eyes did not blink, nor did his brush of tail move. Instead he sat on his haunches as if it did not matter that his head rose well above the sky line, to be sighted from the town. Sander accepted Rhin's verdict of no imminent danger—for the sly intelligence of his kind supplied information no man, with his blunter senses, could hope to gain.

Though he got to his feet, Sander did not remount. Instead he slipped down the ridge, using every bit of cover, Rhin like a red-yellow ghost a step or two behind. Ready to hand, Sander carried his dart thrower, a missile notched ready against its taut string. In addition he loosened his long knife in its leather scabbard.

As they drew closer to the looted town, Sander's nose wrinkled at the stench of burning and of other smells far worse. Rhin growled, sniffing. He liked that scent no better than Sander. But at least, by his attitude, he had picked up no hint of enemies.

Sander circled away from the river bank where lay those blood-stained bundles, heading toward the seemingly unharmed buildings farther inland from the shore. He could hear the pound of waves and smell a new odor, swept toward him by a rising wind—a strange, fresh scent. Was this indeed the sea, not just some larger lake?

As he approached the furthermost of the buildings, he hesitated, something in him willing against this intrusion. Only need for food forced him into an alleyway so narrow that Rhin crowded him with a furry shoulder as they padded on together.

The walls of logs Sander saw were thick and there were only openings set very high, nearly masked by the over-hanging eaves, part of the sharply-pitched roofs. He reached the end of the alley and turned right before he saw any entrance door.

It had been fashioned of heavy planking. Now it hung crazily from a single hinge, plainly having been forced open. Rhin snarled, his tongue sweeping out over his lips. There was a body just within that broken door; between the shoulders was a splotch of clotted blood. The villager lay face downward and Sander had no desire to turn him over.

The stranger was not wearing the leather and furs of a Mobsman, rather a coarsely woven overtunic dyed a nut brown. And his legs were encased in baggy trousers of the same material, laced hide boots on his feet. For a long moment Sander hesitated before he stepped gingerly around the dead man into an interior that showed both search and wanton destruction.

There was another huddle of twisted body and stained clothing in the corner. Sander, after a single glance, kept his eyes resolutely from it. Smashed and near destroyed as the contents of this room were, he could still see that the town dwellers had possessed more worldly goods than any Mobsman. That was only sensible in their way of life. One could not cart chairs, tables, and chests about the land when one was ever traveling to follow the herds. He stopped to pick up a broken bowl, intrigued by the design across its side. It was only a few dark lines against the clear brown of the pottery, but, as he studied them, he could envision birds in flight.

He made his way quickly to the food bins, wanting no more of this chamber of the dead. Rhin whined from without. Sander caught the uneasiness of his companion, the need to be gone. But he made himself examine what was left.

There was a measure of grain flour mixed with chopped and powdered nut meats. Using the broken bowl for a scoop he packed it into his provision bag. He found two dried fish wedged in another over-turned bin. But the rest had been deliberately wasted or wantonly befouled. He was sickened by the signs of relentless hatred he could sense in the room as he hurried out to join Rhin.

Yet Sander made himself approach the next building also. Here again was a forced door but with no body nearly blocking it. However, one glance at what lay inside made him gag and turn hastily away. He could not go any nearer to *that*. It seemed that the raiders, whoever they might have been, had not been content to kill, but had also taken time to amuse themselves in a beastly fashion. Sander kept on swallowing to control his nausea as he backed out into the way that fronted the unfired buildings.

There was one other place he must search for—in spite of his growing terror of this ravaged village. There *must* have been a smith's forge somewhere. He slapped his hands against the bag of tools that was lashed to the back of Rhin's riding pad. What he carried there was all he had from his father. Ibbets would have liked to have claimed those, as he claimed the office of smith with the Mob, but custom had supported Sander to that extent.

Two major hammers and chisels had been buried with his father, Dullan, of course. A man's main tools of trade were filled with his own powers and must so be laid away in the earth when he no longer could use them. But there were some smaller things that a son could rightfully claim, and no one could deny him those. However, Sander needed more, much more, if he were to realize his dream— to find the place wherein those masses of congealed metal, which the traders brought to the Mobs, were concealed, to learn the secret of the alloys which now baffled the smiths.

Resolutely he started on, dodging a charred wall that had fallen outward, closing his mind to everything but his search, holding his nose against the stink. Rhin continued to whine and growl. Sander knew well that his companion wanted none of this place of death and followed him under protest. Yet because there was the brotherhood between them, Rhin would continue.

Rhin's people and those of the Mob were entwined in mutual service. That companionship began during the Dark Time. Legends Sander had heard recited by the Rememberers said that Rhin's people had once been much smaller, yet always clever and quick to adapt to change. Koyots they were called in the old tongue.

There had been many animals, and more men than one could count, who had perished when the Earth danced and the Dark Time had begun. Mountains of fire had burst through the skin of the world, belching flame, smoke, and molten rock. The sea had rolled inward with waves near as high as those same mountains, hammering the land into nothingness in some places, in others deserting the beds over which it had lain for untold ages. Cold followed and great choking clouds of evil air that had killed.

Here and there a handful of men or animals survived. But when the skies cleared once again, there were changes. Some animals grew larger generation by generation, just as distant species of men were rumored to be now twice the size of Sander's own people. That information came from Traders' tales, however, and it was well known that Traders like to spread such stories to keep other men away from any rich finds. They would invent all manner of monsters to be faced were a man to try to track them back to their own places.

Sander stopped, picked up a spear, gruesomely stained, and prodded with that into the ashes of a small building. He swiftly uncovered what could only be an anvil—a good one fashioned from iron, but far too heavy to be transported. Finding that, a sure sign he had found the smithy, he scratched with more vigor.

His delving uncovered a fine stone hammerhead, the haft near burned away, but the best part remaining, then another of a lesser weight. That was all that remained, though there were some traces of metal—copper he was sure—puddled from the heat.

He raised his hand and recited the secret smith words. If the owner, who might lie farther back under the debris

10

at the rear, was still spirit-tied, as men who died quickly and violently sometimes were, he would know by those words that one of his own craft was present. He would not, Sander was sure, begrudge that his possessions be used again, carefully, and to a purpose that might in the end benefit all men.

Sander fitted the two hammerheads in among the tools he carried. He would hunt no farther. Let the dead smith keep all else as grave-hold. But such hammers he did not have and he needed them.

He wanted no more of this nameless village wherein death stank and spirits might be tied to their destroyed homes. Rhin sensed that decision, greeting it with a yelp of approval. However, Sander was not minded to leave the shore of the sea—if sea this was. Rather he passed as quickly as he could among the smoldering buildings, refusing to look at the bodies he passed, to come out upon the slippery sand of the shore.

To prove that he might have reached one of his objectives, he advanced to where the small waves ended in foam upon the sand. There he dipped a finger into the water and licked the moisture. Salt! Yes, he had found the sea.

However it was not the sea alone that he sought, but rather the heart of the old legends around it. It was along the shore of the sea that there once had stood many great cities of old. And in those cities lay the secrets concerning which Sander's father had often speculated.

It was certain that men before the Dark Time had possessed such knowledge that they had lived as might spirits of the upper air, with unseen servants and all manner of labor-saving tools. Yet that learning had been lost. Sander did not know the number of years that lay between him and that time, but the sum was more, his father had said, than the lifetimes of many, many men, each a generation behind the other.

When, at the death of his father from the coughing sickness, Ibbets, his father's younger brother, had denied Sander the smith-right, saying he was only an untried boy and unfit to serve the Mob, then it was that Sander knew he must prove himself, not only to the people whom he

11

had believed kin-blood, but to himself. He must become such a worker of metal that his own number of years or lack of them would mean nothing, only the fact that many things could be wrought by his design and his skill. So it was that, when Ibbets would have bound him to a new apprenticeship, he had instead claimed go-forth rights, and the Mob had been forced to grant him that choice of exile.

Now he was kinless by his own hard decision. And there burned fiercely in him the need to know that he was a better smith, or would be, than Ibbets claimed. To do that he must learn. And he was sure that such knowledge lay somewhere near the original source of the lumps of congealed metal that the traders brought.

Some of the metal could be worked by strength of arm and hammer alone. Other kinds must be heated, run into molds, or struck when hot to form the needed tool or weapon. But there were some metals that defied all attempts to work them. And it was the secret of those that, from childhood, had fascinated Sander.

He had found the sea; now he could go north or south along its shore. There had been great changes in the land, he knew. Perhaps such cities as he sought were long since buried under the wash of the waves, or else so overturned by earth-shaking that little remained. Yet somewhere the Traders found their metal, so somewhere such sources existed—and those he could seek.

It was close to nightfall, and he did not wish to camp close to the half-destroyed town. He pushed on northward. Above, sea birds wheeled and screamed hoarsely, and the steady roll of the waves made a low accompaniment to their cries.

Rhin's head swung around twice toward their back trail. He growled, and his uneasiness gripped Sander in turn. Though it seemed the town was wholly given over to the dead, it was true that Sander had not delved too deeply in the ruins. What if some survivor, perhaps shaken out of his wits by the terror of the raid, lurked there, had seen Sander and Rhin come and go? They might now be hunted by such.

Climbing on the top of a dune, along the sides of which

grew tough sea-bleached grass, Sander studied the still-smoking buildings. Nothing moved save the birds. However, he did not discount Rhin's uneasiness, knowing he could depend upon the acute senses of the koyot to give him fair warning if they were followed.

He would have liked to have ridden, but the slippery sand gave such uncertain footing that he kept on as they were. He angled away from the wave line now, for there lay drifts of wood which looked ready to entrap the unwary. Now and then a shell lay exposed in the damp sand. Sander could not turn away from them, eyeing with amazement the fantastic patterns on these jewels from the sea. He dropped some into his belt pouch. Like a bright bird's feather or a tumbled-smooth stone, they delighted him. He dreamed momentarily of setting them in bands of copper, that metal which so easily answered to the skill he had learned, to make such articles of adornment as the Mob had never seen.

The sand became covered with coarse grass, which in turn changed to meadowland. But Sander disliked this too-open country. He could see, forming a dark line across the horizon, the beginning of wooded land. While his people were of the open plains to the west, they also knew northern woods, and he could see the value of finding cover.

However, he was enough a judge of travelers' distances to be sure he could not reach that forest before nightfall. What he wanted now was a camp site which might offer his some measure of defense, if Rhin's instinct was proven correct and they were to face some danger out of the dark.

He would not dare a fire tonight, wanting no beacon that might draw anyone—or anything—that prowled this country. So at last he settled on a stand of rocks, huddled together as if the stones themselves had drawn close for comfort in an hour of need.

Jerking up handfuls of the grass, he pulled and patted that into a nest. Then he brought out the dried fish and shared with Rhin. Ordinarily, the koyot would have gone off hunting on his own. But it would seem that this night

13

he was not about to leave Sander.

As the young man watched the twilight draw in, felt the chill of the night winds which swept from the sea bringing the strange scents of that water world, his weariness grew. He could hear nothing save the wash of the waves, the sounds of birds. And Rhin, though he held his ears aprick, also manifestly listening with all his might, did not yet show any signs of real alarm.

Tired as he was from the day's journeying, Sander could not sleep. Over him arched the sky in which sparked eyes of the night. The Rememberers said those were other suns, very far away, and around them perhaps moved worlds such as their own. But to Sander they had always seemed more like the eyes of strange, ever-aloof creatures, who watched the short lives of men with more indifference than interest. He tried to think about the star eyes, but his mind kept returning to the horrors of the raided village. What would it be like, he wondered with a shiver, to be suddenly set upon by men out of the sea who wanted to slay, to destroy, to dip their hands in blood?

The Mob had fought for their lives, but only once, in Sander's memory, against their kind. That had been when a terrifying people of light skin and wild pale eyes had come down to raid their herd. Mainly their struggle was against cold and famine and sickness for themselves or their animals, warring against a hard land rather than mankind. Their smiths forged the weapons and the tools for that struggle, not many of the kind meant to drink man-blood.

Sander had heard tales of the sea slavers. Sometimes he had thought that those, too, were inventions of the Traders, who created fearsome horrors to fill the land they did not want others to explore. For the Traders were notoriously tight-fisted when it came to their own profits. But after this day he could believe that man was more ruthless than even a full winter storm. Now he shivered a little, not from the touch of the sea breeze, but because of what his imagination suggested might exist in this wilderness so unknown to him.

Sander put out a hand for the reassuring touch of

Rhin's hairy hide. At the same moment the koyot leaped to his feet. Sander heard a warning growl. Rhin faced not the sea, but inland. It was plain that the animal had decided that there was indeed a menace slinking through the night.

With so little visibility, the dart thrower was no good. Sander drew his long belt knife, which was in reality a short sword. He crouched upon one knee, the rocks a firm wall at his back, and listened. There seemed to be a slight shuffling ahead. Rhin growled again. Now Sander caught a trace of musky odor. He thought he had seen a shadow, moving so swiftly that there was but a suggestion of a shape, out there.

A hissing out of the dark became a loud snarl. Rhin advanced a step, stiff-legged, plainly alert against attack. Sander desperately regretted the fire he had not lit. To face such an unknown menace kindled one of the age-old fears of his own race.

Yet the thing did not attack as Sander expected it to do. He heard that challenging hiss, and he gathered from Rhin's reaction that the koyot thought this unknown to be a formidable opponent. Still, whatever it was stayed beyond the boundaries where Sander might sight it against the lighter rocks. There came a shrill whistle out of the night, followed by a flash of light, which shone straight into Sander's eyes, dazzling him, though he flung up his arm in an involuntary gesture to ward off the blinding glare.

Under the shadow of his hand he watched an animal glide forward, a sinuous body seeming to him more that of a snake than of a furred species. It arose upon its haunches, still hissing, until its head was nearly level with his own. Behind it a smaller edition of itself, much darker in color, hugged the ground. It was neither of that pair who carried the light.

"Stand—" The command from behind the source of the light was an emphatic order, and it was followed by another. "Drop your knife!"

Sander might be very close to death, for he was sure only the will of the speaker held the animals in check, but now he shook his head.

"I do not obey the orders of unknowns who skulk in the dark," he returned. "I am not a hunter or harmer of men."

"Blood cries for blood, stranger," snapped the voice. "Behind you streams blood—kin-blood. If there is an accounting, then it is mine, seeing that no one else lives in Padford now—"

"I came to a town of the dead," Sander returned. "If you seek blood for blood, look elsewhere, stranger. When I rode from the south, there were only the dead within half-burned walls."

The light held steady on him and no answer came forth. But that the stranger had been willing to speak without immediate attack was, Sander believed, in his favor.

"It is true that you are no Sea Shark," the voice observed slowly.

Sander could understand the words. But the accent with which they were spoken differed both from that of the Mob and that of the Traders.

"Who are you?" Now the voice sharpened in a new demand.

"I am Sander, once of Jak Mob, and I am a smith."

"Soooo?" The voice drawled that as if not quite believing. "And where tents your Mob this night, smith?"

"Westward."

"Yet you travel east. Smiths are not wanderers, stranger. Or is there blood guilt and kin-death lying in your back trail?"

"No. My father, who was smith, died, and they would have it that I was not apt enough to take his place. Thus I took out-rights—" He was growing irritated. That he must patiently answer this quizzing out of the dark awoke a small stir of anger in him. Now he boldly asked in return:

"Who are you?"

"One not to meddle with, stranger!" snapped that other. "But it seems you speak the truth and so are not meat for us this night."

The light snapped out instantly. He could hear a stirring in the dark. Rhin whined in relief. Though the koyot could be a formidable fighter when he wished, it was plain he preferred the absence of those animals and whoever controlled them to their presence.

Sander himself felt tension seep away. The voice was gone, taking with it the strange hounds of its hunting. He settled back, and after a while he slept.

Sander's slumber was full of dreams in which dead men arose to face him with broken weapons in their slack hands. He roused now and again, sweating, hardly sure of what was dream and what reality. He could then hear sometimes a soft growl deep in Rhin's throat, as if the koyot scented something threatening. Yet the voice and the light were surely gone.

By the coming of the first gray predawn Sander was ready to move on. This seemed to him a haunted land. Perhaps the unburied dead of the town brought the oppression to his spirit. The sooner he was well away from such an ill-omened place, the better. However, he made a quick survey of the ground where the night before that half-seen beast had reared up in the light.

That truly had been no dream, for there were paw marks deep-set in the soil, pads and claws in clear impression. Beyond, he discovered a single other print, small and distinct, unmistakably human. Rhin sniffed at the tracks and again growled. It was plain from the swing of the koyot's head that he little liked what his own special

18

senses reported. Another reason to be on their way.

Sander did not even wait to eat. He swung up on the riding pad, and Rhin trotted off at a pace that soon carried them well into the tough grass of the lowlands, parallel with the sea. The passing of the koyot stirred into life some birds, and Sander uncoiled his sling, made ready a pebble, brought down two of those fugitives. Once away, where he could light a fire, there would be food.

He headed directly for the distant line of forest, misliking the feeling of nakedness that he had in the open, a sensation that, being plains bred, he had never experienced before. As he rode, he tried to see traces of the path the voice had taken. But, save for the tracks near his improvised camp, Sander found nothing that would lead him to believe he and Rhin were not alone.

Resolutely, he kept from glancing back at the now-distant village. Perhaps his visitor had returned there, since it was plain from the words they had exchanged that the unknown had been in search of those who had despoiled the town. What had the stranger named it. Padford. Sander repeated the word aloud. It was as strange as the accent of the other's speech.

Sander knew so little of the land beyond the Mob's own range. That such villages existed he had picked up from the Traders' guarded accounts. But the herdspeople of the wide lands in the west had no personal knowledge of them. He wished now that he had made a closer examination of the dead. It seemed to him, trying to recall those glimpses of the bodies, that they had been unusually dark of skin, even darker than he was himself, and that their hair had been of a uniform black. Among his own people, who were an even brown in skin color, hair color varied from light reddish gold to dark brown.

The Rememberers often recited queer things, that all men were not, before the Dark Time, of the same kind. Their tales carried other unbelievable statements also— that men could fly like birds and traveled in boats that went *under* the surface of the water and not over it. So one could not believe every remnant of supposed old knowledge they cherished.

19

Rhin abruptly halted, startling Sander out of his thoughts. The koyot gave a sudden shake of body, which was his warning of danger, that he must be free of his rider to confront something. Sander slid off as Rhin whirled about, facing their back trail, his lips wrinkled to show his formidable fangs, the growl in his throat rising to a snarl.

Sander thrust his sling into his belt, whipped free his thrower, making sure there was a dart set within the firing groove. There were no stones to back them here. They had been caught in the open.

Plain to see were two shapes humping along with a curious up and down movement, at a speed Rhin could only equal by short bursts of determined flight. A third figure on two legs ran behind, like a hunter urging on hounds, though the two forerunners bore no likeness to any of the small dogs the Mob knew. Sander dropped to one knee, steadying the dart thrower. His heart beat faster. Those animals, whatever they might be, were agile of movement, continually twisting and turning, yet always advancing. To sight a dart on one was almost impossible.

"Aeeeeheee!"

The cry came as sharp as the scream of a seabird, while the running figure behind the first two flung up both arms as if urging on its furred companions. It was that runner who must be his target, Sander decided.

"Aeeeeheee!"

The foremost of the animals halted and rose on its haunches to stare at the smith. A moment later its mate froze likewise. But Sander did not relax his grip of the dart thrower. The distance, he judged, was still a fraction over what he must have for a telling shot. Rhin's snarl was continual. The koyot was already on the defensive, ready for attack. It would seem that Rhin judged these to be formidable opponents.

The human companion of the pair drew level with them, so the three moved together toward Sander and the koyot. But they no longer ran. Sander rose to his feet, his weapon at the ready.

He stared at what seemed to him one of the strangest sights he had ever seen, for the newcomer was plainly a woman. Her scant body covering revealed that. Like the villagers, she had very dark skin, and her only clothing was a piece of scarlet cloth wound from armpit to knee. Around her neck rested a massive chain of soft, hand-worked gold, which held pendant a disc set with gem stones in an intricate pattern. Her dark hair had been combed and somehow stiffened, to stand out about her face like a halo of black. On her forehead was a tattooed design, much the same as the one Sander himself wore. But while his was the proud badge of a smith's hammer, hers was a whirl he could not read.

She wore boots that reached nearly to her knees, not as well-fashioned as the leatherwork of his own people, and a belt twisted of gold and silver wire from which hung, on hooks, a number of small bags of different colored cloth. Now she walked proudly, as if she were one to whom others paid deference, like a clan-mother, each hand resting on the head of one of the animals.

These were of the same breed, Sander believed, but they varied greatly in coloring and size. One, cream-fawn in shade, was the larger. The smaller was dark brown with black feet and tail. Their long tails lashed back and forth as them came. It was plain, Sander was sure, that they did not have the same confidence in his harmlessness as their mistress did, for they were ready to do battle. Only her will kept them in check.

Some distance away she stopped, her dark eyes surveying him coolly. The animals once more reared on their haunches to flank her, the lighter-colored one's head now topping hers.

"Where do you go, smith?" she spoke imperiously, and at the sound of her voice, he knew that this was his questioner of the night before.

"What matters that to you?" He was stung by her tone. What right had she to demand any answer from him in this fashion?

"The seeing has signed that our paths now run together." Her eyes were very bright. They caught his gaze. He did not like her calm assumption that he was some tribesman under her command.

"I do not know what a seeing may be." With determined effort he broke that linkage of eyes. "What I seek is my own affair."

She frowned as if she had not believed he could withstand her control any more readily than the hissing beasts by her side. That she *had* tried to control him in some unknown manner he was now certain.

"What you seek," she returned, a sharper note in her voice, "is the knowledge of the Before Men. That is what I must also find, that my people may be avenged. I am Fanyi, one who talks with spirits. And these be Kai and Kayi who are one with me where there is need. My protection lay over Padford, but it was necessary for me to go to meet the Great Moon. And while I was gone"— she made a slight gesture with her hand—"my people were slain, my faith to them broken. This should not be!" Her lips drew back in a snarl as marked as Rhin's. "The blood debt is mine, but for its paying I must draw upon the Before Ones. I ask you, smith, have you knowledge of where what you seek lies?"

He longed to say yes, but there was something in her gaze, which, though he would not allow it to bind him, compelled the truth.

"I am Sander. I seek one of the Before cities. Such may be to the north along the sea—"

"A Traders' tale perhaps?" She laughed and there was a note of scorn in that sound, angering him. "Traders' tales are not to be depended upon, smith. These seek always to deceive, not revealing what they deem their own hunting grounds. However, for once, this is partly right. To the north—and the east—there lies a great place of the Before Men. I am a one of Shaman Power—to us remains some of the ancient knowledge. There *is* a place—"

"To the northeast," Sander countered, "lies the sea. Perhaps your city is wave buried now."

She shook her head. "I think not. The sea has eaten deep into the land in some places; in others it has drained from ancient beds, leaving land long hidden once more revealed. But," she shrugged, "of that we cannot be sure until we see. You seek, I seek—but in the end our quest is not too divided. I want knowledge of one kind, you of another, is this not the truth?"

"Yes."

"Well enough. I have powers, smith. Perhaps more potent than you carry in your hands." She glanced at the weapon he held. "But to fare forth into the wilderness alone, that is folly, if there are those who travel in the same direction. Therefore, I say to you—let us journey together. I will share my certain knowledge of where the Before Place lies."

He hesitated. But he believed that for some reason she was in earnest. Why she made such an offer he could not quite understand. She might have been reading his thoughts, for now she added:

"Did I not say that I had had a seeing? I know little of your people, smith, but have you none among you who can foretell, who are able at times to see that which has not yet happened but which will certainly come to pass?"

"We have the Rememberers. But they dream of the past, the future. The Traders—they have said that they have heard of those who foresee not backsee."

"Backsee?" Fanyi seemed startled. "What do they backsee, these Shamans of yours?"

"Some of the Before things, but only small pieces," Sander had to admit. "We came into this land after the Dark Time, and what they tell of is another part, now sea covered. Mostly they remember our own Mob and a past that is ours alone."

"That is a loss. Think what might be done if your backseers could uncover the lost things. But it is much the same with us who foresee—such we can do for only a short way. Thus, I know that we shall journey together, but little more than that."

She spoke with such authority that Sander found himself unable to utter any objection, though he was suspicious of that self-confidence of hers. It was too evident that this Fanyi believed she was conferring some honor upon him by so deciding. Yet there was sense in what she said—he had been traveling blindly. If she indeed had some clue to a definite lost city, he would be far better served to agree to her guidance than to simply wander on blindly.

"Very well." He now looked to her beasts. "But do those agree also? They seem to me to be less certain of the wisdom of our joining forces than you are."

For the first time he saw her lips curve into a smile. "My friends become theirs. And what of your furred one, Sander-smith?" She nodded to Rhin.

Sander turned to the koyot. He exercised no such control on Rhin as the girl apparently did over her companions, nor could he. There was a form of communication between man and koyot, but it was a tenuous one. He was not sure himself just how deep it ran, nor how well in some circumstances it would work. Rhin was willing to share his travels and was an efficient warner against enemies. But whether the koyot would accept close companionship for days with the strange beasts, that Sander had no way of telling.

Fanyi shifted her gaze slightly to meet the eyes of the taller of her furred ones. After their stare had locked and held for a long moment the creature dropped to forefeet and was gone at its backhumping gait, disappearing into the tall grass. Its companion remained quietly where it was, but Fanyi came forward now to turn the same intent gaze up into Rhin's bright eyes. Sander fidgeted, again more than a little irritated at the girl. What right had she to impose her will on his koyot, for that was what she was doing he was sure.

Again she might have read his rebellious thought, for she spoke:

"I do not rule these other ones, smith. It is enough that they learn that we can live together after a fashion, neither imposing wills upon another. My fishers know that if I halt their actions by a will-thought, it is only with good reason. And there are times when I accept their desire as quickly as they do mine. We are not master-slave. No—we are comrade with comrade. That is the

24

way it should be with all life forms. So does the Power teach us who are born to serve Its purposes. Yes, your koyot will accept us, for he knows we mean no harm to one another."

The fisher who had disappeared was returning. Clamped in its jaws was the end of a bundle that it bumped and tugged along the ground until it could be dropped at Fanyi's feet. She loosened lashings to draw forth a square of drab cloth, which had a hole in the center. Through this she thrust her head and then belted the loose folds about her with a woven strip, hiding her scarlet garment and her adornments under the dim gray overtunic.

The rest of her equipment for the trip seemed to be in two separate bags, their strings knotted together. Sander took them from her when she would have slung them across her shoulder and arranged them with his own bags on Rhin. He could not ride while she walked, and the two of them would be too great a weight for the koyot.

Fanyi whistled, sending the fishers bounding away, ranging ahead. For the first time Sander relaxed a little. Those creatures must form an effective scouting force, if Fanyi could truly depend upon them.

"How far do we go?" he asked, finding that she matched strides with apparently little effort.

"That I do not know. My people do—did—" she corrected herself, "not travel far. They were fisherfolk, and they worked the fields along the river. We had Traders come from the north—and more lately from the south. From the south," she repeated and her tone was bleak. "Yes, now I think that those came before the raid to sniff out how helpless we were. If I had not been afar—"

"But what could you have done?" Sander was honestly puzzled. She seemed to believe that her presence, or the lack of it, had sealed the fate of the village. He could not believe that.

She glanced toward him, clearly astounded at his question.

"I am one with Power. It is my thought-holding that walled my people in safety. There was no danger that came to them that I, or Kai or Kayi, could not sniff out and give warning of. Just as I knew, even though I sought with open heart and mind the will of the Great Moon, when death came to those who believed in me! Their blood lies on my hands, that I must avenge—for upon me rests the burden of this deed."

"And how can you avenge them? Do you know those who came raiding?"

"At the proper time I shall cast the stones." Her hand went to the breast of her drab overcovering. "Then their names shall be made clear. But first I must find in the Before Place such a weapon as shall make those who delighted in slaughter wish that they had never been born!" There was a cruel cast now to her generous lips and such a look on her face gave Sander a small, cold feeling.

He himself had never felt such great anger—even against Ibbets—as to death-wish another. When the White Ones had struck he had been only a child of too young an age to be greatly affected by the battle, even though his mother had been one of the victims of it. His whole being had been focused on learning what he could do with his hands. And weapons were only matters of fine workmanship. He rarely thought beyond their fashioning to the uses to which they would be eventually put.

What he had seen in the destroyed village had sickened and revolted him, but it had not touched his own being. For those dead were strangers, none close to him. Had he discovered one of the enemy left behind through some chance he would have fought, yes, mainly to save his own life. But the flame that he knew burned in Fanyi, the implacable dedication to vengeance, he could not quite understand. Perhaps had it been his people who had been so handled, he thought, he would have felt differently.

"What weapons do you believe might be stored in a Before Place?"

"Who knows? The old tales are many. They say that once men slew with fire and thunder, not with steel or dart. It may be that such stories are only tales. But knowledge is a weapon in itself and such a weapon as I have been born to use."

That Sander could accept. He discovered that he had

unconsciously quickened pace a little, as if the very thought that such a storehouse of the Before Days might exist had urged him to hurry to find it. But they dared not, he was certain, count on too much. The churning of the earth during the Dark Time had changed the whole of the land. Could they be sure that anything from Before endured?

When he mentioned this, Fanyi nodded. "That is true. But still the Traders have their sources. And so there must be something remaining. I have this—" Both hands were now clasping her breast where the pendant lay hidden. "I am of a clan-line of Shamans. From mother to daughter, time and again past reckoning, has descended our learning. There are secrets that can be understood only when one is in the presence of that which hides them. What I wear is in itself a secret. Only I can read its message when I hold it in my hand. For no other will this charm work. I seek with it a certain wall—"

"And this wall lies northeast—"

"Just so. Long have I wanted to search for it. But my duty was to my people. Their ills, both of mind and body, were mine to ease. Now it is that same duty which drives me at last—so that I may repay blood for blood."

Her face became such a secretive mask that Sander ventured no more questions. So they journeyed in silence, the fishers playing scout, Rhin trotting at his shoulder.

At noon they halted, and Sander made a small fire while Fanyi stirred together some of the meal he had taken from the village, moistening it with water from his leathern bottle and spreading the result as a thin paste upon a small metal griddle she took from one of her own bags, which she then set to bake before the fire. In a few minutes she dexterously swept off a sheet of near-bread. Sander roasted the birds he had brought down, while Rhin, stripped of riding pad and burdens, went hunting on his own, as Fanyi said her fishers would also do.

The fare was better than the dried fish he had eaten the night before. Fanyi held the water bottle to her ear and shook it vigorously.

"Water," she said. "That we shall need by nightfall."

Sander laughed. "Rhin shall find it. His breed does that very well. I have seen them dig into a bare streambed and uncover what no man would believe existed below. They come from a parched land—"

"Yours?"

Sander shook his head. "Not now, before it was. The Rememberers say we were all from the south and west. When the sea came in, all fled before it, even though mountains spewed fire from their bellies. Some men lived, and later Rhin's people came. They were small once, it is said. But who knows now—so much is told of the Before Time."

"Perhaps there are records." Fanyi licked grease from her fingertips, imparting to that gesture a certain fastidiousness.

"Marks like this—" She plucked a long grass stem and with its tip drew lines in the dust.

Sander studied her pattern. He thought he could see a certain resemblance to similar lines that Traders made on bleached skins when his father had described kinds of metal he wanted them to bring up on their next trip.

"See—this means my name." She pointed out the marks she had made. "F-A-N-Y-I— That I can write. And certain other words. Though," she added with truthfulness, "the meaning of all I do not know. But it was part of my learning because it is of my Power."

He nodded. The smith words were part of his learning, along with the work of his hands. The metal did not run nor harden nor work unless one chanted the right words —all men knew that. Which was why a smith allowed only his apprentice to be with him during certain parts of his labor—lest those without the right learn the work-words of his art.

"Even if you find such marks," Sander asked, "what if they cannot read?"

She frowned. "That would be a mystery one must master, even as one learns the healing art and how the moon works upon men and women, how to call the fish, or speak with animals and birds. It is one of the Shaman learning."

Sander stood up to summon Rhin with a whistle. Shaman learning did not greatly interest him. And whether smith mysteries had ever been reduced to such markings—that he would not believe unless he saw them before his eyes. They were still a goodly distance from the forest, and he had little liking to camp out in the open another night.

He stamped out the last coals of their small cooking fire, kicking earth over the ashes carefully as any plainsman would. The fear of grass fires in the open was one danger that was more real in his mind than such raids as had been made on the village. He had seen the results of such devastation and known the horror of finding two clansmen who had been caught in such and died in the red fury no man could escape.

They plodded on. The fishers were not in sight, though Rhin had returned promptly at Sander's call to assume pad and bags. But Fanyi seemed unconcerned at the absence of her animals. Perhaps they always traveled so.

It was close unto evening when the trees loomed ahead behind a screen of brush. Sander came to a stop, for the first time wondering about the wisdom of his choice. It looked very dark and forbidding under that spread of green that was already beginning to be touched by the flames of fall. Perhaps it would be best to stay in the open for tonight and enter in the morning, rather than blunder into such a gloomy unknown in the dusk.

"Where are Kai and Kayi?" he asked the girl.

She had squatted on her heels and now she glanced up. "They go about their own concerns. I do not rule them, as I have said. This woodland," she pointed ahead with an uplift of her chin, "would be to their liking. They are not usually creatures of the open—but have a taste for trees."

Well, if that was the way of it, what did it matter to him? Still, the more Sander looked into that darkness ahead the less he wanted to enter it with only failing daylight to guide him.

"We'll stay here for the night," he decided, then wondered at once if she would refuse his guidance.

"If you wish," was all she answered, as she got to her feet to lift her bags from Rhin's back.

In turn Sander stripped the pad and his own bags from the koyot, and Rhin padded into the night for the food he would hunt on his own. Neither of the fishers had returned, and Sander began to wonder if Fanyi's control over the beasts was as complete as he had believed. But the girl showed no signs of concern. Instead she slipped out of her drab overdress, and the first flickers of the fire flames turned both her girdle and massive necklace into bands of glitter.

Once more she made the cakes of meal and set them to bake on the thin griddle, while Sander checked his supply of darts carefully. He wanted to enter the dark bloom of the forest with a weapon ready. Then he gathered a pile of wood, gleaned from the edge of the woods, a supply he hoped would last the night.

As she watched her baking, Fanyi began to croon to herself. The words were strange. Now and again Sander caught one that had a meaning, but the rest—it was as if she sang in some tongue that was hers alone.

"Have your people always been by the river?" he asked

abruptly, breaking the somnolent spell that her crooning produced in him.

"Not always—what people has lived always in any land?" she asked in return. "Were we not all shaken, dispersed, sent wandering by the Dark Time? Our story is that we were on a ship upon the sea—driven very far, carried inland by the waters that swept the world. Many of those aboard died or were dragged away by the lick of the waves. But some survived. When the sea withdrew, their ship was left rooted upon land. That was in the day of Margee, who was mother to Nana, and Nana was mother to Flory, and she bore Sanna." Slowly she recited names, more than he could count as she spoke them, until at last she ended, "and I am true daughter to the fourth Margee. The ship's people met with others who wandered, and so was Padford born in the days of my grandmother's mother. Before that we lived by the sea to the south. But we came north because of the evil there, for suddenly there was a new mountain born, even as it was in the Dark Time, and it spewed out fire and running rock so that all life must flee or be utterly eaten up. What of your people, Sander-smith?"

"We came from the south and west, as I have said. Our Rememberers know—but they are the only ones with such knowledge. I am a smith." He held his two hands into the firelight flexing their strong fingers. "My mysteries are not theirs."

"To each man his own mystery." She nodded as she swept the cakes deftly from the griddle and held one out to him. "It is said that the first Margee had the power of healing, and thus she taught those of her blood-line. But also we have other powers." She bit into the round of hot bread, every movement bringing sparkling response from her ornaments.

"Tell me," she said after she had chewed and swallowed. "Why did you take out-rights, cutting yourself away from those of your blood-kin, to hunt what you may never find? Is it because you lost face when your people would not name you smith?"

Somehow she was able to compel the truth from him.

"I was tested and ready—my father would have said so were that not the way it was. But Ibbets was his brother and long had wanted to be smith. He is good enough." Though Sander grudged saying that, he must admit it. "Yet he never seeks beyond what has been done the same way before. I would learn more—why there are some metals that we cannot handle though the Before Men did, what were the secrets that they held that we have lost. My father knew that this lay in my mind, but he said always that a smith has a duty to his Mob. He must not go off a-roving, hunting that which may not even exist. When my father died, Ibbets made the council listen—saying that I was one with a head full of dreams, that I was too young and heedless to be a full smith. He"—Sander's lips tightened—"he generously offered to take me as apprentice. Apprentice! I who had been taught by a far greater worker of metal than he dreamed to be! He was jealous of my father, but in me he saw a way to make sure that the smith magic passed to him. Thus I took outrights. Let me but learn every one of the Before secrets, and I can make Ibbets seem the apprentice!"

"And that is what you wish the most—to humble before your Mob the man who humbled you?" she asked, brushing her fingers together to rid herself of the crumbs of the bread.

"Not wholly that—I want also the smith secrets." The old longing came to life in him. "I want to know how they worked that they could do so much more than we. Were they truly so much greater in mind than we that such learning was easy for them, that where we must seek so hard and long, they knew in an instant of thought which is the wrong way, which is the right? Some of the ignorant —my father claimed them so—speak now of men who learned so much that the Great Power thought to wipe them from the earth, that they were evil in many ways and so must be melted down as one melts a collection of metal fragments to cast anew. Perhaps this may be so. But I seek to know what I can learn—"

"And your Rememberers were of no aid?"

Sander shook his head. "We were not a people who

lived in the great cities. Rather we were scattered in a country that was left much to itself. Always we have been herdsmen, traveling with our animals. Our Rememberers recall the churning of the country and that a handful of our people and a few of our animals fled and survived. But of knowledge beyond that I have only my own clan-line teaching, for we are of a family of smiths, not one with the Mob from its beginning. My first Man came out of the wilderness to join with those wanderers when they had already been roving near the time of a man's life, fleeing ever from the breaking up of all they knew. What we have kept is not clan knowledge, but the skill to use our hands."

She sat with her legs curled under her, her fingers playing with the small bags that hung from her girdle. Now she nodded.

"Knowledge that was needful to keep life within the body, men held to that. But what lay beyond was often forgotten. I wish, however, that I might talk with your Rememberers. There could be more learned from even unknown words that might have meaning. There are such words in many—we do not know for what they stand—things, actions—" She shook her head slightly. "So much lost. Even more will go with those ravening Sea Sharks." Now her rounded jawline set, and she looked bleakly into the fire.

"Life was good in Padford." She spoke as if assuring herself of the past, as if she were no longer aware he existed. "Our planted land grew wider each year. We did not have to depend alone on the bounty of the sea—which can fail at times—as first we did when we settled here. The Traders came in the mid-summer. Twice my mother bargained for books—real books—those records which the Before Men kept. She read them—a little—and what she knew she taught me. We might have learned so much more, given the time." Her hand cupped the pendant on her breast.

"This was given her by him who fathered me. He came with the Traders, yet was not of their breed—rather a seeker for lost knowledge, journeying from a far place.

34

He was making a book himself, recording all that he learned, for his clan was a clan of men wiser than any I have heard of. And he left this necklace so that, if my mother bore a child, that child might seek out the greater source of learning. He taught her its secret—" When she fell silent, Sander could not help asking:

"What became of him?"

"He died," she returned flatly. "There was a sickness and dire pain that came upon him. He knew the secret of it—there was a part within his body that was diseased, that should be cut out. But my mother had no skill to cut to save. So he died. Then she swore by the Great Moon that bore she a child, that child must learn and learn so that the old knowledge would be once more ready to serve her people. But she and I, we were bound to the kin, we could not go a-seeking such learning at our own will. We must be there to talk to the waters at the setting out of the fishing boats, to bless the sowing of the fields so that more grain would grow. It was of our blood line that this was set upon us. Now—I go to seek what this key will open." She still fingered the pendant. "But by the Great Moon, I would that my seeking had not come through such a means!"

The night had gathered in. Only their fire made a barrier against crowding shadows. Sander stood up and whistled sharply, suddenly conscious that Rhin had not yet returned. When the koyot did not bark in answer, he was once more uneasy. Perhaps Rhin had to range far in the hunt. It was not unknown for him sometimes to spend half the night on his own. But in this unknown land Sander wished him closer.

"He is not near." The girl spoke calmly. "They have their own lives, do the furred ones. We cannot demand more of them than they willingly give."

"I do not like it," muttered Sander, though he must agree with her. His association with the koyot was a voluntary one on both their parts. To compel Rhin was to lose him. But he was unhappy now as he settled himself to a doze beside the fire, nodding awake now and then to feed a handful of wood to the flames.

The girl did not settle as quickly in the bed made of her day cloak. Instead, she took from one of those belt bags four small white cubes, each of their sides bearing dots. Smoothing out a hand-sized portion of her cloak, she tossed the cubes with a flick of her wrist, so that they tumbled onto the site she had prepared, and lay one surface up. She bent over them eagerly, scanning the dots that were uppermost, and then frowned. Sweeping them up she tossed again. The result seemed to satisfy her no better, nor did a third try. Her frown was much deeper as she tumbled them back into her bag. She sat for a time staring into the fire, and Sander caught the faintest of mumbles, as if she now spoke words of her own Power, intended for her ears alone.

At last she gave a sigh and curled up on her cloak as if she had performed some necessary action but was not reassured by that. He thought that she slept. If she was as alarmed about the non-return of the fishers as he was about the missing Rhin, she gave no outward sign.

The koyot was not back when Sander stretched the stiffness from his limbs with the coming of light. He was thirsty, and a heft on the leather water bag told him that it was too near empty. Rhin's instinct was what Sander depended upon to locate some stream or spring, and Rhin was not here. Of course, the koyot could easily follow their trail as they traveled on, but Sander wanted him now. Once more he whistled. His call was answered, not by the short yelp he hoped to hear, but rather with the screech of some bird within the wood.

Fanyi sat up. She pulled from one of her own bags a handful of dried, dark red fruit, which she divided meticulously into two shares.

"Your furred one is not near," she said.

"And yours?" he demanded with unusual harshness.

"No nearer. I think they hunt in there." She pointed with her chin at the wood. "As I said, they have a liking for trees."

"Can they find water?" He shook the bag a little to emphasize their need.

"If they wish." Fanyi's reply was calm enough to be

irritating. "But there are other ways. I know some of them. It would seem we must now carry our gear ourselves." She regarded the bags Rhin had borne. "Well, that I have also done before." She spread out her cloak and began wrapping in it the bags she had brought, lashing them into a neat bundle.

Sander finished the dried fruit in two swift gulps. The taste was tart, and the small portion came nowhere near satisfying his hunger. He hoped that somewhere in the forest facing them he could get a shot at meat on the hoof. He needed the strength of such a meal.

Now he made a back pack, using Rhin's pad for its outer casing. The smith tools were the heaviest items, and silently he fretted over the non-appearance of the koyot. Rhin was a formidable fighter, he was also fleet of foot. Foreboding pricked at Sander. They had no knowledge of what might exist in this new country. He had no idea either of how he could trail the koyot and find him, if the animal had fallen into some peril.

The pack weighed heavily on his shoulders. However, he was determined to make no complaint, for the way Fanyi marched confidently ahead into the shadow of the trees was, in a measure, a challenge. Sander went forward with his bolt thrower ready in his hands.

The trees were very large, with a huge spread of limb. Some leaves were already turning yellow or scarlet, a few wafted down now and then to join the centuries'-thick deposit of their kind under foot, a soft carpet that deadened the sound of their own passing.

For the first time Sander was conscious of something he had not foreseen. On the open plains one could fix upon some point ahead and have it as a guide. Here, with one tree much like another, how could one be sure one was heading in a straight path, not wandering in circles?

Sander stopped. Perhaps it would have been better to have stayed on the seashore, using that body of water for a guide. Fanyi paused and glanced over her shoulder.

"What is it?"

He was ashamed of his own stupidity, yet there was

nothing he could do but admit it now.

"We have nothing to follow—this is all alike."

"But there is something. I have been a way in before, and there is a road—a north road—"

A road? Her confidence was such that he could not help but believe that she knew what she was doing. But a road—!

Fanyi beckoned, and, hesitantly, he followed. Already he could look back and see nothing but trees. Nor could he be sure where they had entered this maze of trunks and low-hanging branches. But she showed no bafflement.

And it was only a short time later that they came out onto a more open space. Here the drift of leaves and earth did not quite cover a surface badly holed, fast being destroyed by creeping roots that attacked it from both sides, yet unmistakably still an artificial surface.

It ran straight, and the trees that framed or attacked it were yet young, so there was enough light and freedom to see quite a space ahead. Fanyi waved him on.

"See? It is as I said. This was once a Before Road. Much has been destroyed over the years, but still there is enough to see. Here it bends"—she gestured left to the west—"that way it comes, but from here it goes north—at least what I know of it does."

Sander could trace the old curve; the road must never have been in the open. He wondered why. It seemed to him much easier to build such a highway across the plains than within the grip of the woods. And it was narrower than the two great roads the Mob knew in their ranging (Mattly had once paced across one in measurement). They had been so wide that even the Rememberers were not able to tell how great the armies of people must have been when they used such ways.

The surface here was so rough they had to go slowly and warily that they not be tripped up or catch an ankle disastrously in some vine-hidden hole. But the road did lead them to water.

Sander had caught the sound of a stream before they reached the jagged edge of the span that had once bridged it. Small flies danced over the sun-dappled surface, those in turn hunted by much larger insects. There was a swift current, but the stream was so clear that he could see the fuzzy brown stones forming its bed. Taking the water bottle and leaving his back pack with Fanyi, he scrambled down to rinse out the container, then fill it brimming.

Since the bridge was gone, they made use of some of its blocks, now green-slimed and water-washed, as stepping stones to reach the far side. Heartened by the discovery of water, their most pressing need, Sander began now to look around seriously for a method of relieving their other want, food.

There were birds enough, but they were small and flitted about, hidden, except for sudden flashes of wings, by the trees. He had seen no animals since they had entered this place. And though he watched the stream very carefully now, its glassy surface revealed no movement below. There appeared to be no fish of size enough to show.

Fanyi caught at his arm, nearly knocking him forward into the water. He turned his head to speak impatiently when the sight of her face startled him. She was so plainly listening!

Rhin! A burden heavier than he had been aware he had carried lifted from him. Sander pursed his lips to give the summoning whistle. But Fanyi's hand shot out, pressed fierced across his mouth in a painful silencing.

Now he strained his ears to catch what she must have heard, something, he guessed from her actions, that was a dire warning.

It was not quite sound, rather a pulsation of the air— as if sound had given it birth very far away. He pushed aside her finger gag and asked in a voice hardly above a whisper:

"What is it?"

She was frowning, much as she had the night before when she threw her cubes to read some message from them.

"I do not know," she answered, in a voice even lower than his. "But it is of some Power. I cannot mistake that."

Of her vaunted Powers he knew practically nothing.

Among his people they had a healer. But that one claimed nothing beyond a knowledge of how to set bones, treat wounds, and use some herbs to ease disease. They had also a vague idea that there was an Influence greater than themselves that existed. But that It concerned itself with man was hardly probable. If so, why then had the Dark Time been sent to nearly kill off their species, unless Before Man had in some manner awakened a generation of blood-feud with that Influence. If that was so, the Mob had reasoned during the few times they applied themselves to such speculation, it was better for man now not to appeal to or worship such an Influence.

Sander thought that it might be different with Fanyi. Some of her claims—such as farseeing—were matters strange to him. Also there could be other peoples on earth now, not so wary of the Influence, who might have made some pact with It. From such might come these Powers of which she so confidently spoke. Since this land was of her knowledge, he was willing to be guided by her—up to a point.

"What kind of power?" he whispered once more.

She had gathered up her pendant, held it now cupped in her hand, and was staring into it as if she could read an answer from the points of light glittering on its surface.

As he waited for her to reply, Sander began to wonder if they were even closer to her legendary cache of knowledge, and if this emanation, whatever it might be, was the signal of its being. But whatever Fanyi thought, she was not pleased with what she learned by looking at the pendant. She shook her head slowly.

"It is not what we seek." Her words were decisive. "There is some darkness ahead of us. Yet this is the way—"

"We can go back," Sander pointed out. "It would be easier to go along the seashore. We should have tried that in the first place."

The wood, which earlier had been a promise of cover, now began to take on the semblance of a trap. He wanted none of it—rather to be out in the open where one could see an enemy approaching, even if one was also as naked to that other's sight. "Come on!" As she had earlier caught at his shoulder to rivet his attention, so now his hand closed about her arm.

She gave one more long look at the pendant and then let it fall back against her breast.

"All right," she agreed.

He had half expected an argument and was relieved that she surrendered to his will so easily. Perhaps Rhin's higher sensitivity had already warned the koyot against this place of trees, and that was why the animal had not joined them.

They recrossed the stepping stones and made the best time they dared, scrambling back the way they had come. Always now, Sander was aware of that distant beating. It seemed to him that his own heart thudded heavily in time to it, that he could feel its vibration throughout his body. Nor did it lessen as they fled, rather remained the same, as if whatever caused it kept always at the same distance behind them, slipping steadily along their trail.

It was when they reached the curve in the ancient road that the trap was at last sprung and from a direction Sander had not expected. As they passed beneath the wide-spreading branches of one of the giant trees, there fell over them the tangles of a net. Before Sander could struggle, it was jerked tight, entrapping him past any hope of freedom. The strings of the net were not the braided hide ropes he had always known. Rather they were coated with some sticky substance, which, when it once touched, clung tightly to what it covered. Movement on the part of the captives only wound them more completely in its folds.

He could not reach his knife, he could not even drop the useless dart thrower, which was glued now to his hands. A second sharp and vigorous jerk took him from his feet, landing him face down on the carpet of decayed leaves. He fought to turn his head enough so that his nose and mouth were not closed by that stifling muck and so caught a distorted side view of those who had so easily taken them captive.

Chattering, they dropped from the tree branches, aiding

41

with their strength those already on the ground. They were small, and they were furred in patches. Also, all they wore in the way of clothing were short aprons of woven vines. The fur grew along the outer parts of their arms and legs, in mats across their chest and shoulders, thicker yet on those bellies that bulged a little above the vine cords supporting their aprons. On the other hand, their faces were smooth. But in sharp contrast to the olive skin, which showed a little through and around the dark hair, those faces were red and wrinkled.

Sander could understand nothing of their clicking speech, could detect no weapons save wooden clubs. He saw one of those just as it descended toward him. As the blow fell true, his head felt as if it had burst in an explosion of pain, but he did not altogether lose consciousness.

Bundled in the net, he was being lifted. The sour body odor of the forest dwellers was sickening. They were grunting, perhaps in protest to his weight, as they carried him along. One must have seen that his eyes were open, that he had some awareness of what was happening, for the forest man (if men they could be truly termed) thrust his crimson face closer to Sander's and snarled. Then the stranger shook his club meaningfully directly above the captive. Sander needed no further hint. It would serve no purpose to allow himself to be beaten to a pulp here and now. He obediently lay quiet.

Trussed as tightly as the pack still on his back, Sander found himself pulled aloft. It appeared that their captors were creatures who considered trees their natural roadways. The smith was tense with foreboding as they swung him across wide expanses, sure that sooner or later he must crash helplessly to the ground beneath, while the pain in his head made him dizzy. At last he closed his eyes tightly, determined to hoard his strength for any effort he could make at the end of a nightmare journey.

That Fanyi suffered the same fate he had no doubt, yet he had heard no sound from her. Had they beaten the girl into unconsciousness before they whirled her thus aloft? It was plain that even if she knew something of the woodland, she had not foreseen the coming of these savages.

To Sander's half-dazed mind these were less than men. Nor were they to be numbered among those animals with whom men had established some rapport during the years. The snarling red face, which had been bent over him, had held a mindless ferocity mirrored in its small eyes, while the fetid smell that arose from those pulling him along made him gag.

They were, Sander knew, going deeper into the forest. And that vibration swelled within his body, so that his heart pounded as fast as if he had been running to the point of exhaustion. Not even the Traders had ever mentioned such as these.

Beat—beat—

It still was not a sound, save that it came with the pound of his blood in his ears. Sander felt as if his whole body shook with the force of each great blow—if blows those were. The chittering of the forest things (he would not dignify them with the term "men") grew stronger, much louder.

There came a final downward swing, which ended in a vicious jerk, sending pain red and hot through his head. Then Sander lay flat on the ground in an open place, the sun beaming harshly into his eyes, enough to make him squint them shut again.

When he turned his head as far as he could and cautiously opened his eyes again, it was just in time to see the last of the hairy men swing upward into the trees again on the other side of the clearing.

Had they left a guard? If not—was there any way—? Sander squirmed within his casing of net. He could wriggle a little on the ground, but none of the lashings loosened. In fact, he was sure that they were slowly tightening instead. However, his efforts had moved him so that he could catch a glimpse, through the lashing that held her, of Fanyi.

There was no sign of any of the tree men. The opening in which the prisoners lay was nearly covered with a jumble of blocks. What was paramount in the clearing was a thing squatting upright on a heaping of rocks.

It might have been hacked out of wood, crudely, but with enough skill to represent hazily one of the tree people, though it was three times their size. And it was blatantly female. The ugly face was stained scarlet, and necklaces of polished nuts and seed pods decked the hunched shoulders. Squatting on its hams, its two hands knuckle down on either side, its head was poked forward as if it were looking down upon the prisoners with avid interest.

Then—

One of those small, shiny eyes, which Sander had thought an inset bit of quartz or colored rock, blinked. The thing was—alive!

Sander's mouth went dry. He could accept an image. But that this huge brute thing lived was true nightmare. The nightmare compounded when the vast mouth opened a little to show fangs, one cracked and broken, and the tip of a pallid tongue issuing forth like a loathesome worm.

The thing raised its head a little and hooted—a queer cry like that of some night-hunting creature. From the trees around, though they remained unseen, the forest men answered with a loud chorus of chittering cries.

Here was no resemblance to any speech Sander had ever heard, but it had the power to raise fear in the hearer. He could not fight the net, constricting so fast, crushing his back pack against him, constraining his limbs as if he were held in some giant vise.

"Aeeeeheee!" That cry raised to the height of a scream burst from Fanyi. Sander had a dim memory of having heard it before. Yet he read into it no call for help, rather defiance.

The thing on the rock stopped hooting. It shuffled its paunchy body closer to the edge of its perch, its head swung so that its small eyes regarded the girl. Then, almost negligently, it picked up a round rock lying close to hand and threw.

Only by a finger's breadth did the stone miss Fanyi's head. Sander believed that, had the creature wished, it might well have smashed the girl's skull. The warning was clear. But if so, Fanyi was not heeding it.

"Aeeeeheeee!" Once more she sent that call, which was repeated from the blocks by faint echoes.

Sander remembered now. So had she on the plain called to Kai and Kayi. Did she somehow sense that her companions were nearby?

The huge female grunted, sweeping out a hand in search of another stone. Then she got lumberingly to her feet. Sander gasped. Even allowing for the fact that her perch was above the level of the clearing floor, she was tall enough to top him by far more than a head, her ponderous body that of a giant not only among her own kind but also his.

She descended the blocks slowly, as if she were not quite sure how stable they might be under her weight. When she reached the ground, she stooped to grab at Fanyi. Sander twisted in a last frantic attempt to free himself. He was sure he was going to witness some horrible act of mutilation or death.

But, through the air, as if the fisher had borrowed wings, came Kai, a hissing scream issuing from its fanged jaws. The beast landed true, on the slightly bent shoulders of the giant female, his head darting forward toward her massive neck.

The forest woman straightened with a hooting cry, tried to swing back her arms, tear loose the animal sinking its fangs in her flesh. Now the smaller Kayi appeared in turn, not leaping through the air, but streaking across the ground to clamp teeth into one of those pendulous breasts.

Loud cries from the trees echoed the hoots of the giant. Sander expected to see the forest men drop from the branches to the rescue of their beleaguered female. Yet they did not show, only continued to cry out as she stamped about, striving to pluck away her attackers. She loosened Kayi by tearing loose her own flesh still clamped in the fisher's jaws, flinging the animal from her. But when she sought to reach Kai again, the smaller fisher flashed in once more apparently unharmed by that rough handling.

Suddenly, a fountain of blood burst from the side of the giant's throat. Kai, worrying away, had severed an artery. The forest woman gave a last hoot and sank forward to her knees, while Kayi returned, to snap and tear at her body. She pawed feebly, trying to reach the creature on her back, and then slumped, her terrible head resting upon a block, like a mask of hideous death, while blood ran in a noisome river across the stones. The chittering of her people, still hidden in the trees, sank into silence even as she died.

The fishers backed away from the body, as if, since the death of the giant, they found the scent and taste of her torn flesh noisome. Sander waited, expecting that unseen audience in the trees to burst down upon them, clubbing both animals and their helpless prisoners. He and Fanyi might have escaped whatever particularly grisly fate the giant female planned, but they had certainly not won their freedom.

That beat had stopped. Sander was no longer aware of it. But he could hear rustlings and movements in the trees and braced himself for a final attack. When that did not come, he was even more apprehensive, fearful that they might not be killed at once by the forest men, but rather be the vicitims of some crueler and more prolonged fate.

The fishers crouched by Fanyi, their heads up and turning from side to side as they kept their attention fixed on the trees. Fierce as the animals had shown themselves to be in that surprise attack, Sander thought they would be helpless as Fanyi should the tree men use their nets.

Moments passed. He could no longer even hear those movements. The sun bore down hotly in the clearing and the smell of death was strong.

"They are gone." Fanyi broke the waiting silence.

"What?" Sander tried to raise his head higher to catch a glimpse of what might lie within the curtain of the leaves.

"They have gone," she repeated.

Perhaps they might have for now. But that did not free their captives. The constriction of those ropes around him now was a torment, as he became aware of his own condition rather than of the menace the giant had offered.

"Lie still," Fanyi said now. "I have heard of these vines. There is an answer to them also. But be still—let me try to make Kayi understand what must be done."

He could not move at all now, and his fear took another pattern—that the continued constriction of the rope would slowly cut his body to pieces, crush his back with the weight of his own pack and its smith tools. There was nothing he could do but *be* still, whether at her orders or not.

The heat of the sun on his face brought back the pain in his head, and he longed for water, for the easement of his bonds. Kayi had crouched by the girl, muzzle nearly touching Fanyi's face. They were utterly quiet as they matched stares with one another.

Meanwhile Kai prowled about the clearing, stopping under each tree to gaze upward, as if in search of more prey. Now and then his body, large as it was, was hidden behind some of the blocks. Twice the fisher reared his length against a tree trunk, peering up, his head swinging a little right and then left, as if he sought by scent what he could not see.

Sander looked back to Fanyi and Kayi. The fisher shuffled away from the girl and deliberately dabbed one forepaw and then the other into the pool of blood that had dripped from their dead enemy. With the same care she then scraped her claws into the earth so that loose dust adhered to them.

Thus prepared, she came back to Fanyi and set her filthy claws within the bonds of the net, plainly using her full strength as she strove to tear the mesh.

It was necessary for her to make many trips to recoat her claws against the sticky surface of the ropes. But each time she returned to her task. Sander had some lapses from consciousness. The pain in his head, the steady pressure on his back caused blackouts, and he did not know how long they lasted. He expected any moment the return of the forest men, and now he no longer cared. Finally he passed entirely into that dark world which had been lapping at him.

He awoke, choking a little, liquid spewing from the corner of his mouth. Then, still not quite aware, he swallowed painfully once and again, as more water was dribbled between his dry lips. But he could breathe, the pain in his back was no longer constant. He shifted and

48

knew that he was free from the net. Fanyi leaned above him, pouring the water a few sips at a time into his mouth.

"We—" His voice sounded fuzzy and far away.

"Can you move?" she demanded. "Try! Can you sit—stand—?"

Her urgency reached him only dimly through the haze that wrapped about him. But obediently the smith dragged himself up to his knees, then, with her tugging at him, lurched to his feet.

The sun no longer baked them so fiercely, but they were still in the clearing and the giant's body—Sander averted his eyes hastily.

"Come!" Fanyi pulled at him until he staggered a pace or so ahead. Then he stopped, swaying.

"My tools!" The first truly coherent thought struck him. He would not abandon all that belonged to his past.

"Kai brings them!" the girl snapped impatiently. "Come!"

The male fisher was lumbering along, dragging Sander's pack, jerking at it when it caught against the edge of a block or the branches of a bush. And since Sander doubted if he could stoop to reclaim it and then keep going, he had to be content.

He wavered on, glad to feel strength return as he went, even though the torment of renewed circulation accompanied the motion. His mind began to clear also.

"The tree men—" He strove to find words for his ever-present foreboding.

"They have not returned—I do not know why," Fanyi admitted. "Unless when the fishers slew their great woman they were so in fear that they will not face Kai or Kayi again. Still they may come hunting. But the furred ones will not let them reach us without warning this time."

"Where do we go?"

"There is a path," she replied. "It leads right—eastward. I think we are safer heading for the sea than trying to return through the forest."

To that he agreed. Fanyi had been carrying his dart thrower, now she pressed it back into his hold.

"This is your weapon; have it ready. We know not what manner of revenge these beast-things may plan."

He took it eagerly. If she was right and the fishers could warn them of any future attack by the net, then they would have a chance. He had seen no weapons other than the clumsy clubs.

Since he could manifestly walk alone, Fanyi moved a little ahead, her own pack firmly against her shoulders, Kayi bounding with her, while the larger male formed their rear guard. Sander found himself listening.

The beat, which was more vibration than sound, had been silenced. The whole woods was quiet now, too—no more twittering of birds or any hint that any life beside their own had even ventured under this green roof. It was only then that Sander caught, faint and seemingly from very far away, a yelp he knew. Rhin!

But if the koyot trailed them into this deadly tree trap, he might well be netted as they had been! And Sander had no way of warning the animal not to venture here. Or had he?

The smith paused, drew breath deep into his lungs, and then uttered a cry that bore no relation to the whistle that usually summoned Rhin. Instead this was a deep-lunged yowl—the war call of the great mountain cat. Whether Rhin could catch his meaning he did not know—he could only hope.

Both fishers whirled to face him, snarling. Fanyi's surprise was open. Twice more he sounded that cry, thinking that the desperation which had set him to mimic it had indeed this time produced almost the proper timbre.

"Rhin," he explained. "He must not come and be caught. That is the cry of an old hill enemy. But perhaps unlike it enough in his ears to be a warning."

The girl nodded, already again pushing on. Sander could see that what she called a path must once have been a road. Perhaps not as wide a one as they had followed earlier, but still having remains of paving. Those tumbled blocks back in the clearing—now that he thought about them he believed that they were too regular in outline to be a natural outcrop. Perhaps they had also been set in place by man for some reason.

To his relief Sander now saw that the forest growth was getting thinner. And he caught a murmur that he fiercely hoped was the sound of distant surf. Let them get out into the open on the beach and they would be safe enough—there could be no overhead attack launched there.

They quickened pace. Now the smith felt strong enough to catch up his pack and sling it back across his shoulders as they thudded along. There were blocks of stone poking through the lighter brush. More buildings once? He did not know or care—to get into the open was the important thing.

The growth of trees became much lighter. Bushes and tall grass and heaped stones formed barriers around and over which they had to make their way, the fishers flowing easily but the humans having a more difficult time of it.

Open sun again—but now well down the sky. And the sea! Sander stood on the top of one block he had had to climb, making sure of that. And running along the sand, which spurted out from under his pads as he came, was Rhin! The koyot startled the shore birds, which arose with shrill cries; then his yelp sounded loud and clear.

They pushed through a stand of stubborn briars, and sand crunched under their boots. The fresh air of the beach blew away the last turgid memory of the haunted woods. Rhin reached them, nosing at Sander delightedly, then growling a little, as he must have scented either the forest savages or their nets. His ears pricked toward woods as he growled again more deeply.

"Not now!" Sander told him joyfully. "We're free!"

They had no wish to linger too close to that dark stand. Instead, they turned north again, this time keeping to the beach where one could see for miles anyone or anything that might come.

"Who—or what—were they?" Sander asked that night when they made camp among the dunes, a cheerful fire of driftwood cooking the crabs Rhin had pawed from sand holes. "Have you seen or heard of them before?"

"The tree men?" Fanyi was repacking her bag, having

searched carefully through it as if she feared that some of its contents had suffered from rough handling. "I do not know. I think they must be new-come here, for my people have gone nutting in that wood each autumn and never before have we found such. You ask 'what'—do you then believe that they are not in truth men?"

"I do not know. To me, they seemed closer to animals, lesser than Rhin or your furred ones. And why did they serve a giant?"

"There were many strange changes in both man and animal during the Dark Time. My father," her hand cupped the pendant again, "he had knowledge of such changes. He told my mother some animals now moved toward the estate of men. Perhaps it is also true then that some men drop backward into animals. These forest people are less even than the slavers—though perhaps they are fully akin in spirit." That fierce light was again in her eyes when she spoke of the enemy who had wiped out Padford. "I think that we were intended as offering to placate their female."

Sander did not shiver, but he would have liked to. What might have happened had not the fishers come to their rescue? He did not care to dwell upon that. He noticed that this night neither Kai, Kayi, nor Rhin roamed away from the fire, but were settling down close to its light. Perhaps, they, too, were affected by the strangeness of this world, sensing a menace that lay just below the surface.

He suggested that they watch in turn, being sure to keep the fire lit, and Fanyi agreed at once. But she pressured him into taking the first rest, pointing out that his heavy pack had been such a threat to him in the shrinking net that he had suffered more than she. And, while he would have liked to argue the question, her good sense made his pride seem childish.

When she aroused him, the night had closed in. Rhin lay with his head pillowed on his forepaws, his eyes yellow slits of awareness as Sander went to feed the fire. The fishers were curled into two furry balls, and Fanyi settled herself in a sandy hollow by them.

Above, the stars were very bright and clear, and the ceaseless wash of the waves lulling. Sander got to his feet, motioning Rhin to lie still when the koyot at once raised his head. He walked a little down the beach, gathering more driftwood, feeling too restless to remain still. As he started back, he faced toward that black shadow that was the edge of the woods. Had the forest men come slinking after them? Would those leave the trees to hunt down the slayers of their—what had she been: a chief, mother of the tribe, even a supernatural figure with supposed powers of a Shaman? They would never know. Only that she had had no common heritage with either Fanyi or him, that she had been farther removed from their blood-kin than even the furred ones.

This might be a world of many surprises. It would be best that from now on their party should move with great care, accepting nothing as harmless until it was proven so.

He tramped back to the fire and fed in some wood. Rhin's eyes closed when he saw Sander settle down. Fanyi lay, breathing evenly. In sleep her face looked very young, untried. But she was not. He owed his life to her or at least to her furred ones. Somehow that idea was one he did not altogether like. *He* had blundered around like an untried boy on his first herd ride. There was little for him to be proud of in this day's work.

Frowning, he pulled his tool bag to him, drawing forth the tools, examining them one by one. The two hammers he had found in Padford—those ought to be fitted with proper handles. But there was nothing here except driftwood, and the strength of that he did not trust. When he had time, he would search out some proper wood and see them shafted again. He thought they would have excellent balance, once they were so ready for use.

Now he wondered about the man who had used them. What manner of smith had served Padford? He would like to ask Fanyi. But he thought it better not to call to her mind any thought of her people and their doom.

That made him think in turn of what she sought— some weapon out of the Before Time, one potent enough to wipe out those raiders from the south. Did such exist still? He doubted it. But that Fanyi did have knowledge of some hidden place, that he did not doubt.

Metal—

He thought of copper and gold and silver and iron—those he knew, could fashion to obey his will. But the others—the strange alloys that no man now held the secret of—if he could master those also! His hand curled about the broken handle of the large hammer he had found, and a kind of restless eagerness filled him so that he longed to get up at this very moment and run—run to find the secrets Fanyi promised existed somewhere.

He must discipline his too vivid imagination. Fanyi's idea of what she sought was very vague. He must not count on good fortune until he met with it face to face. Slowly Sander repacked the tools and knotted their bag. It was good fortune enough this night that they were still alive.

For two days they plodded among the dunes. Save for the birds and the shellfish and crabs they foraged for, this land might have been bare of any life. Far to the west showed the dark line of the forest. Between them and it was a waste in which little grew but tough grass in scattered clumps and some brush whittled by the salt winds into strange shapes.

On the third morning they reached a yet stranger desert land. The sea, too, now curled away to the east, so what they faced was a slope leading downward into a land that had once been covered by ocean but now lay open to the air. Here rocks had necklaces of long-dead shell fish, while brittle carcasses of other sea life lay half-buried around outcrops of wave-worn stone.

Sander wanted to alter their path west—hoping to skirt this desert. But Fanyi hesitated, her eyes again on her pendant, in which she seemed to trust so deeply.

"What we seek lies there!" She pointed straight ahead, out into the sea-desert.

"How far?" countered Sander. He had little liking for the path she suggested.

"I cannot say."

"We must be more sure. To go out there—" He shook his head. "We have finished the last of the meal. Even crabs and shellfish will not be found there. Though we filled our waterskin at the pool among the dunes this morning, how long think you that supply will last?"

"And if we turn west, how many days may we be adding to our journey?" she countered.

He surveyed what lay to the west. The beach land they had been following narrowed to a cliff barrier, on which he could see trees. To return to any wood after their experience—no—if there were a way to avoid it. But he had to have some assurance that they would not head into the nowhere of the sea-desert without a better guide than Fanyi's vague directions.

True, he could sight some grass, a few bushes that had rooted out on the old sea bottom. It was not quite so desolate as he had first believed. And there were rocks in that uncovered landscape that would provide them with landmarks, so that they need not wander in circles once they were out of sight of this land that had once been the shore.

"A day's journey," he conceded. "Then, if we find nothing—return."

The girl seemed hardly to hear him, though she nodded. Now she allowed the pendant to drop again and surveyed what lay ahead with an eagerness obviously not lessened by any forebodings.

Rhin trotted confidently along. But the fishers prowled back and forth, venting their displeasure by hissing, following the others only when Fanyi coaxed. It was very apparent that they, at least, had no liking for this open country.

For a space, the bottom was sandy and fair walking. Then there began a gravelly stretch studded with many water-worn stones. This footing shifted and turned under any weight. The land they left must have formed, Sander deduced, one arm to half lock in a great bay in the Before Days.

Sun shone through a huge upstanding fence of wide-spaced rib bones belonging to some sea creature, or perhaps they were the timbers of a ship so overlaid with the bodies of shelled things that all that remained was as if turned to stone. Sander was not sure which.

This sea-desert was not evenly floored, for there were hillocks and dips. In the hollow of one small valley they came upon a little pool ribbed with white salt, perhaps a last remnant of the lost sea.

On and on; now that Sander glanced back he could hardly see the true land from which they had come. And his doubt concerning the wisdom of traveling in this direction grew in him. There was a kind of rejection here—as if the life he represented was resented, hated by the ancient desolation.

At length, they reached a deep cut and looked down its rugged sides. Below flowed a river. How to cross? The fishers were clambering down the side, heading for the water below. He and Fanyi might also do that, but Rhin could not. They would have to go off course—west again, even farther out into the desert, hoping to discover a place where there was an easier crossing.

The river solved one of their problems, however, for Sander saw the fishers dipping their muzzles into the stream, obviously drinking sweet water.

They trudged along the edge of that gorge. Sander's hope was proven right, the rock walls began to sink down while the river widened. They detoured around masses of encrusted objects that he thought were ships, to come at last upon something else, the remains of a wall of massive blocks, which were far too regular in pattern to be the work of nature. Beyond that were other stones that might have once marked the beginning of a road, as well as two great fallen columns, all so overlaid with sea growth that it was plain they were very old, perhaps even old when the Before Time had been. He marveled at the work, and Fanyi traced along the edge of a block with her finger tips.

"Old—old—" She marveled. "Perhaps there was even another Dark Time when the world changed to bring in the same sea that our Dark Time drove out. If we only knew—" There was a wistfulness in her voice that he could well have echoed.

They dared not linger to explore what the ancient sea had concealed, pushing on resolutely to where the river now flowed out to the sea, well away from the Before shore they had followed.

Dusk found them on the new seashore, so once more they camped by the sound of beating waves. Here, too, was driftwood enough for a fire. And the fishers, who had followed the river, came into camp each dragging a large fish. Fanyi hailed their catch, a delicacy her people knew but were seldom able to net.

As the fish broiled on sticks before the fire, Sander leaned his back against a water-worn stone and stared out over the river. There was a current to be sure. But with the bed so much wider and shallower here, he thought they could gain the other side in the daylight without too much exertion. Then following it westward once more they could also depend upon water as long as they paralleled its flow. Though the river had taken them far off the course Fanyi had set, perhaps it was not to be counted a major difficulty after all.

Fanyi laid out a pattern of small shells. "It is a wonder of the sea, Sander-smith, that no two of these is ever quite the same. The shape may be alike, yet the markings —there is always some slight differing. There are some the Traders prize, and those will buy a length of copper wire, even a lump of rust-iron, which still has a good core. I—"

But what she would have said Sander never knew. He had been watching Rhin. Now he made a swift gesture with one hand and reached for his dart thrower. The koyot bristled, his lips drawn back to show his teeth, his eyes near-slits.

Sander listened intently. Fanyi crouched by the fire her hands resting on the backs of Kai and Kayi, who were also hissing softly.

Now came a splashing—from the sea or the river? Sander could not be sure just which direction. Rhin growled again.

"A fire torch!" Sander half-whispered to Fanyi.

Instantly she caught up a thick branch of the driftwood, thrust one end into the flame. When that branch caught, she whirled it around, made the flame-blaze glow. With that in hand, before Sander could stop her, she clawed her way to the top of one of the large stones, swinging her improvised torch outward.

He scrambled up to join her, a dart laid ready to shoot. There sounded a croaking from out of the dusk. Then the light of the torch caught a dark figure standing on the edge of the river, its body glistening as if it had just crawled out of the flood.

The thing stood like a man, erect upon its hind limbs. But for the rest—this was not even as human as the forest men had seemed. Pallid skin hung in folds about its torso, while its upper and lower limbs were flat-seeming. It had a great gaping mouth from which issued the croaking, and above the mouth were bulbous eyes. But—

Around its middle was a strip of something that appeared to be scaled hide. Into that were thrust two long, curved, deadly-pointed lengths that might have been fashioned, Sander thought, of bone, not of any metal.

"Do not shoot!" Fanyi cried out. "It is afraid. I think it will go—"

Even as she spoke, the thing took a great leap backward, sinking into the river. The flame of the torch did not reach very far, so it was almost instantly out of sight as it swam.

"Fire—it does not like the fire." The girl spoke with conviction, as if she had, in those few seconds of confrontation, been able to read the water thing's mind.

Rhin passed below them, racing to the edge of the river, howling madly at the swift-flowing surface. It was plain the koyot had made up his mind that the river dweller was dangerous.

If they were to cross the river to continue their journey, Sander thought, they must plunge into the water in which the thing was clearly at home. He did not like the prospect that faced them with the coming of daylight.

"What was it?" Since this land was more Fanyi's than his, he turned to her for enlightenment. She shook her head.

"Again—such a creature I have not seen before. But there are tales that once something from the sea came and broke the nets at Padford, taking also fishermen who were unwary. It was after a great storm and the water turned red. It stank and so many fish died men had to burn them in great heaps upon the shore. Later there was no more trouble. But that was in my mother's mother's time, and none saw clearly the sea things. It was thought that they were of some intelligence—for the nets were slashed where the cutting would do the most harm."

"It"—Sander slid down to sit on her perch—"the thing did not look much like a man."

"The creature is a water thing," she agreed. "Listen!"

Above the wash of the sea waves, the gurgle of the river, they caught a sound, though distant—a croaking. Was the visitor they had sighted only the scout of a larger party? Perhaps for them to remain near the river was folly. Still Sander hesitated to move out into the dark.

In the end they decided that, with the fire and the sentry duty of Rhin and the fishers, they might stay where they were. As Sander improvised a second torch to aid in hunting more wood, Fanyi brought from one of her belt pouches a thick rod about the length of her own Palm. She turned the bottom of it firmly to the right and then touched a place on its side. Straightway there flashed the light that had transfixed him on their first meeting.

"This is a Before Thing," she told him with pride of ownership. "It was also my father's. But he said that it has limited life and after a while it will die. However, now we can use it to advantage."

Sander shook his head. "If it will die, then it should be saved for a time of greater need. Since you say these water things fear fire, fire we shall use."

With Fanyi holding a torch he made a harvest of driftwood from some distance on either side of their camping place, piling pieces high, hoping this would last the night. The fire itself—unless there was warning of the water dwellers return—they would keep low.

Once more they divided the watch. This time neither the fishers nor Rhin relaxed into deep slumber. Rather they dozed, rising at intervals to pad out into the darkness where Sander believed they were making rounds of the camp.

He himself listened for croaking. However, it had died away. Even when it was his time to rest, he kept nodding awake to listen and watch the fire.

With the morning he went down to the river, carefully judging the chance of crossing at this point. Fanyi insisted that what she sought lay beyond, north and now a little west. If they returned to land, retracing all the way they had covered yesterday, they would still have the river to cross in order to reach their goal, and it could well be patrolled, even back to the edge of the inner country, by the water creatures.

Therefore, dare they attempt to cross here and now?

The river current cut sharply into the new sea. Sander did not like the way pieces of wood he threw to test the strength of that current were whirled so swiftly past.

Secondly, he gauged the river depth with a long piece of wood. Close to the shore he thought it about thigh-high. Beyond that, he believed they might have to swim. And they would have to fight the current also in order not to be swept out to sea.

This meant going back upstream for a distance to allow some leeway. He knew the rivers of the plains. But, except in the spring when they were in spate, none of them had ever presented such a problem as this.

"Can you swim?" he asked Fanyi, when she joined him. His own prowess, he knew, was nothing to boast of. But at least, he thought, he could keep himself afloat by his efforts long enough to reach the other bank. Always providing their visitor of the night before, or his fellows, did not arrive to make things difficult.

"Yes, and you?"

"Well enough to cross this."

"It will be better"—the girl echoed his own thought—"to cross here, I think. If we return we shall lose much time, and it may be more difficult farther back than easier."

They prepared for the attempt as well as they knew how. Their bags were lashed high and tight on Rhin's back; they stripped off their clothing to add to the burdens on the koyot. Staff in hand, Sander gingerly stepped into the water. The flood was chill and his flesh shrank from it. The tug on his body grew stronger as it crept upward from his thighs to his middle. Cautiously he probed the bottom ahead for a possible quick drop in footing that might be disastrous. Rhin plunged in beside him, a little downstream, and Sander could hear a loud splashing behind that told him Fanyi and her companions were following.

He had taken the precaution of bringing a hide rope from his stores. This was anchored to Rhin's back pack, then looped around Sander's waist, the other end in turn knotted to Fanyi's belt.

Now the water was shoulder high, and he had to fight to keep upright in it. A sudden slip of his pole left his threshing without footing. Choking and sputtering, he began to swim clumsily. Within moments his body brought up against Rhin's. The koyot fought to keep his own way, as both of them were borne downstream.

Fear grew in Sander. What if they could not break the hold of the current? Before starting, he had given Fanyi strict orders that, if he and Rhin were overborne, she was to slash the rope that looped them together so she would have a better chance for herself. However, the pull was still taut, she had not done so.

Rhin swam lustily, and Sander made some way beside the koyot, not daring to try to see how much closer to the sea the current had already dragged them. He floundered on, feeling as if he were as much entrapped now by the water as he had been by the forest net.

Finally the koyot found footing and plunged up and on. Sander swiftly linked a hand in the rope making fast the load the animal carried. A moment later one of his feet grazed an underwater rock painfully, and he scrambled on until he could rise once more.

Keeping that hold on Rhin, he splashed and fought his way up the opposite bank. The rope about his middle was so taut as to nearly jerk him backward. He slewed around and caught at it with both hands, fighting to pull it in.

Down in the river, Fanyi's arms flashed into the air and disappeared again. Already she had been carried a little past the point where Sander and Rhin had found footing. Sander nudged the koyot with his shoulder, so that the animal added his strength to the pull.

By their combined efforts, Fanyi's body curved around in the stream. She was at last being drawn up current toward them. Before Sander had time to really assess what might have happened if they had failed, she waded ashore, her mass of hair water-slicked against her head.

Down the bank toward them flashed the fishers. Of the whole party, they had made the smoothest crossing. Now they paused to shake their bodies furiously, sending drops flying in all directions. But Rhin had swung around to face the river, and he snarled.

Sander caught sight of V-shaped ripples cutting the surface of the water. He jerked the rope that still linked him with Fanyi.

"Come on!"

He began to run, pulling the girl along with him, very conscious of his present defenseless state. Rhin trotted abreast of them, but the fishers played rearguard, snarling at what traveled in the depths of the flood.

Sander did not pause until they rounded some blocks of stone that gave him a momentary sense of safety. Then he wriggled free the dart thrower from the burden Rhin bore, loosening the ropes in the process to leave the koyot also stripped for action.

Scrambling on Rhin's back, he climbed from it to the top of the tallest rock. There he lay flat, to survey the back trail. By the morning light he had a clear view. Out of the water trooped a number of the same creatures as the one they had sighted before. Perhaps there were a dozen of them, though they presented a slightly different appearance from the first one, as each wore over his body—or its body—a rounded carapace that might have been fashioned from some outsize shell. Their round heads were covered in the same fashion, and there were even plates strapped about the arms and legs. They had certainly come armored and ready to do battle.

Their weapons were long spears bearing wicked-looking barbed heads, designed, Sander thought, eyeing them like a craftsman, so that those same barbs would break off in a wound. Their croaking sound was more hollow, perhaps because of their helmets, but they kept up a continual chorus as they hopped forward.

Even if they were river dwellers, they were able to handle themselves on the sea-desert, for they did not hesitate to advance. The fishers did not close on them instantly as they had with the forest people. Instead, Fanyi's beasts wove back and forth, just out of spear range, threatening and hissing, yet retreating warily.

Sander took careful aim and fired. His dart struck home, but was partly deflected by a sudden shift of his target, so that it hung in the shell near the "shoulder" of the creature, but missed the vulnerable patch between chest shield and helmet.

Still his attack appeared to shake the enemy strangely. They ceased advancing and bunched. The one who had been his target worried at the dart shaft until he worked it out of his shell covering. Then he held the weapon up as if considering it unique. Their hollow croaking grew stronger, sounding agitated. Or was that only wishful thinking on his part, Sander wondered?

He had already set another dart in the groove. But the river creatures offered such small unprotected areas that he dared not fire again until he was sure of better success. Fanyi, once more clothed, stretched out now beside him. Her hand covered his on the stock of the thrower.

"Let me hold them while you dress," she urged. "Under this sun your skin will burn badly if you do not."

Sander could already feel the heat of the sun. But to leave his post to her—

"Go!" She nudged him hard with her shoulder. "I have

used such weapons as this before." There was an angry note in her voice, as if she resented his hesitation.

By the competent way she handled the weapon, Sander was half-way convinced that she spoke the truth. He laid three more darts on the stone, then half tumbled down to dress.

Back again on the rock's crest, he discovered that the fishers had withdrawn to the edge of the "wall" on which he and the girl lay, while the river creatures had apparently recovered from their surprise over the dart and were determinedly crossing the sand and gravel toward them. The creatures hopped rather than walked as might men, yet they were not slow.

Just as Sander joined her, Fanyi fired. The leader of the water pack dropped his spear. With a loud croak of dismay, he dangled his "hand," a webbed member with four equal-length digits. The dart had pierced that to form another finger set at an angle.

Once more the enemy bunched to examine their fellow's hurt. Sander wondered at tactics that seemed stupid to him. These amphibians were well within range of the weapon, yet they gathered around their wounded fellow, interested only in what had happened to him rather than the party on the rocks. The creatures' seeming disregard of any counterattack by the besieged was puzzling. Perhaps, having spears for weapons, they could not understand a dart that came out of the air. They might even be so stupid or of such an alien way of thought that they did not connect those darts with the party they attacked.

As Fanyi surrendered the thrower to him, she also offered some advice.

"Do not kill unless you are forced to. Death might excite them to vengeance."

"How do you know that?" Sander demanded.

"I do not know—no, rather, it is that I cannot find words to explain." She seemed as puzzled now as the river creatures were over the dart. "It is just as I know what my furred ones think and feel. They are disturbed—they fear. But I believe that they can be roused by hate so that their fear will be smothered. Then they will not care how many of them die if only they can reach us. Now—they are of two minds, they half-believe we are such as they cannot profitably hunt."

Sander could not quite accept that the girl knew this for certain. She must be just guessing. Yet he did not loose any darts even at targets that were tempting. He would wait out this present croaking contest the enemy were indulging in to see what they would try next.

Now that Sander had time to examine more closely their own temporary refuge, he became aware for the first time of the continuity of the blocks of stone on which they rested. This, too, must be some very ancient work of intelligent beings. The sun beat down so fiercely that he squirmed back and forth across the surface on which he lay. To linger here was to invite another kind of disaster.

The party of water creatures moved at last. Two hunched down, holding their spears straight up in the air. The others, including the one with the dart-transfixed "hand," hopped toward the river.

Sander slipped down. The time to move was now. He guessed that the enemy had gone for reinforcements. And he was sure they themselves could handle the two remaining, if they were trailed on into the desert.

Fanyi agreed to his suggestion. She had been standing, her pendant once more in hand, turned northwest, gazing back along the course of the river down which they had traveled the day before.

"We shall have to stay away from the river," Sander cautioned. "Water is their element, and they will make the most of it." Luckily he had filled his bottle this morning before they had crossed the stream. Only, as he surveyed the shimmering heat of the sea-desert, he regretted that there was not a second or third such to sling with their gear.

On the other hand, that bare expanse of sand and stone, open to the full rays of the sun, ought to daunt the water people. If they were indeed the amphibian race he judged them to be, they would not choose willingly a long excursion over this scorched land.

In fact, Sander decided, as he examined the territory ahead with narrowed eyes, it might be well if they themselves chose to travel more cautiously. He was well trained in his people's way of herding under the night stars, using those distant points of light for a guide. At night also they would have fire for a weapon so could travel nearly as well as by day. However, first they must find a place in which to shelter until sundown.

Once more he stated aloud his estimate of their situation. That preoccupied expression smoothed from Fanyi's face and she dropped the pendant.

"Our seamen also steer by the stars," she replied slowly. "And I think that the heat of the day here is such as would make any journey an ordeal. Yes, you have judged rightly."

Again Sander felt a prick of irritation. Of course, he had judged the situation correctly! He did not relish that tone from her, hinting that she must weigh what he said and then agree or disagree. Her statements that her will and power alone had kept her people safe and that it was only because she was elsewhere they had been raided had sounded, and still did, preposterous to him. Shaman she might claim to be, with her tricks of foreseeing and the like, but his people held no faith in anything save their own decisions and actions, and neither did he.

They started off at a jog trot, the fishers bringing up the rear, Rhin once more carrying all their gear except for the bolt thrower Sander held at the ready. The smith had also thrust a half-dozen more bolts into his belt, close to hand. But he wished that he had more. The loss of the two bolts he had already shot was a grievous one when his armament was so limited.

Rhin, in spite of his pack, forged ahead, ranging back and forth as he was wont to do on the plains when hunting. Sander paused frequently at the beginning of their trek to look back.

If two armored amphibians were indeed pursuing, they managed to make such excellent use of the unevenness of the ancient sea floor as to remain invisible. The farther the fugitives ventured into what was increasingly a salt-encrusted and sere desert, the surer Sander became that beings used to living in water could not trail them hither.

That did not make him relax his vigilance as they headed northwest by his recording. Fanyi now and then gazed at her pendant as if it were a sure guide. He himself chose the old method of fixing upon a permanent point, a feature that could not be lost to sight, and aiming at that. Then, having reached that goal, he selected another.

Thirst followed as their boots stirred up a fine dust that was impregnated with salt. To know that the river with its endless bounty was closed to them, unless sheer desperation forced them to its dangers, irked Sander.

He had experienced heat on the plains, and had ridden far during seasons when water was scarce. But then he had also known the country well enough to assess the chances of finding a spring or one of those seasonally dried streambeds into which Rhin dug with the instinct of his kind to uncover seeping moisture. Where in this forsaken land could they find such?

Every time they paused to rest, the smith climbed the nearest elevation to look, not only back but ahead. If they could just hole up, out of this punishing sun and wait until nightfall.

During the fifth such survey, he caught sight of a thing that lay a little to the east of their present course. They were used by now to the relics of ancient ships, their encrusted shapes even furnishing several of the landmarks by which Sander traveled. But this was something out of the ordinary.

In the first place, Sander was sure that he had caught a glint of metal. Secondly, the shape he now studied was totally unlike anything they had sighted before. It was long and narrow, in comparison with the other skeletons of lost vessels, and it lay a little canted to one side, its broken superstructure pointed toward the rock on which Sander balanced.

Also it did not seem so aged. One end was crumpled up against a rise of reef, but otherwise, Sander believed, it appeared near intact. He thought that it might have been left so by the falling of the sea that had uncovered this new land. It offered the best shelter he had seen so far.

If they could find a way inside that hulk, it would be what he had sought for them. And Fanyi eagerly agreed.

As they approached the strange ship, Sander saw that his first valuation of it had been deceptive. It was larger than he had thought. The outline seemed to puzzle Fanyi, for she commented wonderingly that it was not like any ship she knew.

Once at its side they were dwarfed by it. Though the plates that formed it bore streaks of rust, yet the metal beneath had well withstood the passage of time. Sander thumped the surface, judging that under a thin crusting of rust it was firmly intact.

Any entrance must be made through the deck that slanted well above them. He unwound the hide rope that had lashed the pack to Rhin and hunted out one of his largest hammers. This he tied with well-tested knots. Then he bade Fanyi stay where she was, while he rounded the narrow end of the ancient ship to the other side.

There he whirled the end of rope weighted with the hammer about his head and threw. Twice it clattered back, bringing flakes of rust with it. But the third time it caught so securely on some portion of the superstructure that his most energetic jerks could not dislodge it. He began to climb and moments later balanced on the slope of the deck. Facing him was a stump of a tower broken off as if some giant hand had twisted a portion free. There was no other opening he could see.

He crossed the slanting deck to look down at Fanyi. Rhin, released from his back pack, was trotting away. And, though Sander straightway whistled, the koyot did not even look back.

Frustrated, Sander knew this was one of the times Rhin was minded to go his own way. He guessed that might be in search of water. Yet the koyot was heading west on into the desert, rather than east as Sander would expect him to go. The fishers, however, continued to prowl nearby among the rocks, plainly uneasy. Or perhaps they were unhappy at being so far from the green-grown country that was their own.

Sander dropped the rope end, having made very sure the hammer was well wedged into the broken spear of the tower, and Fanyi climbed to join him. She stood there, her legs braced against the tilt of the deck, her hands on her hips, her head turning slowly from side to side.

"What manner of ship was this?" she asked musingly, more as if she meant that question for herself and not for him. "It is surely very strange looking."

Sander edged along to the broken superstructure. Rust streaked its sides, but there was a space to enter within, though dark. Here they needed Fanyi's Before Light, and he asked her to use it. She probed with its beam through the break. He glimpsed the remains of a ladder against one wall leading downward through an opening in the floor. With Fanyi on the deck at the top, shining her light past him, Sander descended, testing each ladder rung as well as he could before he trusted his full weight to it.

He found himself in a confined area, crowded with smashed objects, all sea-stained, that he could not identify. However, the ladder continued. So he went on, reaching a larger room where there were banks of strange-looking cases along the walls. All had been water-washed and were broken. He called and Fanyi lowered the light, then clambered down herself as he held the gleam upward to illuminate those steps. When she stood beside him, she

71

gazed in wonder at the enigmatic fittings along the walls.

"What did they use, these Before Men, to power their ship?" she asked of the stagnant, sea-scented air about them. "There was no sign of a proper mast aloft—nor oars."

Sander was intent on the wealth of metal about him. It was plain that this ship had been the helpless plaything of the great flood in the Dark Time, and waters washing through the hole above had damaged much. Yet most of the metal was still stout. He could scrape away the coating of sea deposits and rust to see it bright and strong underneath.

To his right, behind the jumble of battered wall fittings that made no sense, there was an oval of a door, tight shut. He moved cautiously through the debris that covered the floor to feel about for some latch. There was a wheel there—perhaps one must turn that.

But, though he exerted his full strength of arm, the fitting remained immovable. He drew his hammer from his belt and began a rhythmic attack on the wheel, though the quarters were so cramped that he could not get a proper swing.

At first he merely chipped free an age-long deposit of rust and sea life from its surface. Then the stubborn latch yielded a fraction, feeding his excitement. His blows grew stronger, until, with a sudden give, the wheel moved gratingly. Now Sander delivered a fast tattoo, striking with a smith's eye at the most vulnerable angle.

He had, he believed, brought the wheel to face the notch that would release the door catch. Around the edge of the door were encrustations that sealed it. He turned his attention to chipping them away.

At last he rebelted his hammer and set both hands to the wheel, urging the door open. A puff of odd-smelling air blew out from the dark cave of the interior. Air—under the sea?

Sander snatched the light from Fanyi without any by-your-leave, sending its beam into the room beyond. There was a table there that must have been securely fastened to the floor since all the battering this strange ship had

72

taken in its death days had not loosened it. And it was still flanked by benches. Under them, rolled near to the lower side—

He heard Fanyi catch her breath. They had both looked on death, for that was common enough in their world. But this was no death they had seen before. Those shrunken withered things did not now bear any likeness to man.

"They sealed themselves in," Fanyi said softly, "and then the sea took their ship and there was no escape. Before Men—we look now upon Before Men!"

But these things, still clad in rags of clothing—Sander could not believe that such as these had once been men who walked proudly, masters of their world. The Rememberers had chanted of the Before Men, that they were greater, stronger, far more in every way than those who now lived in distorted lands left after the Dark Time. These—these were not the heroes of those chants! He shook his head slowly at his own thoughts.

"They are—were—only men," he said, never aware until this moment that he had, indeed, always held a secret belief that those ancestors must have been far different from his own kind.

"But," Fanyi added softly, "what men they must have been! For this ship sprang from their dreams! I believe that this is one of those meant to sail under water, not on its surface, such as the legends say men possessed in the Before Time."

Sander had a sudden dislike for this place. What manner of men had these poor remnants been who had sealed themselves in a metal shell to travel *under* water? He felt choked, confined, even as he had in the net of the forest people. Yes, perhaps after all, the Before Men were of a different breed, possessing a brand of courage that he frankly admitted he did not have.

He stepped backward, having no wish to explore this ship farther. They could clear some of the litter out of that upper chamber and shelter there until night. But these remains should be left undisturbed in their chosen tomb.

73

"It is theirs, this place." He spoke softly, as he might if he wished not to disturb some sleeper. "Let us leave it wholly theirs."

"Yes," Fanyi assented.

Together they pushed shut that door upon the past and climbed the ladder to the upper level. As they brushed all they could of the debris in the small compartment down the ladder hole to free floor space, Sander came across lengths of wire, pieces of metal that were hardly corroded at all. He recognized them as something the Traders named "stainless steel," another secret from Before, for such did not corrode easily—neither could it be copied. From these pieces, knowing to his disappointment that he could not hope to carry much, he made a judicious selection. Some of the bits could be worked into dart heads, always supposing they could find a place where he might be able once more to labor at his trade.

Fanyi, for her part, combed through the litter for scraps of material on which appeared lines and patterns that she declared were part of the old art of writing. The most portable of these she tucked into a small sack.

In the end they cleared a goodly space in which, cramped though it might be, they could shelter. The fishers refused to come on deck, though Fanyi coaxed them. The pair settled down instead under the shade of the tilted ship. Of Rhin there was no sign. Nor was there any hint that Sander could see, after a searching survey of that part of the surrounding desert he could examine, of any pursuit by the amphibians.

They shared out a handful each of Fanyi's dried fruit, allowing themselves and the fishers each a limited drink. Then they curled up to await the coming of dark.

The day was hot, but lacked the baking, drying heat of the outer world, so they managed to doze. Sander awoke at last in answer to a sharp yelp, which he had heard for much of his life. There was no mistaking the cry of a koyot. He crawled over Fanyi, who murmured in her sleep, ascending the ladder to the deck.

Rhin reared on his hind feet, his front paws planted against the curve of the ship's side. He yelped again, sharply, with a note of commanded attention. Yet it was not a cry of warning.

Sander swung down by the rope. Rhin nosed at him eagerly. The koyot's muzzle and the hair on his front legs were wet—or at least damp, with an overcoating of the sea-bottom sand plastered there by moisture. Rhin had found water!

"What is it?" Fanyi appeared above.

"Rhin has found water!"

"Another river?"

Sander wondered about that with foreboding. Since their experience with the amphibians, from now on he would look upon all streams warily. But water they must have, or else back trail west completely.

Now for the first time he wished there was some more direct method of communication between man and koyot, that he could ask Rhin a question and learn what lay out toward the east where the other had disappeared earlier. But he was assured in this much: Rhin already knew the menace of the amphibians; therefore the koyot would not lead them into any ambush. He said as much, and Fanyi agreed.

The sinking of the sun removed the desert's direct heat. But they still suffered from the rise of salt dust about their feet. Rhin, once more bearing his pack, trotted confidently forward in a direction that, to Sander, only took them farther from the land. However, his confidence in the koyot was such he was sure the animal knew where he was bound.

Before the moon rose, the fishers suddenly pushed to the fore of the small party, looping forward with their usual sinuous gait until they disappeared into a section of towering rocks that must have once been reefs showing above water. They formed knife-edged, sharp ridges, rather than hillocks that could be climbed.

On the other side of one of these, they came to a second deep drop in the sea-desert floor. But edging this was another tumble of those ancient worked blocks. Among them Fanyi's light (which she had been forced to put to use in this uneven footing) picked out a curving curb. Lying within it was the sheen of water, like a dull mirror that had nothing to reflect.

The pool (Fanyi's light moved in a circular pattern to pick out its circumference) was an oval, far too symmetrically formed to be of nature's fashioning. At one side, some of the curbing had given way, allowing the water to lap over and run away in a small riverlet to the edge of the drop, spinning over it in a miniature falls. The drop there was beyond the power of the light to plumb.

Sander tasted the water. Sweet and fresh. He drank from his cupped hands, dashed it over his dusty face. Small rivulets dribbled down his neck and chest, carrying away the grime of the desert. The fishers plunged their muzzles in deep, sucking with audible gulps. Fanyi followed Sander's example, drank and then washed, uttering at last a small sigh of contentment.

"I wonder who built this," she said, as she sat back on her heels.

Sander brought out their water bottle, dumped its contents into the sterile sand before he rinsed it, preparatory to refilling. A sweet water spring in the midst of the ocean—or what had been the ocean! But long before that, it had been on land. The sense of eons of vanished ages hung heavy about this curbed pool. Men reckoned seasons now from the Dark Time. And the Rememberers had counted some three hundred years from the end of one world and the beginning of this one.

But how long before *that* had this sea land been uncovered for the first time so that men—or at least intelligent beings—raised these stone piles that even long ages had not completely worn away, titanic building that raging seas had not entirely erased? He felt dazed when he tried to think of years that must certainly be counted, not by generations of men, but rather by the slow passage of thousands and thousands of seasons.

There was nothing here of that aura of despair and loss that he had felt in the undersea ship. Not even a tenuous kinship linked him with these ancient-upon-ancient builders. Perhaps they had not even been human as he and his kind now reckoned humanity. He wished that Kabor, the senior Rememberer of the Mob, could witness this, though there would be no hint of memory that the sight could awaken within his well-trained mind.

They drank deeply again, leaving the forgotten pool. Twice they had had the good fortune to find water in the desert. Sander could not be sure such luck would hold for a third time. It seemed to him that they had best now angle back west. There was no game to be hunted here. Hunger could strike them as swiftly and in as deadly a fashion as lack of water. The sooner they reached true land, the better, whether they were able to locate Fanyi's goal or not.

The smith half expected her to protest when he suggested an abrupt swing west. But she did not, though she held her pendant for a long moment or two, focusing the light on its surface, as if by that she could check the path they must go.

Here they could not make good time. The ground was very rough, for the ridges left by old reefs sent them on long or short detours. Their clothing and their bodies, their faces, even their hair, were thick with sandy dust, and the coats of the three animals seemed matted with it. As the night wore on, Sander kept looking ahead for some shelter in which to wait out the day.

After the moon rose, they gained a measure of light; Fanyi snapped off her Before Torch. It was perhaps an hour or so before dawn when Sander felt a sudden drop in temperature. He was sweating so that the chill of this new breeze made him shiver. They halted for Fanyi to rearrange her belongings and put on her overcloak. Now they could see their breath issuing forth in white puffs.

The change had come so quickly Sander wondered if some kind of a storm was on its way. Yet so far there was no clouding over of the stars above. More than ever he was aware they must find some secure shelter.

Ahead a dark mass projected well above the surface over which they advanced at a slow crawl. He strained to see that rise better, wondering if they were approaching a one-time island that now stood as a mountain above the denuded plain.

Fanyi flashed her light, holding her pendant directly in its beam.

"That way!" Her voice rang out as she shifted the light to point ahead, toward the dark plateau. She seemed so sure that Sander, for the moment, was willing to follow her lead without question.

By dawn they arrived at the foot of a cliff. Falls of dressed stone, stained by rusty streaks, made Sander sure that above them now lay the remains of a Before city. The scattered and shattered debris about them gave warning that devastation had hit hard here, and there could be little left of any value above—even if they could make the climb.

If this city had once held the storehouse Fanyi sought, then her quest must certainly be doomed to failure. Sander, too, felt a pinch of disappointment, even though, he told himself, he had never truly believed in her rumored treasure house of knowledge.

When he glanced at the girl, he saw no sign of any chagrin in her expression. Rather she eyed the tumble of stone as if she saw in it possibilities for ascent to what lay above. And her manner was brisk as if she were sure she was on the right trail and what she sought was near.

"This is the place?" he asked.

Fanyi had her pendant in hand again. Slowly she

pivoted, until she no longer faced the cliff, but rather once more the western lands.

"Not here," she said with quiet confidence, "but there." She waved to the more distant shadow of the land.

Sander believed that the city above had been built on a cape projecting out into the vanished sea, or even an island. To reach the true shore of the Before Days one would have to travel still farther west.

They needed food and water. That either could be found in the tangle of shattered ruin above, the smith doubted. He thought that perhaps their best plan was to keep to the sea bottom, heading directly for the land.

However, he had not foreseen the coming of the storm, which that earlier cold wind had heralded. Clouds arose out of nowhere in only a few breaths of time, while the wind became a lash of freezing cold, under which they cringed.

The animals made their decision for them. Like two streaks of looping fur the fishers were already swarming up the fall that formed a vast and uneven stairway to the ruins above. Rhin was not far behind. There was that in the quick flight of all three that Sander found alarming enough to goad him to follow. Rhin's senses were far more acute than his own. In the past he had been saved by the koyot's superior gifts of scent or hearing. If Rhin chose that path, there was an adequate reason.

Both the fishers and the koyot were surefooted on that broken trail. Sander and Fanyi, shivering under each blast of wind, had to go more slowly. Too many of the blocks rocked under their weight, some crashing down under the pull of the wind. They flattened themselves to each stable surface they reached, forcing themselves to grope farther up when they caught their breaths again.

At last they crawled over a dangerous overhang of perilously piled materials to reach a wilderness of mounds from which protruded rusty shells of metal, likely to powder at a touch.

But there was also a show of vegetation, vines withering now with the touch of frost, saw-edged grass in ragged patches, even a wind-whittled tree or so.

Sander's first thought was that they must keep well away from any pile of rubble that seemed likely to crash. He kept glancing overhead as he felt his way along, cautious lest he step on something that would shift disastrously under his weight. Fanyi moved behind him, choosing in turn each step he had pioneered.

At least the force of the wind was abated here by these mounds. And, while the cold was intense, they were not belabored by freezing blasts.

It began to rain. And the rain was as cold as the wind, the force of it penetrating their garments, plastering their hair to their skulls, seeming to encase their shrinking flesh with a coating of glass-thin ice. Sander had known storms on the plains, but nothing such as this.

The wind roared and howled over their heads in a queer wailing, perhaps because it shuttled back and forth through openings in the mounds. Now and then they could hear crashes as if the gale brought down new rock falls. Then, when there came a lull, Sander heard the bark of Rhin.

"This way—" He turned to the girl. But the words he mouthed were lost in the rise of the wind's fury. He reached out to catch her hand.

They rounded a mound, to see before them a line of true trees, now whipped by the storm, leaves being torn ruthlessly from their branches and sent in whirling clouds, to be as quickly borne to earth by the weight of the rain.

Sander staggered forward, away from the treacherous mounds into the fringe of the trees. The branches absorbed some of the force of the rain but not all of it. Rhin paced impatiently back and forth, his head swinging as he looked from Sander to the way ahead, patiently urging the humans to hurry. Of the fishers there was no sign.

They felt underfoot the relative smoothness of one of the paved ways, though the trees and bushes had encroached thickly upon it. Here there were no looming piles of blocks to threaten them as they hurried after the koyot. In a few moments they came out into a clearing where there was a shelter made of wood at one side. Its staked walls met a thatch of thickly interwoven branches. A single door stood open, and there was no sign of any inhabitant, even though this building was plainly of their own time.

Sander plucked thrower and bolt from his belt and waved Fanyi behind him, as he cautiously slipped toward the open door.

It was when Kai poked a nose from the doorway that he knew his fears were needless. In a last dash, the koyot, Sander, and Fanyi reached the opening and scrambled within, Sander jerking the door to in their wake.

It must have been open for some time because there was a drift of soil he had to loosen before he could close it firmly to keep out the fury of the storm. And since there were only slits, high-set under the roof, to give any light, he found it difficult at first to view their surroundings.

This was not the rude or temporary hut he had guessed it to be at first sight, but a large and sturdy building. The floor had been cleared down to a reasonably smooth surface of stone, which might once have been a part of a road. Against the far wall was a wide fireplace constructed of firm blocks, its gaping maw smoke- and fire-stained but now empty. There was a box to one side in which he could distinguish some lengths of wood standing end up.

Fanyi had pulled out her light and shone its circle of brilliance along the log walls. Shelves hung there. For the most part they were bare, save for a small box or two. Under the shelves were the frames of what could only be sleeping bunks. These were still filled with masses of leaves and bits of brush, all much broken and matted together.

Sander caught the faint scent of old fires and, he thought, even of food. But there was also an emptiness here which, he believed, meant that it had been a long time since the place was inhabited.

"This is a clan house," Fanyi said. "See—" She held her light beam high on one wall showing a big metal hook set into the log. "There they hung divide curtains. But this was a small clan."

"Your people?" He had believed that Padford had been the only settlement those had known.

Fanyi shook her head. "No. But Traders perhaps.

82

They live in clans also. They do not take their women or children with them on the trail, but sometimes they have talked of their homes. And this city would be a fine place for their metal searches. They may have cleared this portion of it and moved on—or else heard of richer hunting grounds elsewhere. I think this has been empty for more than one season."

The building was stout enough, Sander conceded. Now that a bar had been dropped into the waiting hooks, sealing the door, he was far less aware of the storm's force. He headed to the hearth, choosing wood from the box. The lengths were well seasoned, and he had no difficulty in striking a spark from his firebox, so that the warmth of flames soothed them as well as gave light to their new quarters. The fishers lay by the fire, licking moisture from their fur. Even Rhin seemed not too large for the long room.

Shelter, warmth—but they still needed food. Fanyi delved into the few containers on the wall shelves. She returned with two on which tight sliding covers had been fastened. These contained a small measure of what looked like the same kind of meal Sander had found in Padford and some flakes of a dried substance.

"They cannot have gone too long ago after all," Fanyi observed, "for this meal is not musty or molded. And the other is dried meat."

Straightway, she shed her square cloak, leaving it to steam dry before the fire. That done, she mixed cakes of the meal and meat flakes, having passed to the fishers and Rhin the major portion of the latter.

Sander prowled about the long room, taking note of its construction. Much work had gone into its erection. He could not believe that this was only a temporary structure. Rather it must have been meant to stand. Perhaps it was intended for seasonal occupation.

In the far corner he came upon a circular piece of metal, pitted and worn, but still solid, set in the stone of the floor. There was a bar crossing its top, and he thought that with pressure applied through that the lid could be raised. Perhaps there was a store room below, with more supplies than the meager amount Fanyi had found.

He went back to the woodbox, chose a length and returned to lever up that strange door. It took some effort, yet at last he could slide the round metal to one side. Crouching low he stared down into thick darkness. There was, he saw as the fireplace flames flickered a little in this direction, the beginning of a ladder of metal. So there was indeed a way into the depths.

Lying belly down, he ran his hands down the ladder as far as he could reach. The steps that formed it had been patched with a crude stripping of other bits of metal. But the smell that arose to him did not, he believed, come from any storage place. It was damp and unpleasant, so much so that he jerked back his head and coughed. The larger fisher had come to the opposite side of the hole, thrusting its head forward to sniff. Now Kai hissed, expressing his own dislike of the unknown. Sander wriggled the cover back into place. He had no desire to go exploring down there in the dark.

Sander took the further precaution of wedging a length of wood through the lifting handle so that it protruded against the hard floor on either side, hoping that this might provide a lock. He had no idea what might threaten from below, but his adventures in the forest and with the river amphibians had been warning enough to take care in any strange circumstance.

Now and again the house shook from a gust of the wind. They had drawn as close as they could to the fire, shedding their soaked clothing by degrees to dry it piece by piece.

The wood box had been well filled, but Sander, fearful that the supply might not last through the storm, had been eyeing the shelves along the wall. He believed they could be battered free and used to feed the flames. Just now it was enough to feel the heat and be sure they had found a shelter, not haunted and dangerous as the ruins might have been, one made by those of their own species.

The roar of thunder was often followed by a distant crash. Sander believed that the gale took new tribute from the rubble mounds. And the small windows high in the eaves gave frame to brilliant flashes of lightning. The fishers and Rhin seemed uneasy, no longer settling in the fire warmth as they had at first.

Sander watched them narrowly. He could not be sure that it was only the wildness of the display outside that affected the animals. Instead, his imagination suggested menaces creeping toward their shelter. Twice he got up, first to inspect the bar across the door, then that other he hoped would seal off the hole in the floor. Both seemed tight enough.

Once they had eaten, Fanyi seated herself near the hearth, her cloak belted about her while she spread to dry her scanter undergarment. Her mat of hair straggled in wild tufts, which she made no attempt to put into order. Instead she sat with her eyes closed, her hands once more clasped over her pendant. There was about her an aura of withdrawal. She might have been asleep, even though she sat straight-backed and unrelaxing. If she was not, she used another method to block out the present, retiring fully into her own thoughts. That this might be part of her Shaman's training Sander accepted.

In time the fishers quietly came to crouch, one on either side of her, their heads resting on their paws. But they were not asleep, for whenever Sander made the slightest move, he could see their bright eyes regarding him.

He was restless, feeling shut out and cut adrift by Fanyi's absorption. Rhin at last lay down between the fire and the door. But Sander could see that the koyot's ears were ever aprick, as if he still listened.

The thunder rolls were dying and the lightning no longer flashed in the high windows. However, the drum of rain on the roof over their heads did not grow lighter. After their trek by night, Sander longed to sleep and he found now that he nodded, started awake, only to nod again. He had no desire to climb into one of the bunks, his wariness keeping him from relaxing entirely. And his vigilance was proven necessary when Fanyi gave a start, her eyes snapping open, her head up as if she listened.

Yet none of the three animals displayed any like unease. "What is it?" Sander demanded.

He saw the tip of her tongue sweep across her lips.

"There is thought—seeking thought—" she answered, but she spoke almost absently, and as if she did not want to lessen her concentration.

Her words meant nothing to him. Thought—what was *seeking* thought?

"There is some one—some one who is shaman trained," she continued. "But this—" Her hands moved away from her pendant. She held them up and out, lightly cupped, as if to catch in her palms some elusive stream of invisible water, "This is so strong! And it is not wholly pure thought —there is something else—"

"I don't understand what you would say," Sander returned brusquely, trying to break through the air of otherwhere that clung to her. "I do not know the ways of Shamans. Do you mean that someone is coming?"

Again he glanced at the animals. But they were quiet, even though they watched. He could not believe that Rhin would allow any stranger to approach without giving full warning.

Fanyi's expression was one of excitement, not fear. It was as if she were a smith and before her lay some problem of smelting for which she now clearly saw the answer. He, himself, well knew the feeling of exultation such few moments could bring.

"It—there is no enemy." She appeared to be choosing words. "There is no awareness of us—that I could read at once. I feel the power of a sending, but it is not my power, and I cannot tell the nature of the matter with which it is concerned. Only there is one who sends. Ah— now it is gone!" She sounded disappointed. "There is no more reach—"

That she believed passionately in what she spoke of, Sander knew. But he could not accept those facts that seemed so much a part of her beliefs. A Rememberer, now, spent long years of "remembering"—of listening over and over again to chants of past events, which it was necessary the Mob be able to draw upon for help in untangling some new problem. The lineage of all the kin was so remembered that there not be too close uniting of birth relationships, weakening the people as a whole. The care of the herd, the very contours of the lands over which they had roamed in the seasons upon seasons since the Dark Time, all that lay in the mind of a Rememberer, to be summoned at will. But this seeking thought——? How could one seek save physically by eye, voice, body?

"The Traders have these seekers?" he asked now. That breed of wanderers with a purpose, who had sought out the Mob, seemed little different from his own people. They were jealous of their secrets, yes. But those were secrets of trails and of the places where they found their basic stocks, the metal that was so necessary for making tools and weapons. They told wild tales of the lands they crossed to bring that metal, yet most of the Mob had been agreed that there was method in those stories—— meant to warn off any curiosity on the part of outsiders. Traders had been known to kill lest some favorite supply place become open to those not of their own particular clan. But they said nothing of this mind-seek.

"I have never heard that such was so," Fanyi replied promptly. "The Traders who came to Padford"——she shook her head again——"they were no more nor less than any of the villagers. Yet we have already seen strange peoples who are not of our blood. Think you of the forest savages or of those who swarm in the river. This world is very full of wonders, and he who travels learns."

"The Traders tell wild enough tales, but those are meant to afright men and keep their own secrets safe."

"Or so we have always said," she returned. "But perhaps there is a small seed of truth at the center core of such."

Sander would have laughed, but then he reconsidered. It was true that he had been shaken out of his complacency in the domination of his own species by their two brushes with forest and river dwellers. Though the Mob had never met any except herdsmen like themselves or the far-ranging Traders, could they say that those were the *only* people left in the world? The fishermen of Padford differed in coloring and life ways from his own kin. And he had heard of the Sea Sharks who made up the slaving bands from the south, though no man had ever understood why they collected the helpless to take into captivity. Those, too, were men—of a kind.

Now he began to recall some of the Trader stories. Suppose she was right? Suppose there *were* armored beasts of giant size roving elsewhere, slaying any man they met; flying things that were neither man nor bird but mingled something of each in an uncanny and horrifying way, their talons raised against normal man? It was easier to believe that the earth still bubbled and boiled in places, that if any ventured too far into such tormented country they died from the poisons filling the air or sank by inches into a steaming mud from which they could not fight free.

"You see"—she smiled now—"I have led you to re-think what you have heard. Therefore, perhaps it is also reasonable to believe that elsewhere there are Shamans to whom I am as but a small child, still unlearned in even the simplest of the healing ways. What"—she flung her hands wide as if to garner in against her breast some thing that seemed precious to her—"what marvels may exist in this world, open to our finding if we only have the courage to seek for them! If someone has learned to mind-seek—then I shall also do this! Am I not of the kin-blood to whom such knowledge is as meat and drink? Young and untried I may seem to such ones, yet I can say in truth—we are of one kind of mind, therefore let me learn of you."

Sander watched her excitement, troubled. Yes, he could understand her thirst for learning, was it not also his? But what he wanted was a learning that brought concrete results, that did not deal with such unreasonable matters as thoughts that were loosed, as it were, to roam. Rather he wanted to know more about what he could make with his two hands when their skill was well harnessed by his mind. It gave him a queer feeling to think of using thought in some other way, not to accompany physical action, but in place of that—if he had guessed aright what she hoped to gain.

"I believed"—he strove now to return her to the obvious —"that what you sought was a weapon of vengeance for your people."

"And do you not know," Fanyi flashed, "that thought itself can be as able a weapon, if it is skillfully used, as those forged darts of yours? Yes, I have a debt to the dead; do not believe that I have ever forgotten that." There was a flush rising beneath her dark brown skin. "Now—" She rose to her feet. "I say we should sleep. My fur people, your Rhin, they shall play our watch."

"The fire—"

Away from the hearth it was cold.

Fanyi laughed. "Do not worry. Kai knows much." She laid her hand on the head of the larger fisher. "He shall watch the fire, and well. This has he done for me before."

She chose a bunk along the nearer wall, taking her now dried and warmed under-robe to twist about her. Sander watched her settle in before he followed her example. The last thing he remembered seeing was the larger fisher lifting a piece of kindling from the box, catching the length between his powerful jaws and pushing it into the fire with the dexterity of one who indeed had performed that same act many times in the past.

So Sander settled himself to sleep. And he was deep in a dream wherein he trudged through a long dark tunnel, drawn ever by the sharp tap-tap of a hammer on metal, seeking a smith who had all secrets and from whom he must learn.

A cold touch on his cheek brought him out of that corridor before he ever caught sight of the so-industrious smith. Rhin loomed over him, and it was the koyot's nose that had touched his face. The animal lowered his muzzle for a second such prod as Sander came fully awake and sat up.

The sound of the wind, the heavy pelt of the rain, was gone. It was so still that he could hear the sound of his own breath, a faint crackling of the fire. But the fishers no longer lay by it. They were ranged one on either side of the barred door, facing it. And when Rhin saw that Sander was fully awake, he looked in the same direction.

Sander sat up and reached for his boots. They had dried after a fashion, but he found it hard to force his feet into them. While he struggled to do that, he listened.

He could pick up nothing, but he relied fully on the warning of the animals and he did not doubt that there was someone or something near enough to arouse their instincts of alarm. The Traders returning to their house?

That need not be a real matter for fear. The laws of hospitality, which were scrupulously kept save among the Sea Sharks, would excuse their intrusion here in such a storm, jealous as the Traders were. Sander hoped furiously that this was the case.

Still, he caught up his dart thrower, loosened his long knife in its sheath, as he padded, as softly as he could, across the room to lay his ear tight to the barred door.

$\mathbb{T}$hat Sander heard nothing did not mean that the alarm was false. Now he reslung his weapon in his girdle and turned to the wall on which hung the shelves. They might be used as a ladder, allowing him to peer out one of the high windows.

Swiftly Sander cleared the remaining containers from the shelves he selected, tested the anchorage of the boards by swinging his full weight upon them. Though the wood creaked protestingly, they held firm. He scrambled up, to crouch perilously on the narrow top plank, struggling to retain his balance as he reached farther overhead and caught at either side of the narrow window opening.

These had been covered, sealed against the air, by pieces of glass, a refinement that surprised him. Had glass, the most fragile of inheritances from the Before Time, actually existed in this rubble in pieces large enough to be salvaged?

Sander brought his face as close as he could to that surface. He discovered that the glass was not clear, carrying within it bubbles and distortions, as he tried to peer outside. Yet those imperfections did not prevent a good sight of the clearing immediately before the house.

The darkness of the storm was past. It was, he judged by the angle of the pale sunlight that struck full against the door, late afternoon. But it was not time he was interested in—rather what might be prowling out there.

A wide expanse lay clear immediately before the door. The brush, which formed the first rank of the wood growth, stood some distance away. On the ground was a light skiff of snow and that was not unmarked!

The snow must have fallen near the end of the storm. Already it began to melt under the direct rays of the sun, especially around the edges of numerous tracks. Through the bubbled glass Sander could not make out any clearly defined print, but they were larger than those made by any animal he knew.

Shapeless as they seemed, there was something about their general proportions—Sander would not allow himself to speculate. Nor could he even be certain that more than one creature had left its signature there. A single unknown thing might have scented them, plodded back and forth for a space.

Sander shifted on his narrow perch. He could see where those tracks had emerged from the wood, but no sign they had returned thither. Was the creature prowling about the back of the house now?

At that moment the silence inside and out was broken by a high, wailing cry, startling Sander so he almost tumbled from his spy post. He heard from below the answering growl of Rhin, the hissing of both fishers, then a soft call from Fanyi:

"What was that?"

"I do not know." Sander twisted his body around, striving to see farther both right and left. "There is something prowling outside. But I have not yet sighted it."

His last word had hardly left his lips before a bulk shuffled into the sun, coming from the left as it had just completed another circuit of the house.

The thing halted before the door, its out-thrust head nearly on a level with the window from which he viewed

it. What was it? Animal—? Yet it walked upright. And now that Sander studied it more closely, he thought that its covering of matted and filthy-looking skin was not part of its own hide, but rather clothing of a sort.

Clothing? This was a *man*?

Sander swallowed. The thing was as huge as the forest female had been. Its head, hunched almost against its shoulders suggesting that its neck must be very short indeed, had an upstanding crest of stiffened hair, the ends of which flopped over to half conceal small eyes. Now it impatiently raised a vast clawed hand, or paw, to push the hair away.

They had felt no kinship with the forest people, and this was an even greater travesty of the human shape. The legs were short and thick, supporting a massive trunk. In contrast, the arms were very long, the fingertips scraping the ground when the creature allowed them to dangle earthward.

Its jaw was more a muzzle than the lower part of a true face, and a straggle of beard waggled from the point of it. Altogether the thing was a nightmare such as a child might dream of to awake screaming for comfort.

Now it shuffled forward, planting one wide fist against the barred door, plainly exerting pressure. Sander heard the grind of the wood against the bar. Whether that would hold—?

He dropped hastily from his perch. The creature outside now aimed blows against the door, and the bar might or might not continue to hold, while the snarling of the koyot and the fishers grew into a wild crescendo. It was plain that they had reason to fear the attacker.

"It is—" Sander gave the girl a quick explanation of what he had seen. "Have you heard of such before?"

"Yes, from a Trader," she returned promptly. "He said that these haunt the lands of the north and are eaters of men. You see, smith, here is one of their tales indeed proven true."

The crashing against the door was steady. The bar might hold, but would the pins that supported it prove as stout? For them to be caught within— As far as he

93

had seen, the thing carried no weapons, but with those mighty hands what more would it need?

No wonder the builders of this place had set it above that floor bolt-hole. Sander crossed quickly to that, jerking the wooden latch he had inserted with such care. As he levered up the round top, the whole house began to tremble under the assault from without.

"Get a torch!" he ordered Fanyi. She had warned him of the limited life her own light might have, and he had no wish to be caught in some dark run below.

The girl ran to the fire, snatched up a long piece of wood, and thrust one end into the flames. Silken fur swept past Sander's arm. The fishers were already flowing into the opening. Rhin—could Rhin make it? Stripped of his burdens, Sander hoped so. The koyot trotted to the smith's side, dropped his head to sniff into the opening.

Then he turned his rump to the hole, cautiously backed in. As the outer door cracked down its middle, Rhin disappeared as if he had fallen. A moment later he yelped reassuringly from below. Sander tossed down the bags Fanyi handed to him, held the torch while the girl swung onto that patched ladder.

After she was well down, Sander wriggled the cover back halfway over the hole, leaving but a narrow space to squeeze through. He lowered the torch to her reaching hand, lying belly-flat to accomplish that exchange, then sought the ladder himself.

Partway down, he tugged at the metal cover, making a last great effort at the sound of breaking wood from aloft. In the flame of the torch he could see now a metal bar fastened to the underside, a crude piece of work that must have been added long after the Before Days. With a last frantic lunge he sent that across, locking the lid above his head into place.

They had descended to a large round tunnel, he discovered. There was no sign of the fishers, but Rhin waited. The koyot whined softly, plainly liking none of this place, now and then audibly sniffing the ill-smelling air.

If they advanced from here, the koyot must drop to

his haunches and crawl. Fanyi had stuck the torch up-right in a ring set roughly into the wall. Now she was busy knotting their gear into back packs, since it was plain Rhin could not transport it along these confined ways. Sander hoped desperately that the tunnel grew no smaller or the koyot could not force a way through it.

"Look!" Fanyi pointed with her chin as her hands flew to tighten knots.

The piece of wood she had brought from the house was nearly consumed. But, leaning against the wall under the hoop that held it, were a number of better-constructed torches, their heads round balls of fiber soaked in what Sander's nose told him must be fish oil.

It would seem by these preparations that the builders of the house had forseen emergencies when it would be necessary for them to take to these underground ways. Was the presence of the beast now above the reason why they had left their well-wrought shelter?

Sander lighted one of the torches, divided the rest, giving half to the girl. Then, bending his head a little, he started down the tunnel, hearing the complaining whines of Rhin as the koyot edged along with Fanyi behind him.

There was no way of telling how long that piece of tunnel was nor even in what direction it ran. Part of it had collapsed, been redug, and shored up. Finally they came to a hole hacked in one side and struggled through it into a much larger way, one in which Rhin could stand upright. The floor of this was banded by two long rails of metal that came out of the dark on one side and vanished into it again on the other. The fugitives paused, Sander unsure whether to turn right or left.

"Aeeeeheee!" Fanyi gave her summoning call to the fishers, and she was straightway answered from their left.

"That way." It was plain she had full confidence in her companions. "They have ranged on, now they believe they are heading out—"

The smith could only hope her confidence was well placed. Torch in hand and held at the best angle to show them the uneven footing, he turned left.

There seemed to be no end to this way under the Before City. Though Sander was almost sure that the thing that had besieged the house could never squeeze its bulk through the opening in the floor, even if it could tear loose the lock on the lid, he kept listening intently for any hint they were being pursued.

His torch picked out trickles of slimy moisture down the walls of the larger tunnel. Yet it seemed quite intact otherwise, with no fall of roof or sides to threaten them. Then the light picked up a mass that nearly choked it.

As Sander drew nearer, he saw that that this was not composed of any slippage of the walls, rather it was rusting metal that filled the opening top to bottom, leaving only narrow passages on either side. Those the fishers had undoubtedly been able to venture through. And he and Fanyi could undoubtedly do so also, but he doubted if Rhin could force a way.

Handing the torch to the girl, Sander shrugged out of his pack and brought from that his tool bag. He chose the heaviest of his hammers and went to face the rusty mass.

Under the first of his blows the metal crumpled, some of it merely a dust of rust. Whether it could be treated so, to open a passage, he could not be sure, but he would try. In spite of the chill damp his exertions brought the sweat running so heavily that he had to stop and strip off his shirt as well as his hide jacket. And his back and arms, having foregone the discipline of daily work for too long, ached.

Still, he swung and smashed with a rhythm that speedily returned since he had known it for so long. Foot by foot, he cleared a wider passage to the left. Luckily not too much of the obstruction needed to be beaten away. Rhin pushed carefully along behind Fanyi, who held the torch high. Midway through, that brand was exhausted, so she lit a second from the supply she carried.

The metal was very brittle. Sander guessed that erosive damp had brought on the consuming rust. He studied the wreckage when he paused for breath, trying to guess what it had been. It had, he decided, probably transported either men or supplies beneath the surface of the city.

They coughed as the dust from his hammering arose, until Fanyi tore strips from her clothing and tied them over their mouths and around Rhin's muzzle, wetting them from the water supply in their bottle.

The crashing blows of the hammer made Sander's head ring. If the monster had followed them down, it would be in no confusion over which direction it must take to follow them.

There was a final subsidence of a last metal plate and once more they faced the open way. Sander was hungry as well as dry-mouthed with thirst. But any remedy for that state still lay before them, and all they could do was to struggle along as quickly as they could.

Not far ahead was a branching of the way. Once more Fanyi sounded her call to the fishers. But this time there came no answer. And though they pushed the torch close to the surface of the ground, they could detect no tracks. Sander turned to Rhin. For the first time the koyot moved out with more assurance than he had shown since they had taken to this underground way.

He lowered his head to sniff along the edge of those rusted shells of rails and to search the ground between them. Then he gave a sharp yelp of command and trotted along the inner of the two ways. Luckily they came to no more of those plugs of metal. But the passage sloped downward, and there were spreading patches of wet upon the walls, signs also that at one time water had risen to a point within a hand's-breadth of the roof.

Sander watched those walls. It could well be that they had been loosened with the passing of the years, that even the small disturbance made by the passing of their own party could bring about a fall, entrapping or killing them all. Under his urging, they made the swiftest passage that they could. Yet that seemed to him to be agonizingly slow, and he listened tensely, not now for the monster that had attacked the house, but rather for any sound of shifting over their heads.

Fanyi called out and pointed ahead. There was a pile

of the same rubble as he had seen in the mounds above. And this choked the whole of the way. But over it was a jagged hole in the roof, under which the debris made an unsteady platform.

A head hung in the open, eyes staring down at them. It was plain that the fishers had not hesitated to try that escape route, as dubious as it looked. Kai's head disappeared as Rhin moved forward.

With caution, the koyot placed his forepaws, one after the other, part way up the mound of crumbling stuff, which sent a trickle of gravel and small stones thudding down as he so moved. He stood still, nosing ahead at the next portion of the rise, as if scent could assure him whether or not it would bear his weight.

Sander and Fanyi edged away as Rhin made a slow climb. The koyot panted as he went, his tongue lolling out of his half-open jaws, drool dripping from its tip. He planted each paw with delicate precision.

Up again, and another cascade of finer rubble. Only one more length and his head would be out of that hole. Sander crept to the edge of the mound, held the torch as high as he could to give Rhin all possible help.

Once more gravel rolled, bringing with it that same coarse sand that had slipped under their feet when they crossed the sea-desert. Now Rhin's head and shoulders were out into the opening. His muscles bunched as he lunged up, scrabbling furiously on the edge of the opening with his forepaws.

Sander jumped back to escape the slide the koyot's efforts caused. Now Rhin showed his head once more in the hole, looking downward and uttering a series of barks as if urging the humans to duplicate his feat as soon as possible.

The smith lit a second torch and then a third. These he planted butt down in the pile so they threw full light over that treacherous shifting surface. He shed his pack once more and pulled forth his coil of braided hide rope before he spoke to Fanyi.

"I am going up. When I make it, lash our packs, then stand well clear until I pull those up. After that I'll drop the rope. Make it fast to your waist, and take all the time you need for the climb."

With the rope's end tied about his middle, he faced the slope. That last slide of gravel and small stones had luckily uncovered the edges of a few larger rocks that promised more stable footing. He tested the lowest of them as best he could and then cautiously scrambled up on it.

The space was narrow, hardly wide enough to afford room for his toes as he felt above, his hands slipping through loose material twice, before, under the moving stuff, he could locate a firm block. Wriggling carefully along, he managed to reach the second perch. Rhin gazed down, his yelps increased in volume. It was plain he was offering his full encouragement.

This last bit was even more tricky. Rhin's emergence had broken the edge. In order to reach the crumbling remains, Sander must squirm forward over what looked in the limited light to be a very uncertain bit of surface. He remained where he was for a long moment, trying to breathe evenly, to steady his nerves before he moved out. Though he had never admitted this weakness, Sander had never taken joyfully to any scramble up a height, even when the surface he sought to climb was more hospitable. He did know enough not to look back, to concentrate only on what lay immediately ahead. He could not remain forever where he now was; there was nothing left to do but trust to fortune and his own strength and make this last attempt.

Now he dug both hands into the mass, seeking some better support. His nails tore, and he felt sharp pain in his fingers, ground between moving stones. But at last, he tightened his hold on something that did not shift as he slowly exerted more and more weight.

Sander pulled himself up as the whole surface under him appeared to crack. Somehow he got a firm brace under one knee, used that to push out farther ahead. He was still inches away from the edge, and he feared more than ever to trust any hold.

Rhin's head had swung. Without warning the koyot

snapped, his jaws closing on the hide jacket that strained tightly over Sander's shoulders. The fangs in those jaws grazed skin as well as covering, and Sander gave a startled yell.

Rhin's unexpected move brought him up, and he surged, much as the koyot had before him, out, skidding free across self-encrusted ground under the full light of a large and glowing moon.

After that it was easy enough to jerk up their gear, find a convenient small rock to weight the rope, and drop it once more to Fanyi. With a line lashed about her, and Sander's strength added to hers, her ascent was far easier and speedier than his struggle had been.

Once both were aloft, they had a chance to look about them. To the west rose the lines of a sloping beach. To the east was the plateau that once must have been an island, holding the near vanished city. The tunnel they had followed plainly had once run under the arm of the sea to connect the island with the main continent.

But where they were was certainly too open. That monster had perhaps not followed them into the lower ways. But if it or perhaps its fellows were denned in the city, one such could sight their small party here in the open and be on their trail again.

Sander found his body trembling as he stopped for his pack. His exertions in the tunnel, his hunger, and the tension of that last climb were taking their toll. To reach the one-time shore—to somehow find a shelter there—that he must force his body to do.

At least they could give the packs back to Rhin here in the open. Sander fumbled with the rope, packing and lashing the gear. They had the rest of the torches still, but it was better not to light them and so mark themselves to any hostile eyes. They must make the moonlight do.

Stumbling often, Sander walked beside Rhin, Fanyi on the other side of the koyot. The fishers had again vanished. The smith supposed they had headed toward the beach.

He wavered as he walked, trying to control the shaking of his hands, ashamed to display his fatigue to Fanyi.

Luckily the terrain sloped upward gradually. There was

no cliff to climb. Once up on the shore, they were ankle-deep in beach sand, faced by a wilderness of rocks, with grass growing among them. Sander lifted his head enough to look for the wood that had masked this same shore to the south where they had left it what seemed a very long time ago.

However, there was no dark line of trees. This land was far more open, though here and there were the same mounds of rubble that had marked the island. It was plain that this city had been a place of great extent, its buildings spreading also to the mainland.

"Let us find some shelter quickly." Fanyi's voice held a note of strain. "I cannot say how far I can now go or how long I can keep my feet."

He was grateful to her at that moment, he did not know how much longer he could keep going either. Yet some inner pride kept him from making the same confession.

In the end they both hooked a hand in the ropes that held Rhin's burden, so that the koyot was more than half supporting them as they reeled into a fairly open space, a hollow where some bushes had rooted.

Snow had fallen here and still lay in small patches, reflecting the moonlight. But the punishing wind had died, and the night was very still. Sander shivered. His fingers were stiff and numb as he fumbled with the knots that fastened their gear, letting it thud to earth. Out from behind one of the hillocks that marked the ruins flashed the fishers. Kai carried a limp body in his mouth, dropping his burden at Fanyi's feet. He had brought in a very large hare.

Rhin, now bare of back, sniffed once at the game, made a low sound in his throat, and trotted off purposefully, intent, Sander knew, on providing his own food. The smith studied this hollow they had chanced upon. At least two of the rubble hills stood between them and the arm of the sea-desert. They could not spend the night without warmth and food.

He knelt to hack at a wiry bush. The dry and sapless

growth broke easily under his touch. Moments later he had a small fire ablaze and was able to turn his full attention to skinning and gutting the hare.

For two days they kept to the campsite. There was no threat here of any of the dangers they had met elsewhere, no sign that the monstrosity from the old island had its kin here. Sander went hunting, using his sling to knock over hares and a kind of runt-deer that was smaller than even Kayi. These animals were so bold Sander believed they had never been hunted—a further proof this land was safe for the wayfarers.

The days grew colder, their nights were spent between fitful dozing and care of their fire. Snow fell again, not heavily, but enough to cover the ground. Sander disliked the fact that their tracks to and away from their camp were so well marked across that white expanse. He tried every dodge known to disguise these, only to admit that he was unsuccessful.

There was no way of adequately curing the hare skins. But they scraped them as clean as they could, then lashed the pelts together in a bundle. Sander already knew that their clothing was not heavy enough for this climate, so they might soon be reduced to using those hides, smelly and unworked as the pelts were, for additional warmth.

Fanyi sat for long spaces of time, the pendant clasped tight in her hands, so entranced that she was little aware of what was going on about her. Twice she reported that she had again encountered what she persisted in calling the "seeking mind." Neither time, she was sure, had that thought been aware of her. Nor was there, to her infinite disappointment, any way of her tracing it to the source. Which was just as well as far as Sander was concerned. His mistrusted her accounts of what he still could not accept as possible.

During his hunting he also prospected for metal. But if any had been here after the Dark Time, it must have been mined long ago by Traders. And he did come upon holes recent enough to suggest that they had not been made during the catastrophe, which had changed the world, but were due to burrowings since that time.

The sheer size of this expanse of debris-strewn wilderness was amazing. How many Before people had lived here? Far greater numbers surely than any Mob could count. Sander had followed Rhin to the bank of another river, this one half-choked with fallen stone, which must wind to the now distant sea on the other side of the raised island.

Man and animal were both wary of the water, one standing on guard while the other filled the water bag. However, so far Sander had neither heard nor seen any evidence of amphibians. There were some fish—he took one with an improvised pole and line—a long narrow creature that startled him with its likeness to a snake and that he quickly loosed again, knowing he could not stomach its clammy flesh.

It was near the river that he found the head. Not the head or skull of any creature that had lived, rather one wrought in stone. Big as his two fists balled together, it was clearly very old, the neck being broken raggedly across. And it was the head of a bird, with a fierce proud look about it that somehow attracted him.

He brought it back to show to Fanyi. She turned the

carving around in her hands, examining it closely.

"This," she pronounced firmly, "was an emblem of power or chieftainship. It is a good omen that you have found it."

Sander half laughed. "I do not deal in omens, Shaman. That is not the way of my people. But this is a thing that was well made. If it had a special meaning for him who wrought it, then I can understand why he dealt so well in its fashioning—"

She might not have heard him; that withdrawn look had returned.

"There was a great building," she said. "Very tall—very, very tall. And this was part of a whole bird with outspread wings. Above the door was that bird set—and—" Fanyi let the lump of stone fall to the ground, rubbed the back of her hand across her eyes as if to push something away. "It had a meaning," she repeated. "It was the totem of a great people and a far stretching land."

"This land?" Sander glanced around the heaped mounds. "Well, if it were such a totem, then its power failed them in the end."

Slowly Fanyi reached forth a hand once more and touched the broken-off head. "All totems failed in the Dark Time, smith. For the land and sea, wind and fire turned against man. And what can totems do to stand against the death of a whole world?"

She took up the head once again and set it on a stone, wedging it upright with smaller pebbles. After she had made it secure Fanyi bowed her head.

"Totem of the dead," she said softly, "we pay you honor again. If there lingers any of your power to summon, may you lend us that. For we are the blood of men, and men fashioned you as a symbol to abide in protection above their strong places." Her hands moved in gestures Sander did not understand.

Let Fanyi deal with unseen powers and totems; he was much more interested in the here and now. Yet looking upon his find, Sander thought that he would like to enwrap it in clay, bake from it a mold into which

105

he could run, perhaps, easily worked copper, and so fashion a symbol tied with the past. But the head was too heavy to carry with them now. It was far better he cling to the scraps of metal he had found in the wreckage of the ship.

He grew impatient. They had rested here long enough, gained their needed supplies, for he had dried some of the meat in the smoke of the fire. To remain longer brought them nothing.

"Your guide—that thing you wear," he said to the girl. "Where does it point now?"

Again she turned her head to northwest. But to go in that direction meant trailing through more remains of the city. He would have felt freer and more at ease had they headed straight west where he guessed these graveplaces of Before man's holdings might sooner cease to show.

Sander, in spite of his impatience, allowed two more days to add to their supplies. The weather was clear but colder each morning. However, there were no more such storms as had struck at them earlier. Finally, on the fifth morning after their winning to what had been the old shore line, they started off. Above, the sun was bright as it climbed, giving a warmth they welcomed.

As usual the two fishers slipped away and were soon hidden from view by the mounds and walls or rubble, leaving here or there a pawprint to mark their going. But Rhin was content to accompany Sander and the girl.

Fanyi had the pendant ever in her hand. Now and then she pointed out a direction with such certainty that Sander accepted her guidance. He wished that he could examine for himself that oval with its winks of what he took to be shining stones. That the Before Men could have fashioned a true direction finder he did not doubt, but neither did he believe he could fathom its secret now. However, at last he asked.

"How does that thing speak to you, saying we must go right or left?"

"That I do not know; I know only a little of how to

read what it has to say. See?" she beckoned him closer, "look, but do not touch. I do not know how another's spirit might influence this."

The pendant was oval, but not flat, having a thickness of about the length from the tip of his little finger to the first knuckle, while the metal from which it had been fashioned was bright and untarnished, probably one of those mysterious alloys the secret of which baffled all those of his calling. Set in a circle stood the stones, round and faceted. These were of different colors and there were twelve of them. But, bright as they were, Sander's full attention was caught by something else. In the metal moved a visible line of light, which was not steady.

"Watch," Fanyi bade him. She swung her body abruptly to the left. On the pendant the lined moved also, so it still pointed in the same direction that it had previously, save that now it touched a different one of the stones.

"My father," she said softly, turning again so that the short bar of light touched the same stone it had formerly, "knew many things. Some he was able to teach my mother and later she taught me. But he died before I entered this world. This was his great treasure. He swore by some magic of the Before Men it could guide the one who wore it to the place from which it came. The closer one approaches that place, the brighter will grow this pointing line. And that is the truth, for I have seen it do so each day we have traveled. I know that which we seek is a place of great knowledge. Perhaps the Before Men had some warning of the destruction of their world and were able to prepare a storehouse that even the great upheaval of the Dark Time could not destroy."

Sander was impressed by that band of light. It was true that it did swing when Fanyi moved. And he could believe it was meant for a guide. What manner of man had her father been? A Trader, who had hunted through the ruins and chanced upon such a cache as he had not believed existed? Or some other, whose tribe perhaps possessed a Rememberer with a greater store of Before

Learning than any the Mob knew?

"Your father—was he a Trader?"

"Not so. Though he traveled with the Traders to Padford. He was a searcher, not for metals, but for other men. Not to enslave them as do the Shark ones, rather to learn what they had kept from the Before Time. He had recorded much, but"—she looked un-happy—"when they made his grave barrow, my mother placed within his hands that book he had used to set down what he had learned. A book is of writing—much writing marked on pieces of smoothed bark or cured skin. My mother knew that was his greatest treasure; therefore it was meet that it be laid in the earth with him so in the Afterward he would have it as another would have his tools and weapons. For my father said that words so marked down were the greatest tools of all—"

Sander shook his head at that. The saying was foolish. How could marks such as she had made in the dust with a bit of twig be more to a man than the tools with which he wrought something out of little or the arms with which he could defend his very life?

"So my father believed!" Fanyi raised her head proudly, as if she might have caught Sander's thought. "But if his records lie with him, I have this." Her fingers closed tightly about the pendant. "And I think it is only a small part of other wonders."

During their journey that day Sander took a chance now and then to glance over Fanyi's shoulder at the pendant. They had to detour, sometimes even to back track, around piles of ruins. Each time the line of light changed course, so that it ever pointed in the same general direction, no matter which way they went.

It seemed to Sander that there was no end to this city. Whence had come so many people; how long and hard had they worked to bring hither this stone to raise buildings? His wonder intensified.

During the ranging of the Mob, they had at times found remains of old cities. Mostly they had avoided the piles of debris, for there was a taboo because such were sometimes the source of a sickness-to-death. The younger men had once or twice prospected a little for metal. However, what they found was so rust-eaten as to be of little account. It was better to depend upon the Traders, who apparently were ever ready to risk any danger to secure the lumps they brought to the mobs.

No city Sander had seen went on forever! Or near to that. But if there had been any metal worth the plundering here it had been taken long ago. Birds nested among the bushes that cloaked the sides of the more stable piles of rubble, left white smears of droppings down weather-worn blocks. At this season the nests were deserted, but they could be seen because the leaves were stripped from the branches by the wind.

Twice Sander used his small sling. And once was lucky, bringing down another of the giant hares. This they roasted at nooning, saving their dried meat for later. They had seen nothing of the fishers. Rhin sniffed at some of the stones and now and then growled low in his throat, as if he caught some faint scent there he did not like. Each time Sander tensed, searched the ground nearby for any track. He feared most a monster like unto that of the one-time island.

Still, whatever traces the koyot picked up must have been old, or perhaps not of the lumbering creature. And there were no trees about to attract the forest people.

In his searching for wood at their night's camp Sander stumbled on a discovery that shook him. A huddle of bones lay in a small hollow, and not the bones of man. The leering skull, its jaw supported by a rock, was twice the size of his own. And he saw, driven into one of the eye holes, a dart.

Cautiously, he freed the missile. In pattern it was not too different from his own. The metal had been well worked, the handicraft of a trained smith. But it carried no marking Sander recognized. He squatted down to examine the skeleton more closely.

This must certainly be the remains of one of the monsters. However, he believed the kill more than one season old. He wondered why the slayer had not retrieved his dart. Such were not to be wasted and each hunter thought first, after bringing down his prey, of reclaiming his weapon. Perhaps the monster had been shot at a distance, then still living, but wounded to the death, had reached here before it collapsed.

Sander made a careful circuit of the surrounding territory, to come upon a second find, a gaping hole in the side of one of the mounds. A later landslip had nearly refilled it, but the original opening was not so concealed that it could not be distinguished. Traders perhaps, intent upon uncovering some treasure here, had been attacked by one of the half-beasts. He could almost reconstruct what had happened.

Perhaps the men had suffered so grievously from the monster's onslaught that they had fled, taking their dead and wounded with them. This evidence of a battle, old though it might be, was alarming.

He pried loose the dart. The point showed a small film of rust, but that he could scour away with sand. And any addition to his own supply was useful.

Sander was not yet satisfied. With a whistle he summoned Rhin. The koyot, once he sniffed the skeleton, growled fiercely, showing his fangs. But when Sander urged him past the collection of bones to the hole, he showed no great interest. Whatever scent had hung there must have long since disappeared. Now Sander sighted something new, beyond a ragged pile of rubble—deep lines rutted in the earth.

There was only one interpretation for those. A cart had been brought here, a slightly smaller one, Sander estimated, than those the Mob used for their plains travel. And it had been loaded heavily, enough to impress this signature of the wheels deeply into the soil. So the diggers had not been entirely routed, they had taken away whatever they had found.

But if this land was the hunting ground for a band of Traders, his own party could be in danger. Even though they had not the outward appearance of seekers for metal, no carts and only the koyot and the fishers who might serve as burden carriers, yet so jealous were the Traders they might attack any intruders in what they considered their own territory, without waiting for any explanation of the trespassers' business there.

This site was old, judging by the condition of the landslip and of the monster bones. However, that did not mean that the explorers who had left that excavation were gone from the ruins. So large a city as this would prove too rich a ground to be forsaken quickly.

So now they had a new element to guard against. Sander knew that Rhin would not accept any stranger unless he himself vouched for such a one. Even Fanyi might have been attacked at sight had it not been that the fury of the fishers had won her protection until Sander had accepted her in peace. Therefore, they must depend upon the koyot to give them both protection and warning. The smith had no wish to trade darts with any Trader. He needed the knowledge, the supplies those could uncover, too much. The ones he had met were amiable men, though shrewd in bargaining. They were not like the Sea Sharks with whom all men had a quarrel from the moment of sighting. He hoped that if any exploring party did cross their path, Rhin would give warning early enough so that they themselves could make plain their lack of threat.

When he reported his findings to Fanyi, she did not seem disturbed.

"It could even be the men of Gavah's kin. It is he who comes down coast in the spring—did come down coast"—she corrected herself bleakly—"to deal in Padford. Our Smith, Ewold, swore his metal was very good."

"What did you trade in return?" The Mob had offered dressed leather, woven wool from the herds, both of which the Traders appeared pleased to accept. He wondered what Fanyi's kin had produced that had moved the Traders to carry their metal hither. To his mind the village had not seemed productive of much that would lure any speculators to their doors.

"Salt fish and salt itself," she returned promptly. "Our men went out to the sea-desert for that. And we had sometimes a surplus of grain and always dried fruit. My

111

mother offered herbs that their healers did not have. We were not so poor a people as you believe, smith!"

"Did I say that?" he countered. "To each people their own way of life."

"Perhaps you did not speak it, but it lay in your mind," Fanyi replied with conviction. "The Sea Sharks took more than kin out of Padford in their raid. I wonder why do they so prey, snatching those of their own species to bear away captive on their ships?" She asked that question as if she did not expect an answer. "We have heard of them, not only from the Traders, but from our elders. In the south they preyed upon us also. We were once a more numerous people, but we lost youths and maids to the Sharks. That is part of *our* memory, smith, though we have none of your Re-memberers to call it forth at will."

"I have heard of the Sharks only from Traders," Sander confessed. "At least they keep to the coast, and we have not seen them inland. Unless the White Ones were of their breed—"

"The White Ones?"

"When I was very young, they came. They were a strange people, charging to instant battle as if their lives depended upon our deaths. We were not able to parlay with them to establish the boundaries of grazing lands as we do with other Mobs. No, they killed all—child, woman, man, koyot even—for they had a queer dread of them. Out of the north they traveled with their wagons. To draw those, they had not koyots but creatures like deer, save they were very large and carried on their heads weights of branching horns. They acted as if they wanted all the world for theirs alone, to clear out all the Mobs of the plains. When my people learned of their blood-engorged madness, Mob linked with Mob, together we met them on a field where they and their beasts died. For when they saw that we would triumph, the women slew their own children and themselves. They put edge even to the throats and hearts of their beasts. It was such a slaying no one of the plains shall ever forget.

"We found strange things among their wagons. But it was decided that all they carried must be accursed because they acted as mad men. Thus their possessions were piled in great heaps. On those we laid their bodies and the bodies of their beasts. They were fired until at last there remained only ashes. Then did all the Mobs who had gathered to defend their land decide in council that a Forbidding was to be laid upon that place, one set in all our Rememberers' minds. Thus, none of any clan-kin there gathered would ever visit that field again.

"Our own dead we buried in hero barrows along the way to the place of blood, so that the earth-spirit part of them might watch for us. Though some men believe," he added, "that men have no earth-spirit part, that just the body, like wornout clothing, remains of a man when breath is gone from him. But there were enough of those holding otherwise that this was done. Now when any of the Mobs range to the north with their herds, the new-sworn warriors, the maids near to the time that they will choose a tent mate, all ride with a Rememberer to the line of the barrows. There he chants the tale of the White Ones and their madness."

"Why were they called White Ones?"

"It was that their hair, even among the young, grew very pale, and their skins, though they rode under the sun, were also bleached. But it was their eyes that betrayed the greatest strangeness, for those were of one color, having no pupil—being only like balls of polished silver. They wore the forms of men, were not like those we have seen in the forest, or that thing that battered into the house, so in that much we could call them kin. But for the rest—no, they were not of our kind."

"Whereas the Sea Sharks are," Fanyi said firmly. "They wear the forms of men like ourselves, but they have inner spirits of devils spawned from the dark."

She was anchoring the sticks holding their meat at just the right distance from the fire to broil. Twilight was already drawing in. Rhin had vanished. But Sander could not deny the koyot that chance to fill his stomach, even with so many possible menaces ranging in the

113

dark. The smith gave a start, his hand instantly on his dart thrower, as there was movement in the shadows. Fanyi's fingers closed about his wrist.

"It is Kai and Kayi," she said. "Though one may mistrust all shadows here, yet some can hold friends." She crooned softly to welcome the fishers.

Fanyi caught the head of the first one, Kai, and then Kayi, holding them between her palms as she gazed into the eyes of each fisher in turn. Then she spoke:

"They have found no sign of others here. In this much, fortune continues to favor us."

Perhaps fortune favored them, Sander decided somewhat grimly, yet he was still uneasily aware that in this broken land a whole Mob might move silently and hidden. There was no reason to relax their watch.

Again they shared out sentry duty for the night. As he sat in the early morning hours, feeding the fire now and then, he watched Rhin, listened to the sound of the river below, to noises out of the dark.

The attack came suddenly—between one breath and the next—not springing from the shadows, but somehow within his own mind. Sander could not even cry out against that invasion, and he had no defense to raise. Instead he felt as if he stood in another place, the features of which were veiled from him, even as he could not see the one—or thing—that had summoned him, overbearing

115

his will as easily as a man might overbear in strength a child.

This was a sensation he could not find words out of past experience to describe. His very thoughts were seized upon ruthlessly, to be shifted, drained of what the other wished to learn. Sander had confused metal impressions of scenes—broken buildings, movement in and among those. Yet when he fought to see clearly any part of that, all faded, dissolved, changed.

Then there was only the fire with the night beyond. Yet Rhin's head was up, the koyot's eyes blazing with reflection from the flames. Beside him the fishers had reared, all turned to face Sander. Alone of their party, the girl still lay quietly asleep.

Sander heard Rhin growl softly, deep in his throat, the light hiss of at least one of the fishers. The smith raised his hands feebly to rub his forehead, feeling weak and frightened. No hint that such could happen to any man had ever come to his people, been hinted at by a Rememberer. He had been in two minds over Fanyi's claim of unseen, intangible power—was this what she had meant by "seeking thought"? Who had so sought *him* and for what purpose? Sander felt violated by that invasion of his mind.

Kai hissed, baring teeth in Sander's direction. The smith flinched from the beast's open enmity. Rhin—Sander glanced quickly to the koyot. There still came that low growl from the animal. Yet, when Sander's eyes met Rhin's squarely, the sound died. The smith, who had never tried to communicate with the koyot after the same fashion Fanyi used with her fishers, had now an impression that Rhin had been alerted to the mental invasion but now accepted that Sander was again himself.

The smith longed to shake Fanyi awake, to demand of her what could have caused this attack that was certainly of some Shaman's brewing and not of normal man. As his first fright and dismay faded, he knew a rising anger. No one must know that he had been so used. He sensed there had been contempt in that exploration of his thoughts, that he was deemed to count for little in the

116

estimation of whoever had netted him for a moment or two with that invisible mind control. No, he would not ask her.

Instead, Sander began to rummage in his smith's bag. As he did so, he repeated mentally one of the secret working chants. Dimly he was recalling something his father had once commented upon. There were supposed to be places from the Before Time where strange influences could seize upon a man, bend him to an unknown service. But there was an answer to such, a defense that was part of a smith's own secrets.

Sanders fingers closed upon some of those lengths of wire he had ripped loose in the old ship. Measuring them, he began to wind the strips into a braid as tight as he could pull them. Then he fitted the loop around his own head, so that a portion of it crossed his forehead directly above his eyes. That done he pulled it free once more to weave the ends and make it firm.

Iron—cold iron—had a meaning reaching from the Before Times. It could be a defense when worked in certain ways. He had never had reason to test that belief (though many of the Mob wore amulets of cold iron; some he had fashioned himself according to their desires). Then he had secretly thought it a baseless superstition, only in favor because to have such toys about them gave men a feeling of security within their own minds, though it had no truth.

Now—now he could accept the idea that there were enemies—or an enemy—here who were in some way to be more greatly feared than monster, White One, or jealous Trader.

Having finished his crude diadem of rusty metal, Sander set about weaving some smaller bits into a complicated knot that he strung on the thong of hide. This for Rhin. He did not know whether the koyot might be influenced by the same invasion that had shaken him, but what precaution he could take, he would.

There remained Fanyi and the fishers. The animals, Sander believed, might not let him near them. They were an aloof pair, tolerating man and koyot only because of the urging of Fanyi. While the girl—she had seemed excited, even pleased when she had caught a suggestion of that "seeking thought," making it clear she welcomed contact with any who could use it. He supposed that was the result of her Shaman training. But if such contacts were accepted as normal and right by the Shamans—! If he had his way, he would leave her at this moment, strike out into the dark.

Outrage and fear pulled him strongly. However, such emotions he would not yield to. No, they would continue to travel together until—until Fanyi might give him reason to believe that she was far more akin to that—that seeker —than she was to him and his kind.

The metal pressed harshly against the skin of his forehead. Sander still repeated mentally the words of power that must be said at the fashioning of any tool or weapon. Now he fed the fire again. The fishers settled quietly once more beside Fanyi. Whatever influence had invaded their camp to strike at him must have withdrawn.

Sander lashed shut his smith's bag, stowed it with his gear. He could see the dawn light slowly creeping up the sky across the cliffs that banded the river, and he hoped this day's journey would bring them to the end of the city, or, if not that, to the goal Fanyi sought. He had begun to dislike heartily this maze of mounds and wreckage. If earth-bound spirits did exist, then surely the dead walked here in the hundreds. And since perhaps no man had done them honor at their burial, they would be answerable to no restraints.

Sander shied away from such thoughts. He did not believe in any earth-bound part of the dead. And he would not now be reduced to a child who fears the dark because his imagination peoples it with monsters. No—no—and no!

Fanyi stirred, opened her eyes slowly. Her expression, Sander noted with a return of uneasiness, was much like that she wore when she fondled the pendant at intervals and seemed so to retreat from the outer world.

"It is there—he is there—" Her voice trailed away. She blinked as if throwing off the last remnants of a vivid dream. Then, as she sat up, her face was alight with an eagerness he had never seen before. The excitement she had shown when she had caught the "seeking thought" was but a pale illusion compared to this.

"Sander—*it* is there! Do you hear me?" She caught at his arm, shook him with a fierce energy. "I have had a foreseeing!" Her face was still alight with excitement and joy. "We shall come to it soon—the secret place. And there will be someone there, someone important."

"Who?" he asked flatly.

A small shadow of bewilderment crossed her face, driving out the joy.

"I—do—not—remember. But—this was a true fore-seeing. We shall find what we seek!"

Her enthusiasm daunted him. Had she had reservations all these days behind the confidence she seemed to draw from her pendant? Was it that she truly had not been sure that it *would* lead her—them—anywhere? He guessed so, but said nothing. It was plain that she now was very sure indeed of success.

"What," she asked, "is that you are wearing?" Her gaze was fastened on the band he had braided. "It is made of metal wire. Why did you make it? Why do you wear it?"

"That is my own secret," Sander answered stolidly. He had no intention of letting her know what had happened. "A smith's secret."

She accepted that. Nor did she question it when he fastened about Rhin's throat the other bit of twisted metal, though he knew she was watching him closely.

The fishers flowed away with their usual speed. And after eating, Sander reloaded the koyot, making fast the back burden in such a way that not more than two jerks of a single cord could loosen it. If they were to face danger, Rhin was not to be handicapped at the onset of any fight.

Fanyi led out, her eyes ever seeking the pendant. The mounds of rubble were thinning, with more space between them to give room to a stronger growth of first brush and then trees, the latter thickening in girth the farther they

119

went. They continued to parallel the river bank and gradually the land sank, so that the cliffs which hung above the water were no longer so high.

Not long after leaving camp they came into a wide, open stretch rutted with the marks of carts. Rhin lowered his nose to sniff, but he did not growl. To Sander's trailwise eyes, these all looked old, made some time ago. But there were so many of them, crossing and recrossing, that it was plain in the past there had been a great deal of traffic in and out of the city. Also the deep-set impression of most ruts hinted at heavy loads.

He caught no sign of any koyot pad tracks mixed up with the cut of cart wheels. Rather there were others—those of the famous greathounds of the Traders. For the first time since they had left their night camp, Sander broke the silence, though he believed Fanyi had been so intent on her own thoughts, perhaps mulling over the dream she termed a "foreseeing," that she had hardly been aware he and Rhin were with her.

"If your sign points us in this way," he observed, "we may not be the only ones to find your storage place. The Traders, or whoever has combed this city, seem to have passed here in force."

The girl shook her head. "I do not believe that any Trader knows of what we seek. It is not metal, the work of Before Hands, it rather is work of their minds. I know of no Trader who would concern himself with such."

"Do you know of all the Trader clans?" he countered. "We, on the plains, have contact with four bands who come regularly, nearly thirty men in all. We have never seen their women. How many came to Padford?"

"I can remember twenty," she answered promptly. "And my father—but he was no Trader. There may be others like him, seekers of knowledge."

"Yet he traveled with the Traders," Sander pressed. "And it is known that that is not their way, to allow any not of their kin to follow their trails."

"My mother said that those who brought him treated him oddly, almost as if they feared him in some manner. Yet he was not a man who carried his weapons loosed or who quarreled easily. She said she was sure that the Trader chief was pleased when they left and my father chose to remain behind for the winter. Yet he said he would go with them when they came again, for he thought to travel even farther to the south to learn what lay there. And they did not refuse him when he spoke."

Sander grew a little tired of this mysterious father who had been laid in his grave place before even Fanyi was born. He seemed to have made such an impression on the Shaman mother who had taken him to her house that she treated him with a reverence and awe that was not usual among her sex.

The women of the Mob chose their mates. Yes, and discarded them if they were not satisfied with their bargains. His father had been chosen twice. But the latter time he had declined the proposal, for he already had a son to learn his mysteries. And no smith wanted to divide his power when the days came that his own arm was no longer strong enough to swing the greatest hammer. Sander had been raised mainly in a household of men: his father, his uncle, who had so sharp a tongue and narrow a mind that no woman had ever looked upon him with favor, himself who was apprentice.

Any tenthold was eager to supply a smith with clothing well-worked, a portion of baked meal cakes, blankets woven from the wool of the herds, in exchange for what his father could fashion in return. Those of their own tent had never gone empty of belly or cold of body, even though no woman's loom nor cooking pots rode in their travel wagon.

But a man owned only his weapon and his tools for the most part, all else belonged to a woman. It was she who fitted out her daughter, when the maid came to choose, and counseled her to choose wisely and with an eye for the future, mainly among the older men and not the youths whose skills were yet unproven.

Was this custom also held among Fanyi's people? If that were true, and Sander expected it was, then the women of Padford could well have drawn aside from a stranger such as her father, seeing no security in such a union, bound to be a short one. However, their Shaman had welcomed him, spoke of him with unusual respect, nursed him to his death. The unknown traveler must indeed have had some force of character that this had been so.

"It is not usual," Fanyi continued, "for a Shaman to wed. Her powers should not be limited by showing favor to any one man. Yet it is also necessary that she breed up a daughter to follow her in her craft. Therefore, when my mother chose a far traveler, the village was content. Only she found him to be much more than she supposed. And when he died, her mourning was not of ceremony only but from the heart."

"You say"—Sander felt a little uncomfortable at that note in his companion's voice, as if he had walked into the private portion of a tent without being so urged by its owner—"that a Shaman must bear a daughter. But what if there comes a son—?"

Fanyi laughed. "That will never happen, smith. We have our own secrets and in some things we can even outwill the ways of nature. The first of my clan, she who survived the Dark Times, had a learning new even then. And this she gave to her daughter, and from daughter to daughter that was passed. *We* do not breed sons, only daughters—and only one to each generation. For that is our will—though it can be altered if we are minded, only we are not. For there is no place for a boy-child in a Shaman's house."

As they were journeying, the land had opened out before them. The outline of an abrupt rise ahead showed such sharp pinnacles, such knife-edged clefts as Sander had never sighted before. Here the river rushed faster, with a roar. They rounded a point to see before them a mighty falls, a mist half-veiling the falling water, spinning out in filmy threads to hide the full length of that downpour.

On the other side of the river the land lay more level, those nodules of saw-edged rock less discernible. Sander halted in some dismay as he sighted plainly what lay ahead. Some great force had twisted and rent this land.

Flows of lava had caught blocks of stone, tangles of warped metal, now rusted and eroded. The landscape was such a gigantic mixture of things made by man held captive by nature, frozen into what was, at the first glimpse, an impenetrable barrier, that it was daunting.

Yet the ruts of the cart tracks headed directly forward into a country they would have sworn no wheel could cross. Fanyi started at that jumbled barried across the land.

"A wave—a wave that swept in from the sea," she murmured. "A wave as high as a mountain. A wave that carried with it most of the city—a wave that broke here and so lost its hold upon that which was heaviest. Such a wave as it is said carried the ship of my people inland. Now I marvel that they survived—unless their wave was smaller."

"It does not matter how this was made." Sander came directly to the point. "We are concerned with finding a way through, if your guide still tells us that must be done."

She studied the pendant and then nodded. "The indicated path still lies straight before us. But these"— she pointed to the wagon ruts—"say that others must have found a road, one large enough to take their carts."

Sander did not point out that to travel such a well-marked path might well be inviting ambush. For the moment he could see no other chance of penetrating that unbelievable mass ahead.

"Look!" Fanyi pointed. "A building!"

For a moment he was startled by what she pointed out. Then he saw the wreckage was not a complete building, merely blocks still perhaps connected by the metal sinews the Before People used to tie together their masses of stone; but enough of those blocks were intact to make a shell of sorts hard-rammed against a pinnacle.

The hugeness of the disaster that had left its own monument here was overpowering. He had accepted all his life the tales of the Dark Times, of the titanic forces that had overpowered the Before World; he had seen the rubble of tumbled cities, the sea-desert. But not until he stood before this breath-taking crumbled mass that had—

must have—been thrown by the force of a raging sea upon tormented and shaken earth, there to be rooted at the retreat of the rea waters, had it ever been directly brought home to him what fury had been loose upon his kind and their world. As Fanyi had said, it was hard to believe that any man could have escaped what had struck in the Dark Time. Even the chants of the Rememberers did not reveal the deep despair of those who must have fled, only to be licked away by water, engulfed when quakes opened the very land under their feet.

Fanyi had covered her face with her hands.

"It is—" She could not find words, he realized. Any more than he could summon them at this moment.

He put his arm about her shaking shoulders, drew her against him, two small humans standing before the death sign of a world.

At length Sander, with difficulty, wrenched his gaze away from that incredible wall.

"Do not look at it," he told her. "Watch the ruts; maybe you are right and those will guide us through."

Resolutely, he stared down at the rough marks on the ground. Here and there were bared lumps of stone over which the wheels must have grated. The way turned farther from the cliff edge, away from the falls. Those, too, Sander would not look upon. There was a kind of horrible fascination about the down-dash of that water, as if a man observing it too closely might be led to leap, following the flow. The thunderous sound beat louder and louder in their ears as they half stumbled, half fled along the path.

Sander noted that Rhin was now running, nose to the ground, as if on a hunting trail. The koyot did not even appear to notice the horrible mountain range of debris. Of course, the smith understood, to Rhin's mind, intelligent as the animal was, it would have no meaning. Only to man who had lost so much would the sight deliver a hard blow out of the past.

Now the wagon track narrowed. They drew opposite the falls, and the sound was such they could not have heard each other, even if they had tried to exchange some form of encouragement. There was a single set of tracks

124

and those ran perilously close to the drop. Sander edged his back to the wall of the heights, facing out, drawing Fanyi with him. Their clothing, hair and faces, were wet with spray as they moved along crabwise, as far back from the edge as they could push. Rhin had bounded ahead, but they moved by slow degrees. Sander felt giddy, he fought a desire to leave that mass of stone and tangled debris behind him, to advance to the water side. If he did that, he believed, he would be lost.

Fanyi with the fingers of one hand gripped his furred overjacket so tightly her knuckles were bleached pale. In her other hand she had palmed the pendant, and her lips moved as if she recited some Shaman's words of power.

Their journey seemed to last forever. Twice they dropped to their bellies and crawled in order to continue to hug the side wall, for masses of stone or rusty, broken metal projected outward. Yet the wagon ruts continued, and Sander knew a vast respect for those who had dared to drive along this way, or else the others had done this so often that the first surge of terror in the face of the overwhelming disaster of mankind had been long since forgotten.

To the right, now that they were at last past the falls, there spread a lake, dotted with islands of rock and a reef or two of congealed and long-cooled lava. On the far side of the lake, which they could only just sight, was an opening that must lead to another river, as if the lake had two outlets.

A second wall of debris began to rise, this time between them and the lake. Here Sander saw evidence that the road had been opened partly by man's labor, using tools that had left marks on stone blocks, or cut away masses of metal. The space so cleared was hardly wider than a wagon, a small wagon, while the labor it must have cost could only make Sander believe there must lie at the end of this trail some rich reward equal to such effort. Having passed the falls, Sander began to trot, Fanyi running lightly on beside him. He sweated as he went, his heart pounding as he refused to look any higher than the surface of the very rough way before them. It began to slope downward.

They had passed beyond that portion where the road had been cut by man. The way opened out again. Ahead they could see that this slope continued down nearly to the level of the lake's water.

On their side of the lake there was no sign of vegetation. This grim and deadly mass supported not even the most stunted bush. But across the lake the yellow and red of trees in fall leaf showed, and a green line along the shore as if it gave rootage to reeds.

It was as they dropped down into this lower way that they met Rhin and the fishers. All three animals stood barring their path as if in warning.

Rhin gave a summoning yelp, and Sander began to run, though he watched his footing that he might not crash by catching a foot in one of the deeply worn ruts. The koyot's stance suggested excitement, also a certain wariness. Now Rhin's pointed muzzle swung to the heights where the gigantic flood had deposited what it had carried inland.

When the fishers saw that the two humans were coming, they humped away to be lost among the crannies and pit holes of the distorted range. Rhin gave a last warning yelp, scrambled off in the same direction.

Among these fantastic heapings of stone, twisted and broken spikes of metal, some caught in congealed lava pools, there were plenty of places one could take refuge. The boom of the falls was loud behind them. Though he strained his ears, Sander could catch no sound which arose above that, since Rhin had given tongue. The smith climbed a spur of wreckage, testing each step above before he put his full weight upon it, then turned to reach down a hand to Fanyi.

Together they reached a place where a jagged pinnacle had split off from the mass of parent rock. Jammed into the cleft between the two was a mass of debris that looked none too steady. There were far too many sharp-ended bits to afford them any but a precarious perch. Yet here the fishers had flattened out, clinging to their choice of support with their claws. Rhin crouched, his belly tight against the uneven rock and metal, frozen into immobility. So well did his gray-brown coat fade into the background that Sander knew the koyot was practicing one of his hunting tricks. He could thus lie for patient hours intent upon the burrow of a hare or a deer trail that led to water.

There was barely room enough left for Sander and the girl to crowd in beside the koyot. Once there Sander made ready his dart throwers. Rhin gazed back down trail, the way they had come. His ears pricked forward, and Sander could feel the vibrations of a growl the animal did not voice aloud.

Sander leaned closer to the girl so his lips nearly brushed the now unkempt hair above her ear.

"Do your fishers know what danger comes?" Not for the first time he wished that he and Rhin had a more complete form of communication. He believed that Fanyi could read the thoughts of her two furred ones, or at least guess more accurately what their action indicated.

She wriggled about to gaze steadily up at Kai. The fisher's fangs showed in wicked promise.

"Something comes," she made answer, "and from more than one way. See how Kayi faces forward, while Kai faces back? We are between two sources of trouble."

Sander grimaced. This was all he needed. He had perhaps ten bolts, and there was his sword knife, also the sling with which he hunted. A pebble propelled by that might be useful and dangerous in its own way, but it would be necessary to aim with great accuracy. He laid his darts ready to hand, then jerked loose Rhin's burden, leaving the koyot free if there was to be a fight.

For a long space it seemed that the alarm had been false. However, Sander knew the range of the animals' hearing far exceeded his own. They might even have scented what prowled along that narrow road. Then—

The sound that filled the air whirled him back in time to his childhood. With it came a stab of fear as acute as a real sword point thrust into his flesh. Such a clamor had long ago tortured the ears of the Mob so much that they had stuffed in bits of grass to deaden their hearing.

It was the battle horn of the White Ones! No one who had ever heard could forget it. Now that bray pierced the roar of the falls as easily as if the clamor of unleashed water did not exist.

In turn the horn was answered by a croaking, a booming series of cries, which were even more startling. For they did not proceed from any human throat.

Up the trail from the lake they came in great hops, those weird amphibians who were like the river dwellers in the desert. Their bodies were encased in the same shell-fashioned armor, while each held a wickedly barbed spear. The huge shells from which they had made their helmets so overhung their countenances that, from the perch where Sander's party hid, they could see nothing but the shells themselves.

As the amphibians came into sight, they broke ranks, climbing into hollows and crevices, squatting there on their haunches. Like Rhin, they carried with them an inborn camouflage that made them nigh invisible as they burrowed into their chosen nooks, preparing an ambush, Sander was sure.

Once more came the sound of the battle horn. One of those huge antlered beasts, such as had served the White Ones who had died on the plains, came into view. This time the creatures did not pull a trail wagon; rather, it carried a rider, his boot toes tucked within a band lashed about its middle. The White One who so rode advanced with caution, his mount picking a slow way. Only two or three steps did the antlered one take into the open. Then it shied back, giving vent to a deep grunting.

There was bared metal, a sword twice the length of the knife Sander wore, in the hand of the rider. His head, covered by a peaked hood of hide, swung slowly right to left and back again. Only when the battle horn boomed again, delivering an order, did he urge his mount on. Fanyi reached up, laid one hand on each of the fishers' muzzles, to quiet them. Once more Sander felt the vibration in Rhin's body. But they all froze without a sound.

A second of the huge deer (if deer those were) advanced into the range of their vision, with more behind. However, the riders moved with such caution Sander was sure they expected trouble. Not one of the amphibians had moved. In fact, when Sander glanced in their direction, even though he had seen them settle in, he could distinguish only one or two of them, and these only because he recognized the crevices they had chosen.

The White Ones' eyes searched the ragged walls. As the last one pushed out into the descending trail, Sander saw the long sweep of the war horn now slung across his back. Their party was small, only a half-dozen. They could well be scouts for just such an invasion as the Mob had defeated when Sander was a child.

Their outer coats were of long and shaggy fur, matted and filthy. Binding the coats tightly to their bodies were wide sashes of stained and dirty cloth. They did not appear to speak to one another as they drew to a halt, but their hands were upheld, the fingers moving in quick jerks, which perhaps conveyed meaning.

It was apparent that they disliked what they saw or sensed ahead, yet some strong need pressed them forward. The leader urged his mount on, his hand ready on his sword. However, the spears of the hidden amphibians were twice—three times the length of that weapon. Any of the water creatures could bring down such a rider before he would be in range to retaliate.

Sander, now watching the enemy, saw a movement of one of those shafts, a readying for battle. At that moment an impulse arose in him to cry out—to warn the White Ones. Only his knowledge of what had happened on the plains more than ten years ago kept him dumb. Then the White Ones had been like demons, slaying without any mercy, finally killing themselves lest they have any contact with his own people. Their utter ruthlessness was

130

so much a part of his clan tradition that normally he would have had no wish to raise a single finger in their behalf. But they still wore the guise of men of his own species, while those waiting to spear them down had no part of any world he knew.

Fanyi's hands fell on the smith's shoulders. She exerted force to pin him in place, cramping his arms so that he could not have launched a dart without a struggle, which would betray them to both parties.

Her lips formed a distinct "no." He had a flash of dislike and fear. If Fanyi could read his brain, as she might be doing, he did not like it.

The leader of the White Ones paced warily on. Then a spear whirled out of nowhere. Only a swift swerve of his mount kept the man from impalement. The amphibians boiled out of hiding, hopping forward, spears forming a wall of points. It was apparant the White Ones could not hope to attack, having only the weapons Sander saw in their hands.

The man bearing the horn, riding several lengths behind the swordsmen, now made the first move. He swung the horn around, setting the rounded mouthpiece to his lips, steadying the length of dull metal against the neck of his mount. His cheeks puffed and he blew mightily.

The shock of sound sent Sander's hands to his ears. He felt Rhin quiver, as if the high notes were a lash laid across the koyot's muscular body. Fanyi loosed her hold on the smith. Instead, she pressed a hand again on each fisher's head, though those animals twisted and writhed.

As much as that blast had affected their own party, it had an even greater effect on the amphibians. Two dropped their spears and fell to the ground, where they lashed out with arms and legs, as if in torment. Their fellows retreated, a retreat that became a rout when they reached what seemed a safe distance from the swordsmen. The White Ones booted their mounts into a trot and rode after the fleeing water creatures. Now the leader of the riders leaned over to strike at the necks of the two amphibians on the ground, stilling their writhing bodies. Both parties then vanished in a whirlwind of dust, round-ing the turn in the trail up which the amphibians had come earlier.

Sander made no move to lead his own party out of hiding. He still suspected that the White Ones were a scout squad and behind them toiled such a tribe as had come down on the plains.

However, Rhin relaxed and the fishers squirmed from Fanyi's hold, uttering cries as if to urge their companions on. Thus Sander was forced to accept the idea that these White Ones were not being followed, at least not closely. If that were true, the sooner he and the others were away from this debatable land the better.

He paused by one of the fallen amphibians, though he did not look, or want to look, closely, under that mottled brown shell helmet, at the thing's face, now slack in death. But he picked up the spear and trailed it with him.

The shaft was far too long, but he believed it could be cut to a shorter length. The barbs that crowned it were so cleverly wrought that, against his inclination, he paid tribute to the smith who had fashioned them. The material was not metal, rather bone, skillfully carved. He shuddered at the thought of how such a head would tear into flesh. The barbs were slender. Undoubtedly they would break were the spear to be withdrawn, leaving fragments to fester within the wound.

Released by the lifting of Fanyi's will and hand, the fishers humped around the curve of the trail and disappeared, following both the White Ones and the retreating water creatures. Sander remained in two minds about the wisdom of continuing. If there *was* another company of White Ones somewhere behind them, they could well be caught in a pinchers consisting of two deadly teams of fighters. But for the same reason he could not suggest retreat.

If they could be as fortunate the second time to find a hiding place among the chaos of the rocks, they might have a chance to escape. But a man should not risk his life easily on the turn of fortune alone.

The mass of storm wrack still towered over them. As they went, no more shattering blasts from the battle horn

132

sounded. However, when they turned a curve, to see before them the shore of the lake, they witnessed the last of that engagement.

The White Ones rode up and down along the shore. Plainly they were not tempted to follow into the lake those who swam there with the ease of creatures in their natural element. The escaping amphibians left tell-tale vees of ripples, showing very little even of their heads above the surface.

The land, which was level here, widened out. Sander made a quick decision to leave the road and turn left to skirt the edge of the heights. A quick climb aloft there might be their own salvation if the White Ones sighted them.

In this manner they crept along, sometimes traveling on their hands and knees; Rhin also crouched. Stone cut through their garments, bruised their hands; yet that hardship was nothing if they could pass unseen as far as riders and swimmers were concerned.

To the north the White Ones seemingly gave up their hopes of attacking those in the lake. The riders drew together, and Sander caught the flutter of their hands as they conferred in soundless language.

Finally the party of mounted men broke apart. Two booted their antlered beasts back the way they had come, sending Sander, Fanyi, and Rhin flat against earth behind the nearest outjut of the heights. The smith lifted his head cautiously. In so much his fears had been proven right. Those riders heading east must be going either to report or gather reinforcements. His own party's salvation was to make their way as quickly as possible past the other riders settling down on the lake shore.

Keeping to the broken foothills was the best answer. The enemy mounts, larger and much heavier than Rhin, needed room in which to maneuver. They could not crawl along the ground as the koyot now prudently moved.

Still, to hug the side of the heights was to make only a very slow advance. The one advantage was the many hiding places the rough exterior of the slopes offered.

Luckily, the White Ones appeared to have no thought

of immediate exploration here. Perhaps they feared other opponents besides the water things they had so easily routed. This land was made for ambushes. A handful of the Mob, had they darts enough, might crumble the whole of White Ones' tribe into swift death. Sander was sure he had not sighted any dart throwers among that band. Certainly, if the riders had had such weapons they would have loosed them at the amphibians.

Their creeping carried them well past the riders at last. Now Sander waved Fanyi and Rhin to their feet. A screen of debris, studded with outthrust masses of stone and eroded metal, stood as if it had been truly intended as a barricade. Behind that, though they could not hurry, at least they made much better time.

Twice Sander climbed the crest of the barricade. It was really a vast layer of completely fused material, which must have broken from the heights behind it, to form a jagged foothill. From cover there he could survey the back trail.

He marked the ruts of the road, which still ran along the bank of the lake and the riders now following it at a slow walk. It was plain the White Ones were not pushing their pace any.

Finally, the leading rider slipped from his beast, the others following suit. Their mounts clunked out into the shallows of the lake where, even on this side, some green of water plants not yet stricken by frost now showed. Dipping their heads, the animals wrenched off great mouthfuls of the vegetation, champing lustily. The men had taken up their position beside a large jutting rock and were opening their saddle bags.

Sander realized that he, too, was hungry. But they could not linger here. The more distance they put between themselves and those scouts, the better pleased he would be.

His party worked their way on, discarding no caution, through great masses of refuse crushed by the ancient waves and left by the draining sea. Sander longed now and then to test some bit of metal he saw embedded in that debris. With this at hand—why had the Traders ever sought the more eroded and destroyed city? Or had that trail been meant to lead here in order to plunder this huge chaos?

Yet there were no signs of any delving about. In fact, Sander believed, it would be very chancy to try it. Now and again, even as the mounds had been trimmed by a brisk wind in the city, masses broke loose and came crashing down. So he kept one eye overhead, to avoid passing near any height that looked unstable.

They halted at last because they were so tired they could not keep going. Sharing out their meat and water, Fanyi gave a great sigh. Rhin lay panting heavily after he had gulped his portion. Their boots had suffered from the broken ways over which they had come. Sander cut loose the bundle of uncured hare skins and tied them around their feet, fur side in, hoping by so little to cushion and protect what was left of their boots.

Fanyi rubbed the calves of her slim brown legs. "Never have I traveled such a trail as this," she commented. "Those ruts were bad enough, but this scrambling up and down is far worse. And how long will it last?"

He knew no more than she. The crumbled stones, the lava-engulfed wrack of the ancient sea, was everywhere. Some peaks of rock rose mountain-high, plainly up-thrust from the earth's crust at nearly the same time the sea had swirled in. It was a nightmare land, and Sander gave thanks to fortune that they had traveled it so far with no more than scraped skin or a bruised and battered hand, to show. It was plain that they must hole up before the coming of night. Even Fanyi's precious Before light could not guide them over such rough ground.

The lake, which was of such extent that even yet with all their traveling, they had not reached the western end, tantalized him every time he climbed to view a path before them. But he had been warned by the adventures of the White Ones. To go near that occupied water would be an act of folly. They must keep to these harsh, broken lands for safety.

Some time before sundown they chanced upon such a place as Sander thought would serve. Two massive slides from the heights had spread into the lower land, now forming walls of fused fragments. Between these lay a stretch of relatively smooth ground. They dared not light a fire, even if they could have found wood. Fanyi had recalled the fishers, and she curled down between their furred bodies, perhaps warmer so than she might have been by a fire. Sander had Rhin.

The animals rested quietly, displaying no unease. They ate quickly, with signs of relish, the chunks of dried meat Sander doled out, though the fishers were so easily satisfied the smith could believe that even in this desolate land they had found game during their earlier roaming. However, none of the three appeared wishful to vanish again as the night closed in. When the dark was really thick, Sander borrowed Fanyi's Before light. Shading that with one hand, he made his way down to the edge of the slip that formed the western wall of their refuge.

There he snapped the light off and stared intently eastward. If the White Ones still followed the wagon trail, they might not be adverse to setting up a camp with a fire. But he caught no sight of any flame.

It was only when he turned again west, ready to grope his way back to their own hollow, that he sighted a spark of what could only be firelight, not a star. He was sure that the White Ones had not ridden past them during the afternoon. Therefore those scouts had not lit this beacon. For beacon it appeared to him, so high was it set. As he watched, it began to blink, slowly, in a pattern of off-and-on.

Just so did the Mob send warnings across country when there was danger to the herds. Only those blinks bore no resemblance to the code in which he had been trained. Sander whirled around, facing east again.

Yes, he had been right with that guess! There was another high-placed spark of light that blinked in answer. White Ones? Somehow he doubted it. The men who had scattered the amphibians this morning had the appearance of those riding a new, unknown trail. But who else would signal among these tormented hills?

Traders? That seemed far more of a possibility. All that Sander knew concerning the strictly kept secrets of

136

their own places arose in his mind. They could well have posted sentries in the heights, sentries who had marked both the coming of the White Ones and Sander's own party. Were the White Ones as much enemies of the Traders as they had proven to be for the Mob on the plains?

At this moment he fervently hoped so. That fact would make his own position and that of Fanyi much the stronger. A mutual enemy could draw together even unfriends in a time of peril.

The light to the east gave a last wink and vanished. As he turned his head, he saw that that to the west was also gone. He crept carefully back to their camp and settled down beside the koyot. Fanyi's breathing he could hear through the dark, even and peaceful. He guessed that she was already asleep.

But Sander did not follow her swiftly. There was something that seemed to loom over him, spreading outward from the congealed storm wrack. This had been a place of death, not only of men, but also of their ambitions, their dreams, all that they had fashioned. If any earth-tied spirits existed, where better could one hear their broken whispering, their pleas for life, their fear of a death that had come in such terror that their own minds could not conceive its vast blotting out of their world?

Some of that horror that had gripped him in the morning, when he and Fanyi had looked for the first time upon this place, stirred in him now. He was cold with more than the chill of the night. Almost, he could hear screams, shouts of those lost and long gone.

Sternly, Sander set himself to the regaining of good sense. His lips moved as he recited the power words of the smith. A man made tools and weapons with his hands —after a pattern his mind sketched for him. Those who used them in time died and were laid there in their barrows. This was the natural way of life. The dead who might have perished here in the Dark Times—they were long gone. And the things they fashioned were not the things Sander understood. He might be of their distant kin, but he was not of their clan; they had no hold on him.

He fought imagination, put out of his mind as best he could that memory of the fragment of a building he had seen still partly intact and plastered against the cliff. The Before Men had had great knowledge to serve them, but it had not helped them escape the Dark Time. What good then was all their special learning when the earth and sea turned against them?

Slowly, he considered the quest that had drawn him here. Very far in the past now lay the taunting words of his uncle. They no longer awoke a flame of anger within him. Below these tormented mountains, his own life seemed very small, near meaningless. Yet it was *his* life. And if there lay ahead what Fanyi had promised, the wisdom of the Before Men that he could take himself, then he would not be as small either. His fingers flexed as he lay, thinking of patterns he had long carried in his head, things he would do if he could work the unknown metals—

It would not even matter much whether he returned to face down those elders of the Mob who had decided that he was too untried and young to take his father's place. No, what would matter most was the fact that he would *know*—know and use skills he had dreamed of but never found.

He pillowed his head against Rhin's haunch, resolutely shutting out the terror of the heights, intent upon what lay here and now.

With morning they circled down to the lake where Sander filled their water bottle, Fanyi and the fishers keeping watch. Here the water had a queer, metallic taste. But Fanyi pronounced it harmless, saying that the minerals in it might well be beneficial, for she brewed such for healing. There was no sign of the amphibians. However, Sander noticed on one of the rocky islands, well out from the shore, a mound of set stones in which a dark hole of entrance gave directly upon the lake. He believed that this might mark a home of the creatures.

They turned away again from the easier surface of the wagon road, to scramble along at the edges of the hills. The open space was slowly narrowing again, sooner or later they would be forced back closer to that rutted track. Sander kept listening. Their own feet, muffled by the hare pelts, and the pads of the animals awoke little or no sound. But even the slip of a stone seemed to echo far too loudly!

Once more the road began to climb. Here some of the ruts had been filled with stones, and the debris had once more been cut back on either side. They must now return to that cut, for to climb jagged rocks on either side offered a risk Sander did not want to contemplate. There was too much danger of a fall.

He forced the pace, wanting to be quickly out of this gap where they were so clearly visible. Somewhere in the battered heights above, that light he had sighted in the night must mark a sentinel's post. He had no doubt that they had already been marked, spied upon. Yet the challenge Sander continued to expect did not come.

Beyond this second narrowing of the level land, the heights sloped once again. And from the peak through which ran their road, they caught a good view of what lay ahead. There were some rises, but none as tall as those behind, and far less of the battered wrack of the waves had been planted here.

Instead, below was a growth of grass, scattered trees wearing scarlet and gold, some stands of pines showing dark green. And—Sander paused, startled—

There was what appeared to be a cross between the village of Padford, with its wooden and stone walls, and the mobile tents-on-wagons used by the Mob. In short, a deep ditch had been dug into which some water from a river feeding the lake seemed to have been diverted. Beyond that ditch, earthen walls were mounted high and crowned with a wall of tree trunks, their tops hewn into points like a defensive stake barrier, save these trunks were larger and more firmly set than any such wall he had ever before seen.

Clustered within were tents-on-wagons—much larger than those the Mob hauled to form their own temporary clan-towns up and down the plains. The tents-on-wagons circled an open space wherein stone had been used to construct a rough tower, standing perhaps twice the height of the tents about it. From cooking places before each tent arose trails of smoke. There was a stir of people coming and going, and a band of loose animals, herded by one mounted man, trotted out of the enclosure, across a bridge which could be lowered or raised to span the ditch.

Hounds! Then this must be a Trader stronghold. Unlike the people of the Mobs, the Traders bred different animals. The hounds, as they were called, were akin to Rhin, yet different, in that their ears did not stand erect, but flopped on either side of their heads. And instead of uniform coloring, they were splotched, spotted, had white and red-brown patches or feet, no two ever looking alike. The Traders seldom rode on their long treks, but used these beasts to carry their stock. However, Sander had never seen them in such number before.

Surrounded by the trotting hounds was an inner core of deer-like creatures, larger than those Sander had long hunted. Having left the village, the hounds were spreading out, still guarding the deer, their noses close to the ground, coursing off in different directions much as a koyot would do when released to hunt. Their herder kept on, riding alone straight after the deer in the general direction of the gap.

The fishers, reared on either side of Fanyi, began to sound their hissing battle cry. But she instantly had a hand on each. It was plainly her will, not her light hold that restrained them. Rhin watched with interest but did not growl. He knew Traders of old and had fraternized with the hound pack-bearers they had brought with them.

The hound that bore the rider suddenly gave tongue and began to run. And behind Sander came a voice, sharp and clear:

"Stand! Or do you want your throats torn out, fools?"

That question was asked in such a tone that Sander did not doubt the questioner was quite ready to enforce his command. He allowed his hands to drop into full sight, his weapons still in belt and shoulder strap. Inwardly, he was deeply ashamed to be thus easily taken by a hidden sentry.

The rider arrived swiftly, for the hound ran at top speed, while the fishers snarled in open rage. Still Fanyi kept them under control. Rhin yelped, the hound answered with a deep bay.

Sander longed to turn to see who kept watch behind,

but he knew the folly of making any move, which might bring instant hostile reprisal.

The rider pulled to a halt before them. He wore the leather breeches and furred overjacket of a plainsman. But his face was half-hidden by a black beard trimmed to a point, and his ear length hair was mostly covered by a cap of yellow-white fur. His hands held a thrower ready, dart in the slot, and there was no welcome to be read in his expression.

"Who are you?" His demand was abrupt, as he eyed first Fanyi and then Sander, though, Sander noted, he kept shooting wary glances at the fishers.

"I am Sander, smith. And this is Fanyi, Shaman of Padford—" Sander answered with an outward show of confidence, which he hoped he could continue to assume.

"A smith and a shaman," returned the rider. "And why do you wander? Or are you outriders of some Mob?" His two questions were frankly hostile.

"You are Jon of the Red Cloak," Fanyi spoke up in return. "I have seen you in Padford. That was five seasons ago."

"I was there. But a Trader goes many places during his travels. And what does the Shaman of Padford do here? You are tied to your people by the Great Will you obey. Do they of Padford then wander?"

"Not so. Most lie dead, Trader Jon. How many the Sea Sharks might have taken, I cannot number."

Though he still held the dart thrower steady, now the man gazed intently at the girl.

"Sea Sharks, eh? You say they raided Padford?"

"They killed, they burned, they took," she repeated with emphasis.

"But he—" The thrower moved a fraction to indicate Sander. "This smith is not of your people. How came he, and why, to this land? No Mob favors leaving their plains, except for good reason.'

"I had good reason," Sander returned. "No Mob has two smiths. Therefore I come to seek knowledge—more knowledge of metals."

The man's gaze grew fiercer. "You are bold, smith, to

say thus you come to steal our secrets!"

"I care not," Sander answered, "where the metals are found. It is the working of them that means much to me."

"So," commented the Trader, "any man might say, were he found where he has no right to be."

"Do you then," Fanyi asked, "claim all this?" She indicated the land about them.

"What it contains is ours by right of discovery. You," he snapped at Sander, as if by any prolonged conversation he weakened his case, "loose your gear"—he pointed to the bundles on Rhin—"and let me see what you have stolen—"

Though he had no idea of the strength of the force that might stand behind him, Sander refused to play meek any longer. He knew enough of Trader ways to realize that if one did not stand up to them and bargain, one was completely lost. He folded his arms across his chest.

"Are you then chief here?" he asked. "You are not head of *my* Mob, nor even a Man of First Council, unless you so declare yourself. I do not take orders—I am a smith, one with the magic of metals. Such are not to be ordered about by any man without reason. Nor," he continued, "does one so address a Shaman."

The man made a sound that might have signified scornful amusement.

"If she was Shaman of Padford, and Padford is no more because of the Sharks, then is her claim of Power false. As for you, smith," he made a taunt of that title, "more than words have to prove your worth."

The fishers growled, Rhin echoed them, while the hound bristled and showed his fangs in turn.

"Control those beasts of yours," ordered the Trader, "or else look to see them dead. Move on, carefully. We shall see what the Planners make of you."

Fanyi glared at Sander. He read warning in her look. The fishers were still growling, but they had gone to four feet again and she walked between them, her hands resting on their backs as they moved, flanking her, down toward the town.

Sander followed. There was little else he could do. He

143

heard a scrabbling behind him and realized that his caution had been right as three riders on hounds moved forward to box him in as he went.

Some of the loose hounds came bounding closer as the party followed the rutted road toward the ditch bridge. They bayed and growled. Rhin and the fishers, their fangs showing, made ready answer to the challenges the other beasts offered. But there was no attack, for the riders sent the hounds off with a series of cries not unlike barks.

Men issued from the village to await them. It was one of these who called to their captor:

"Ha, Jon, what have you gathered in? These are no Horde stragglers."

"They are invaders no matter what they look like," the rider returned. "But if you want to trade blows with the Horde, those also come. The signals have been seen."

Fanyi stopped short of the bridge. "Trader, my companions will not enter here. Bring out your Planners."

"Dead animals can be easily transported—"

The girl raised her hands and brought them together in a loud clap. Her eyes caught and held the eyes of the threatener. He looked as if he were struggling vainly to make some further statement or give an order, but something had locked his lips.

"I have spoken, and the Power is mine, Jon of the Red Cloak—know I not your true name? Thus, I can command you to do this thing. Get hither one of authority that we may speak together."

Sander believed the rider struggled between his own will and that of the girl. His expression was one of furious anger, yet he slid down from the back of the hound and tramped heavily over the bridge, those gathered there making way for him.

Fanyi's face bore that look of concentration that Sander had seen her wear when she had sat with the pendant in her hand. Though he found it hard to believe in her reputed "power," it was plain at this moment a man, who was not even conditioned to accept her decisions as her own people had doubtless always been, was obeying her orders against his own will.

144

There was a closed look about the men who surrounded them. Though this was obviously a well-established town, which had been in existence for some time, no women or children showed in that silent crowd. Sander did not like the inferences one could draw from their quiet and from their set expressions. The jovial, open friendliness the Traders displayed when visiting the Mob was gone. All those warnings concerning their jealous guardianship of their own territory were now, to Sander's thinking, made manifest by this lack of welcome.

In a world where strangers, unless they were openly hostile like the White Ones and the Sharks, were made guests and asked for stories concerning their travels and lands farther away, this suggestion of hostility was new to Sander. However, he was a smith, no one could deny that. And in any civilization a man of such skill must be truly welcome. He glanced from face to face among that assembly, striving to see a forehead tattoo matching his own. Was there no smith here at all? As fellow members of a craft that had its own secrets, he could claim acceptance from that one man at least in this village.

But he could not sight on any stretch of skin the blue hammer brand. Still he rehearsed in his mind the workwords by which he could prove his claim to the metal mysteries.

There came another parting of the crowd and Sander saw Jon again and with him a much older man. The newcomer walked haltingly, sticks which he dug into the ground to support his forward-leaning body in each hand. He held his head at a stiff and what must be a painful angle. For all his crookedness of body his gait was swifter than Sander would have thought possible, so he nearly matched Jon's strides in spite of his own more limited length of step.

Alone among the Traders did the newcomer bear a forehead marking, and for a moment Sander thought that here must be the smith he had sought. Then he realized that no man so frail of body could carry out any but most easy metal work. And his tattoo was not of a hammer, but one that had a strange familiarity. At first, Sander could not remember where he had seen before the profile of that fierce-eyed bird head. Then he recalled the broken bit of stone he had found along the river, the symbol Fanyi said had once stood for a great and proud country.

The bird-marked man stopped before Sander and his group. For a long moment he studied each in turn, both people and animals. Then he spoke in a voice deep and rich that seemed almost too powerful for his thin body.

"You"—he singled out Fanyi the first—"are of Power. You"—now he swung his head around a little to look at Sander—"are a smith of the plains people. Yet you travel together with these who are your companions. What matter brings so strange and diverse a band together?"

"I am of Padford," Fanyi replied. "But Padford no longer is. The Sea Sharks came and—" She made a gesture of negation.

"I have heard it said," the other said, "that the Power of a true Shaman can wall in those people who believe."

"It was the time of the Great Moon," Fanyi answered steadily, though her face was bleak. "I answered the call of my need. It was at that time they struck."

The old man's lips and jaw moved a trifle as if he chewed upon words in some manner that he might thus test truth by the taste of them. He made no comment, only swung a second time to Sander.

"And you, smith, as you name yourself, what brought you out of the plains, away from your Mob and kin?"

"My father died." Sander gave him the truth, seeing no reason to disguise it. "I was young, my uncle claimed too young to be full smith, though my father had named me so. There is no place in any Mob for two smiths—therefore I claimed out-right."

"The impatience of the young, was that it, smith? You could not bend your pride, but rather chose to live kinless?" There was, Sander believed, a note of derision in that query. He held his temper manfully.

"There was also the wish for knowledge."

"Knowledge!" That sharp word cut him short. "Knowledge of what, smith? Of some treasure trove you could plunder to buy your way back to your kin? Was that it?

146

Hunt metal for yourself so that Traders cannot make their living!"

A growl akin to Rhin's rose from the crowd about them. Before Sander could answer, the other continued:

"And what treasure have you looted, smith? Turn out your gear."

Sander wanted to balk, but he knew that he would thus only provoke a struggle that would do no good. Sullenly he went to Rhin, unknotted the bag holding his work tools and the small bits of metal he had pried and broken loose in the ship. As he unrolled the covering, Jon pounced on one of those lengths of battered wire.

"See, he has—" the Trader began with a kind of triumph, then he held the wire closer to his eyes. Dropping that length, he pawed over the rest of Sander's small store. "Look you, Planman!"

The Trader held a fistful of the ship's stuff closer to the old man.

"Whence had you this?" the latter demanded.

"There was a ship, one caught in the sea-desert. This came from the inside of that," Sander explained. The Planner must be half-smith himself, or have an eye smith-trained, else he would not have seen that it was any different from what they might find in a ruined city.

"And this ship was of metal?" demanded the Planman.

"All of metal. There were dead men within its belly, and they were not bones."

To his surprise the Planman nodded. "It is then like unto the one Gaffred uncovered in the mountains last year, one made to travel under the surface of the water."

That, to Sander's incomprehension, appeared to convert the Planman from suspicion to at least the first stage of offering hospitality. Fanyi repeated that her animals would not enter the town, which for a short period raised again a chorus of doubts from the Traders. But at length it was agreed that Sander take housing with their smith (who had suffered an injury, which had left them for a space without a worker), while Fanyi would be allowed to stay without, camping in one of their trail wagons now parked for the season.

Sander did not like being separated from the girl. She had left these people with the inference that they had been drifting along together, two lost ones without kin, saying nothing of the strange storage place she sought. He had followed her lead, as after all hers was the claim on the site to which that finder of the Before Time served as a guide. But he thought that the Traders believed there was some deeper tie between them than just expediency and so considered him hostage to warrant Fanyi's presence.

Sander knew that to be untrue. There was nothing to prevent the girl from going off by night. And if she did so disappear, his lot among the Traders was going to be anything but easy. There was also the knowledge of the White Ones heading this way. But when he mentioned them, he discovered the Traders were confident of their own means of defense.

Kaboss, the smith, greeted Sander's arrival with a hardly enthusiastic grunt. He surveyed the plainsman's kit of tools, not quite with a sniff of disparagement, but with the air of a man who had in the past discarded as unworthy very similar pieces. The bits of ship wiring, however, intrigued him. And he put Sander through a most exhaustive examination concerning everything he had observed about that stranded hulk.

One of Kaboss's own heavy hands was wrapped in bandages, and when once or twice he flexed his fingers without thought, he gave an exclamation of pain. He allowed Sander to eat—such a bowl of well-seasoned stew as the plainsman had not tasted since he left the Mob— and then bore him to the smithy where he pointed out a pile of repair work that had stacked up there because of his injury. Like any Trader he haggled over terms, but at last Sander struck a bargain that was satisfactory enough and went to work with a will.

Rhin had been quartered in a stable and given a gorge-feed of dried meat. Now after licking his paws, sore from the travel in the mountains, the koyot had gone to sleep.

Sander paid close attention to his work, though the time for it was short, since the day had been well advanced before they had reached the Traders' town. Yet also he tried to think what might come next. That Fanyi would calmly settle down as a part of this clan, even if she were granted full kin-right, he did not believe. And neither would he stay if she went.

Kaboss was full smith and would take over again entirely once his hand healed. Sander had left his own people rather than be counted apprentice for more years. He had no intention of playing that role among strangers. And in spite of what he continued to tell himself was reasonable common sense, he did believe that the Shaman knew something when she talked of a storage place of knowledge. The pendant had more than half converted him to her point of view. He had never heard or seen anything like that before.

Kaboss's household was small. His housemate was a silent woman, looking older than her chosen man, her hair streaked with gray, though she was dressed in a manner to show the importance of their household, wearing a thick necklace of much burnished copper, four silver rings, and a belt of silver links about her dull green robe. She did not speak often and then only to the serving maid, who scuttled about, an anxious frown on her face as if this were a mistress no one could hope to please.

There was no sign of an apprentice. Then Kaboss mentioned that he had such, a younger son of his brother, but he had been gone for some days now on an expedition scouting for metal to the north.

Under questioning, Sander told something of their trip, their meeting with the amphibians, and the attack of the monster upon the house on the one-time island. Kaboss was much interested in that portion of his tale.

"Such are still to be found then!" he commented. "They were once so great a danger that we could not hunt lest they corner us. Then we had a great roundup, calling in the clan of Meanings and the clan of Hart, and that day we killed full twelve of them. Since, they have troubled us no more, so we thought them all gone. Now come these you call the White Ones, also to cause danger. The stream

149

people—they are of little account. One can handle them easily enough on land."

The woman suddenly leaned a little forward in her cushioned chair. She stared intently at Sander, as if she heard nothing Kaboss had said, or if she did, it meant but little. Now she pointed to their visitor.

"Tell me, stranger, why do you wear iron in that fashion about your head?"

He had forgotten the twisted wire he had set there in hope of not repeating that experience with what Fanyi termed the "seeking thought." Now his hand went up to touch the band in half-surprise.

The woman did not wait for his answer but continued:

"You seek the protection of the 'Cold Iron,' is that not the truth, stranger? There has come to you something you cannot understand, something no man seeks, is that not so?"

Kaboss stared from questioner to Sander and back again. Now he edged a little away from the younger man.

"Spirit-touched!"

The woman smiled, not pleasantly. "I wonder that you did not see it for yourself, Kaboss. Yes, he is spirit-touched. And such I will not have under this roof. For it can be he might open a door for what we cannot see or feel. Take him forth and leave him with that other, who frankly says she speaks with that which is not. Do this for the safety of not only this house, but all our clan."

"Planman Allbert sent him here," Kaboss began.

"This house is mine, not that of Planman Allbert. And I think if any discover you have sheltered such a one, you will find we have more un-friends than friends."

Reluctantly, Kaboss arose and beckoned to Sander. "The house is hers," he said heavily. "So any choice is hers. Come, stranger smith."

Thus did Sander find himself again in exile, a whispered explanation to the gate guards enough to send him and Rhin packing out into the night.

Still bemused by the rapidity of what had chanced, he started for the tent-wagon that had been assigned Fanyi. He was not in the least surprised to find it empty, even her pack gone. Slinging his own burden up on Rhin, he impressed upon the koyot a need for trailing. And mounted, his koyot's nose sniffing the trail, he rode out once more.

That Kaboss had expelled him so easily from the village without referring to the Planman made Sander uneasy. As he rode on, he pondered what appeared too quick a change of attitude. The woman had certainly made clear her own feelings—which suggested that perhaps the Traders themselves had encountered just such a brain-touching invasion as Sander had met. They knew the meaning of "cold iron," which had been for a long time a legend. Sander had never known it to be invoked among his own people. Perhaps this circlet would have awakened questions had he worn it while with the Mob, but here the trader-woman had instantly named it for what it was —a protection against the unseen.

But the Planman had been so emphatic that he remain with Kaboss.

Had the old Trader been slightly too emphatic on that point? Sander's thoughts coasted away in another direction. Suppose the Traders suspected that it was not chance wandering that headed Sander and Fanyi in this direction. Being constituted as they were to think first of

the discovery of hidden treasure, they would readily accept a suggestion that these trespassers had some such
search in view. But, rather than try to force a secret from
them, the easier way to discovery would be to loose both
on some pretext and then trail them.

Sander did not doubt in the least that the Trader
hounds could scent with the same efficiency and expediency as Rhin. Already men might be mounting, to skulk
behind.

There was, however, the matter of the White Ones.
Would their invasion be feared enough so that the Plan-
men dare not detach any of their fighting force to hunt
down Sander and the girl? The smith had nothing but
guesses to add together, but he thought that the sum of
them was enough.

For himself, he saw no need for secrecy. If there was
any knowledge to be had, why should it not be open to
all comers? He would not deny the Traders their share.
But what if it were the White Ones who came after
them? Sander shook his head firmly as he rode, though
there was no one to witness. No, he wanted no enemy to
benefit by anything Fanyi might uncover.

Rhin was plainly following a trail that was open and
fresh-set. For the first time Sander considered Fanyi's
attitude. She had made no attempt to wait for him. Did
she value his possible aid in her quest so little that she
had shrugged him off? He felt a pulse of anger at that. It
was as if he were inferior, one who was of no use to her
now. Perhaps the pendant had given her some secret sign
that she was close enough to her goal to make his company no longer necessary. He resented the idea he might
have been used and then so easily discarded.

Half believing this, he did not urge Rhin on, hot as
the trail was. The fishers were too-formidable opponents.
And if he had been only a temporary convenience as far
as Fanyi was concerned, there was no reason to think the
girl would not use the animals against him. They had no
kin ties—she and he.

Now and then he glanced back at the dark blot of the
Trader village. There was certainly no stir there yet. How-

ever, that did not mean that he was not under observation. They might want him well ahead before they began their hound-mounted pursuit.

There was no cover in this part of the valley. The village was situated closer to the heights on one side, while to the north curled the river. Rhin trotted toward the water, sniffing now and again at the ground. The night was frosty-clear. Sander huddled into his fur overjacket, drawing the hood, which usually lay between his shoulders, up over his head, pulling tight its drawstring.

He was tired, and his arms and shoulders ached dully from the unaccustomed labor of the afternoon when he had exerted his best efforts to impress Kaboss with his skill. Before that had been the tension and fatigue of their struggle through the heights with the alarms along the way.

Sander knew that he could not fight off sleep too long. Even as he rode his head nodded until he would snap fully awake again. How could Fanyi have gone so steadily, though of course *she* had not labored at a forge for part of the day past.

Rhin reached the river bank and paused, nosing the ground a few paces right and then left. Finally the koyot barked, and Sander realized that those he followed must have taken to the water here, though he wondered at Fanyi's recklessness since she knew that this flood in the lower regions was occupied by the amphibians.

Did the trail here go west or north? Sander tried to push aside the heavy weariness of his body and mind to decide. Ever since they had reached the land from the sea-desert, the pendant had pointed continually west. He could not believe that the direction had now changed so abruptly.

Therefore, Fanyi and the fishers had taken to the water in a simple move to confuse any hounds set behind them. If he prospected up stream, he might come across the trail where they had issued forth again. Only the point of emergence could be on the other side of the stream; if so, he would have only half a chance to find it.

With knee pressure he urged Rhin west, paralleling the

154

river. There was a moon tonight. But it was on the wane and its light was limited.

As he rode in and out among a growth of brush, Sander suddenly jerked entirely awake. That band he had set about his head—it was warm! No, hot! And getting hotter! His hands went up to jerk it off, and then he hesitated. That was what the unknown wanted. Cold iron. No, hot iron, iron that could blister and sear. The pain was to force him to rid himself of his defense.

It was iron heated in a strong blast of air-fed flames. Impossible for it to be this way in the chill of the night. It could not be! Sander began the chant of the smith's work-words. The band about his head burned like a white-hot brand, only that was what the other wanted him to think! Somehow Sander realized that. So the heat was only an illusion—a dream—that was sent to rob him of his first protection.

If this torment was only a dream—then that heat did not really exist. Determinedly, he kept his hands down, fought against the agony of the branding. This—was—not —*real!*

Now Sander singsonged aloud the smith's chant. He had not believed in Fanyi's boasted powers. But he had to believe that *this* existed, or he would not feel it. Yet he stubbornly told his shrinking, hurting body, it is *not* true! There was no fire, no forge, therefore there was no heat in the thing he wore. Cold iron—*cold* iron—

Those two words became mixed with the others he spoke. *Cold* iron!

He was not quite sure when the heat began to ebb. For by that time he was only half-conscious, clinging to one thought alone, that the iron was truly *cold*.

Within his overjacket, his coarse wool shirt was plastered to his body by the sweat of pain. He wobbled so that he could not have stayed on Rhin had he not seized with both hands upon the koyot's hide where it lay in loose rolls about the animal's neck. The iron was cold!

Rhin stopped—or had the koyot been halted for long moments while Sander fought his battle for survival? The smith did not know. Only, he realized, he was slipping from the saddle pad. On hands and knees, he dragged himself under the down-looping branches of a pine, his hands sinking nearly wrist-deep into a drift of ancient needles. There he huddled, passing quickly into exhausted sleep from that unimaginable battle.

Sander's sleep was dreamless, and when he awoke, a shaft of sunlight illumined the part of the river he caught a glimpse of between two bushes. His first memory was of the strange attack. Quickly he slipped off the band, his fingers searching his skin for the tenderness of a burn. But there was no mark there. Soberly, he once more put on the band of wire. Perhaps, if he had allowed belief to settle in his mind, he *would* have been scarred. It was still hard for him to accept the fact that such things could happen.

Yet who knew what marvels the Before People had controlled? Fanyi's pendant was more than Sander had ever imagined could exist. There was Fanyi's father—that stranger she had never seen—the man who was not a Trader, but one who, of his own will, traveled to seek out new knowledge of the world. Sander knew of no other man who was so moved. A Mob crossed plains lands because of the needs of the herds on which their wealth was based. The Traders made their long treks for gain. But a man who roved merely to see what lay on the other side of a hill or beyond a valley, such Sander could not yet understand.

Rhin! Sander stared around. The koyot was not sharing his sleeping place as they always did when on the trail together. They were no paw prints in the needle carpet. And Rhin must still be burdened with all of Sander's gear. Cautiously, the smith edged down the river bank, onto a stretch of coarse gravel. He knelt, threw back his hood to splash chill water over his face. The shock of it brought him completely awake.

Because he had no other choice, Sander loosed the whistle the koyot would answer if within voice range. But, though he listened, there was no yelp, no matter how distant. Only one thing remained, lying on the pine needles—the knot of iron he had made for the koyot. Caught in it was a tuft of yellowish fur, as if Rhin, in some agony like to his own, had pawed it free.

Had Rhin run before the hounds of the Traders? One hound the koyot could have met fang to fang. However, if those of the village had loosed their pack in full, it could well be that the koyot had fled before a collection of enemies he dare not face by himself.

If so, why had Sander not been captured by the Traders? His hiding place under the pine was certainly not so secure a one as to be overlooked by any of their hounds.

That Rhin was gone on a hunt of his own—perhaps. Though deep inside, Sander doubted that. The smith drew up his hood once more, lashed it tight. He had his dart thrower, his belt long-knife—and little else save the clothes he wore, which by now, his nose told him, should be discarded for fresher. His gear, tools, food—all else had vanished with the koyot.

Sander had no intention of returning to the Trader village. He might lack the koyot's nose for a guide, but he had a strong feeling that westward lay the answer. Also such a trail carried him from that haunted land where both the amphibians—now he gave a wary glance to the river, striving to sight any suspicious disturbance of the water in view—and the White Ones could lay ambush.

Sander drank deep, striving so to somewhat satisfy the hunger he felt by filling his empty stomach with water, then climbed the low bank. There was no sign of any trail, so he strove to keep the river in sight in order to make sure he was not wandering heedlessly. Now and again he gave his summoning whistle, hoping against hope that the koyot would either return or answer.

As the sun grew warmer, Sander unlaced his hood. Being a plainsborn man, he did not like this wooded country, thinly set as these trees were. He remembered, with shame for his own heedlessness, how back by Padford he had thought that the forest could provide shelter and what that tree-shadowed land really held.

Now he strode along, thrower in hand, dart set in the groove ready for firing, his hearing strained to catch the least sound. A light wind shifted leaves from the trees, and once or twice Sander caught the call of a bird. But he might have been the only man crossing a deserted country—until he sighted a streak of mud where a clump of sod had been pushed aside.

There, in the clay, was the print of a half-hand—a small one. Once his eyes were so alerted, he discovered other indications that here Fanyi must have emerged from the water, slipped on the clay, and thrown out a hand to support herself. That she had made no attempt to hide such traces argued to Sander that for some reason the girl had not feared any pursuit this far from the village. Or else she was now in such a hurry that haste meant more than concealment.

Realizing that she could not be too far ahead, he searched for other signs of her passing and found a few— a branch tip broken, twisting from the stem, a smear of leaves scuffed up from last year's carpet. The trail angled away from the verge of the stream, heading more to the south where trees grew thicker on upward-sloping ground.

Sander passed through young woods onto the surface of an ancient road. There was no trace here of the wreckage stretched behind. Perhaps in this small pocket of the earth there had been less havoc wrought during the Dark Time. The road, to be sure, had breaks in its surface, was drifted with soil in which grass and weeds, now fall-dried, rooted. But it was an easy path. In that soil Sander read not only of the passing of Fanyi and her fishers, but imposed over those in two places was an unmistakable paw print which could only belong to Rhin! That the koyot had deserted him to follow the others shook Sander.

He knew that Fanyi exerted a greater measure of control over the fishers, or perhaps one might say she was able to communicate more fully with them, than he did with Rhin. But he would never have believed that the Shaman could have such influence with the koyot as to deliberately draw the animal away from Sander himself. Unless, he corrected himself, she saw in this action one way of defeating pursuit.

To discover that Rhin must have been tolled away

only made stronger his own determination to hunt Fanyi down. He plodded ahead, not with speed, but grimly, not now to be turned from the way.

Those he followed had kept to the old road, going as openly (as far as he could judge from their tracks) as if they had no reason to believe that any would pursue. The road climbed more steeply a grade that nearly equaled the stark heights behind.

Sander was hungry, but that no longer mattered, though once, when he came across a place where nuts were being gathered avidly by bustling squirrels, he picked up enough of the tough-shelled harvest to nearly fill his hood, pausing to crack a number that he picked free and munched as he went. They tasted good, but they were hardly as satisfying as the stew he had eaten in Kaboss's house, a meal that seemed now like some long-past dream.

The smith reached the crest of the slope, could look forward down a long descent. A light haze hung in the air, yet he did not sniff smoke, only saw that tendrils seemed to cloud the distance. However, there was no mistaking what did lie directly ahead and to which the old road ran. Here once more were ruins, yet these had not been reduced to mere mounds of rubble in which one could not discern any features that said they had once housed men. Nor were these those battered fragments a storm had flattened like the ones he had viewed yesterday. No, there was enough form left here and there to show distinct structures. It seemed to Sander that, even as he studied them, an odd haze began to descend upon a topless wall, a shattered front, ever thickening to hide more and more.

That this must be the place Fanyi had sought, of that he was convinced. He lengthened his stride, trotted down the broken road with a desire to reach the ruins as soon as possible. His aching legs, his empty middle, as well as the westward-reaching sun told him that the day was fast on the wane.

As soon as he approached the ruins closely, he could see that the road was choked in places by barriers of fallen stone, and no attempt to clear them had been made. In

159

fact, he spotted several large chunks of metal undisturbed, and wonder grew in him. This certainly was within easy range of the Trader village. Why had they not come mining here?

The very fact that such treasure lay in the open awoke his caution. Sander hesitated, searching the ground for tracks of those he had followed. When he saw nothing, he retraced his own steps until the claw marks of one of the fishers (Kai's he decided judging by the size) drew him to the right. There a second road opened, narrower than the other, which turned north sharply, heading away from the main mass of the ruins.

Trees and bushes narrowed in, reducing the surface to perhaps a quarter of its original expanse, so the way was hardly wider than a foot path. But pressed into the leaf mold and soil there were tracks, clear and deep, openly left to be traced. Fanyi, the fishers, and Rhin. Sander could not tell whether the koyot had already joined the girl or still was simply following her.

The roadway curved twice, then ended in an expanse of pavement that reminded Sander of that on which the Trader house had been built back in the lost city. There were three buildings, or the remains of them, windows watching him with hollow eyes, nothing behind the forewalls now but emptiness. These bounded three sides of the square, the road having led into the fourth.

Sander took one step out onto that surface and swayed, falling forward to his knees. The pain in his head, shooting inward from the iron band, was so excruciating that he could feel nothing but its agony, he could not think at all. Instinct alone made him throw himself backward. Then he lay gasping with the shock of the pain, though it was now gone as suddenly as it had struck.

Some time later he squatted on his heels at the mouth of the pathroad to study the scene before him, thoroughly baffled. He had fought through tough brush and around trees, making an outward circuit of the place, only to discover that there was placed there an invisible barrier that could react on his "cold iron" viciously and instantly, dared he attempt to approach past a certain point.

No legend from a Rememberer's vast store, no tale of any Trader, mentioned such an experience as this. There was, to his sight, no movement, within that protected area. Yet Fanyi, the fishers, and Rhin had certainly come this way.

Upon intent study he had noted several tracks across the disputed space where he dared not venture without being literally swept from his feet by a force generating sheer agony in his head. So he had that much proof that they were here. But why he could not follow——?

Sander believed he need only remove his self-wrought protection and step out. But an inner core of caution argued against any such act. To surrender to the unknown so completely was not in his nature.

Though he had tried the same trick he had used on the trail, striving to make his mind dismiss the onslaught of the pain attack, that did not work here. This force was infinitely greater, and perhaps his own power to withstand it had been sapped somewhat during the first bout.

Go——he had to go on, that he knew. But he could not, wearing the band. His choice was as simple as that. And now his dogged desire to find out what lay behind all this would not let him retreat. Slowly, with a feeling that he was surrendering to an enemy, Sander worked the wire circlet loose, stowing it in the front of his outer fur jacket beside the knot he had made for Rhin.

Arising to his feet, he approached the open, moving with the caution of a scout in unknown territory, his weapon ready to hand. Still, he had a conviction that what he might find here was not to be brought down by any dart, no matter how well aimed.

Out he went, stopping where he had been struck down before. For a moment there was nothing—nothing at all. And then—

Sander stiffened, set his teeth. That thought—the thought that was not his! Now he had no escape, for it held him enmeshed as securely as had the web of the forest men. Against his will, his most fervent desire, he

161

marched forward, straight toward the middle of the three buildings.

Was this the answer to Rhin's desertion, to the open trail he had followed? Had Fanyi, all three of the animals, been so compulsively drawn in the same fashion?

Sander wavered as he went, his will battling against his body in a way he would never have believed possible. Was this a taste of the "power" Fanyi had so often spoken of? But he could not believe that the girl he knew generated *this*.

He was not being compelled toward the tottering walls of the building he saw. Rather, he was pointed directly at an opening in the pavement to one side. That this was not of the same construction as the ruins he could see, for the edging of the cut, though fashioned of blocks of stone, was very rough and crudely made in comparison to those ruins that had not entirely collapsed.

The thought of going underground gave him a spurt of additional strength to battle the will controlling him, but not enough to break its hold. Nor could he raise his hand to the iron circlet he had so recklessly put aside.

Sander reached the crude-faced opening. He could see the end of a ladder, and his body, enslaved by that other's will, swung over and began to descend. This must have been a tight fit for Rhin, but undoubtedly the koyot had come this way, for Sander caught the acrid scent of the animal's body in the enclosed space.

This burrow was not dark, there was no need for torches. So Sander saw when he reached the bottom of the ladder to look down a corridor. There were cracks across the walls, which were a dull white in color, but none had split open. Set at intervals along those walls were rods giving forth a glow of light. Not all of them were burning; several were twisted and befogged. But enough were in action to give full sight.

Save for those bars of light, there was nothing else along the hall, not the break of a single door, while the way appeared to stretch on and on. Only, at not too far a distance down its length, that same haze that had half veiled and distorted his view of the city hung again, so he could not be sure what lay behind it.

He was given no time to pause, for again his feet moved him forward, passing between the first two bars of light, heading on and on. When he screwed his head around as far as he could to look back some moments later, Sander discovered that the distorting haze had closed in behind him even more thickly, so he could no longer see the ladder at all.

The corridor was wide enough for a half-dozen men at least to march abreast, and high enough so that Rhin would not have had to crawl on his belly to transverse it. And the coating of the walls was slick, shining in the subdued light, but the footing was not slippery, being made of small red blocks fitted tightly together.

Sander breathed in air that was fresh, carrying no such taint as had that of the tunnel under the city. Now and then he was sure he could detect a faint current against his cheek.

Then the way ended in a cross hall, wide and well lighted in the same fashion. This ran both right and left, its sources hidden by the haze in either direction.

No decision was allowed to Sander here either. His path was already decided for him. Mechanically, he swung left and walked steadily ahead.

Though side openings showed both right and left, Sander was held to the main passageway. Eventually he reached the head of a stairway, one again leading down. There was evidence that some of the ceiling had fallen. Props of metal had been rammed in place against the walls; beams of the same crossed overhead, supporting cracked masonry.

Once more Sander descended. Had some of the Before People waited out the Dark Time in underground burrows? The stories he had heard of the rending of the earth itself by quakes could not have made any such plan a safe one. Here in this broken portion most of the wall lights were dark, leaving only an eerie glow at intervals. There was no change, except for the cracking in the walls themselves.

He counted the steps as he went down—twenty of them. And he could only guess at how deep this way now lay below the surface of the outer world. The props, rough as they looked against the remnants of the smooth wall, had been well set and braced. There had been a great deal of work down here to insure that these passages would continue to be usable.

By whom? The Traders? All the metal-hunting Sander had seen evidence of had been carried on above surface, while the fact that so many of these reinforcing beams and braces were of solid metal made him wonder. To so waste a highly marketable product (for it was apparent that this array of braces was singularly strong and un-eroded or rusted) was not the way of the Traders.

The mist that had floated the upper ways was missing here. Instead, where the lights still existed, the monotony of the corridor showed clearly. The will that was not his continued to force the smith ahead.

He passed a small wagon (if wagon the object could be named where there existed no method of harnessing any beast to it) against the wall. There were two seats in the front, and a fifth wheel, small, not touching the ground, was mounted on a post before one of those seats. The thing was completely wrought of metal.

In his excitement at the profuse use of a material so rarely found in an unbattered or non-time-bitten condition above ground, Sander could almost forget for an instant or two that he was as much a prisoner as if his arms were lashed to his sides and he was jerked along by a rope.

The first horror of his predicament had dulled a little. He no longer struggled uselessly against the compulsion, rather yielded, conserving his strength, his mind busy with questions that perhaps never could be answered, but among which might just lie some suggestion that would serve him later.

No Rememberer's tale had ever hinted at an unbeliev-able situation where the will of another could take over the rule of a man's body, compel him to action. But the knowledge that a Rememberer carried from the Before Days was admittedly only fragmentary.

Sander's people had not even been natives of this part of the world in that legendary time. Therefore, no man, even then, might have known what was being accomplished elsewhere. That someone could activate very old machines, such as the wagon he had just passed—yes, that he could accept without question. For the work of one man's hands might be repaired with patience and the proper tools. It was that very hope of accomplishment that had brought him north.

But the tampering with another's thoughts—that was another matter. To him such an invasion by mind was as alien as the monster on the ancient island. He decided now he had but one possible chance—to allow whatever force was summoning him now to believe that he was wholly docile, until he could learn what lay behind his capture.

The wall braces were no longer in evidence. Sander had passed beyond the section of corridor that had been threatened. Here the walls showed no cracks at all under the lights, none of which were dark here, all glowing equally. By their light Sander saw a doorway at the end of the hall, with further radiance beyond it.

Then he heard something—Rhin's sharp bark! The sound was the same the koyot always gave when greeting Sander after any absence. In so much he had been right— the koyot was waiting for him. He stepped through the door and blinked, for the light within was far greater than that which had lined the corridor.

He found himself in a room of medium size, but an odd room, for the side walls ended just above the level of his head, sprouting pillars to rise farther, ending against the ceiling well above. The room was empty, not only empty, but without any break in the walls at all, save that door through which he had just entered. Yet he was sure that it was only part of a much larger space.

At that moment the compulsion that had led him here vanished with the swiftness of one snap of a dry stick. Yet Sander was sure that, should he try to retrace his way, he would not be allowed to do so.

He had heard Rhin's bark, and it had come from this direction. Therefore, there must be a way out of this room, leading beyond. Methodically, Sander turned to the nearest wall. Though his eyes could detect not the faintest line of any opening, he began running his fingertips over the slick surface. Squatting down, he began a search upward from floor level, rising up to stretch his arms near to the wall top in a careful sweep of touch.

The construction was not of any stone that he had ever known, for this surface was far smoother than any rock could be worked. And it was chill to the touch. Yet in some places he chanced upon a slight radiated warmth. Some of those spots were hardly larger than the fingertips exploring them, others expanded so he could span them with a flattened palm.

And they occurred only on the wall directly facing the door, he discovered, after he had made a complete circuit of the small chamber. Since these were all he had found, Sander returned to them, tracing their positions carefully.

Hands—they were set in hand patterns! If one laid one's palm so, fitting into the larger space, then one's finger tips, if the fingers were spread as wide apart as possible, just touched the small spots. One hand was directly right and one left, but to fit them properly one had to stand with one's body pressed to the wall, arms extended to the farthest limit. Sander took that position and pressed his flesh into the warmth of those invisible holds.

Heat flared. He had wit enough not to snatch away his hands. In a second he knew that this radiation was not as hot as it first seemed. But he was equally startled when a disembodied voice spoke out of the air overhead, as if some invisible presence now stood directly behind him.

What it said was gibberish for the most part. But to his vast amazement Sander grasped words out of the smith's chant, words that were the deep secret of his own trade. There was an interval of silence, and once more the same stream of sounds was uttered.

Sander moistened his lips with his tongue. A—*smith*—? One of his own calling? Well, he could only try. With his hands still on those hot areas, he raised his own voice, to send, echoing hollowly through the space, the work chant, that which contained those words he was sure he had heard.

And the wall—the wall turned! The section of flooring on which his boots were planted swung with it, completely

167

around, carrying him to the other side. This was so far away from all his past experiences that he could not move for a long moment, loose his touch of the wall that had behaved in so improbable fashion, to look about and see where it had transported him.

Shivering a little, the smith forced himself to face around. He stood in another room, perhaps slightly larger than the first. However this one was not bare. There was a table, its top clear as glass, only he had never seen any fragment of glass so large, its legs fashioned of metal tubes. There were two stools fashioned of the same material, clear-topped, metal-legged.

In the center of the table rested a box about the length of his full arm, the width of his forearm. While on the top of that a number of small knobs were raised, each of a different coloring or shading of coloring. Again there was no door. And when he ran his hands over the wall that had so unceremoniously delivered him here, he could no longer locate those warm places for his hands.

Baffled, he approached the table cautiously. On the small surface of each box knob there was a marking, akin, Sander was sure, to that "writing" Fanyi boasted she knew. But the purpose of the box he could not guess. Gingerly he bent over it to study those knobs. Perhaps this controlled another door; anything was possible here. He no longer doubted that Fanyi had discovered the end of her quest. There were certainly marvels gathered in this place unlike any found in the outer world.

One line of knobs was red, shading from a very dark crimson to near pink. The second rank displayed shades of green, the third yellow, the last brown, which ended in one near white. Sander touched each line very lightly. No heat here. But that this had an important purpose he did not in the least doubt. And he wondered gloomily how many combinations of the various colors could be worked out.

Since the compulsion had released him, he felt very tired, and he was hungry enough to ache with the emptiness. Unless he could somehow force this box to yield its secret, he might well be a prisoner here indefinitely.

168

How long did it take a man to starve to death?

Stubbornly, he refused to be beaten now. If the way through another wall lay with this machine, then he was going to find it!

Begin with the first row—then the second, then combine—pushing the buttons on those two in every pattern he could think of. After that try the third and the fourth rows. Sander did not allow himself to be shaken by the thought that what he would try might take hours of effort.

He seated himself on one of the stools and leaned forward, exerting strong pressure with his forefinger on the first button in the red row. He was halfway down the line when there was a response. But it was not the one he hoped for. No wall slid aside, rose or sank into the flooring. Instead the button, upon pressure, snapped down level with the surface of the machine, did not rise again.

Sander looked hopefully at the walls hemming him in, no longer intent upon the box itself. Therefore, it was only at the sound of a click that his eyes were drawn back to it. There was an opening in one end, from which slid a brown square, and then another, both about the length of his little finger. Now the button flashed up again into line with its fellows while Sander stared questioningly at the two objects lying on the table.

It was the odor arising from them that startled him the most. Meat, roasted to a turn over a fire under the care of a most attentive cook. But why—what—how?

Warily he picked up the nearest square. It was warm—having the texture of perfectly browned crust. He could no longer resist the odor and recklessly bit into the biscuit-like offering.

As it crunched between his teeth, he could not have truly named it—a kind of bread? No, for the taste was like its scent—that of well-done meat. Yet it was plainly *not* the roast both smell and taste proclaimed it.

And though it might be loaded with some drug or fatal herb, Sander could not refuse to finish it after that first taste, any more than he could have, in his present state of dire hunger, thrown a grilled fish from him. He finished the biscuit in two bites and eagerly bit into the second.

169

Oddly enough, though the morsels were small, two of them gave him a feeling of repletion, though they added to his thirst. Now he eyed the remaining untried buttons, wondering if this box also had an answer for that need.

He went at the matter methodically. Another red button gave him a stick, darker brown, but of somewhat the same consistency of the square, which smelled like baked fish. The green line produced three different wafers, unlike in shades. These he put aside with the fish stick. The yellow had only one button in working order. But it, the box offered him a small cup of some thin, shiny material that was filled to the brim with a semi-soft, pale cream substance. A touch of his tongue informed him that this was sweet. The last row—at the next to the last button—slid out to his hand a slightly larger cup, a lid of the same substance creased tightly over it. When he had worked that off, Sander held a measure, not of water, but of a liquid with an aromatic odor he had never smelled before. He gulped it down though it was hot. Like the cream stuff, it was sweet to the taste but it slaked his thirst.

Carefully, he put the fish stick and the wafers inside his coat. The cream substance, for want of any spoon, he licked clean of its container.

Would the same knobs work again, providing him with extra provisions? Once more he tried the same combination of pressed knobs, but no more supplies appeared. Did it only then work once? Had there in the beginning been food delivered from each of those buttons—but now that abundance had failed through the long seasons, so only these were left—and perhaps he had exhausted the last of what the box had to offer?

The thing was a machine of some kind, of course, but how it worked he could not guess. It was certainly too small to hide, within its interior, supplies to be cooked and offered. Sander got down on the floor, looking up through the transparent surface of the table at the box's underside. But it was entirely solid.

He was no longer hungry or thirsty, but he was still a prisoner. The stool on which he sat—if it were moved against the wall, would it give him extra height so he might reach the top of the partition?

When he tried to shove it, he found that it could only be drawn back from the vicinity of the table far enough for some one to be seated, no farther.

Sander shrugged. He suspected there were no short cuts here. It would require patience and all the wit he possessed to learn the secrets of these rooms. Rhin—if he could win an answer from the koyot, he would at least know in which direction he must advance, which of the three walls was the barrier to be crossed.

He whistled, and the sound seemed doubly loud and strong. Listening, he could hear nothing but his own faster breathing. Then—from afar—came the yelp. However, it was so echoed within the area, he could not pinpoint the direction.

Once more he began a patient and exhaustive search of the wall surface. He knew what to look for now. Only this combing of the walls was fruitless. No warm spots were to be found, even though he made that sweep twice.

Finally Sander returned to the table, flung himself on the stool and rested his elbows on the surface, which supported the box, holding his head in his hands as he tried systematically to think the problem through. There were none of those mysterious handholds on the walls, that he would swear to. He had leaped several times, trying to catch at the top of the same barriers. But so slick was the coating there, his hands slipped from any grip he tried to exert. Then—how did he get out?

For Sander was very certain that there was a way out of this room, doubtlessly one as cleverly hidden as those handholds had been. What was the purpose of this place? It seemed that whoever had constructed it (unless that mind was either entirely alien or warped) had intended to make it difficult for any one to travel through. The situation had elements, Sander decided, of some kind of testing.

Testing—he considered that idea and found that he liked it, that such an answer fitted what small facts he knew. The purpose of the testing, unless it was to gauge the imagination or intelligence of the captive, he could not now know. But its former purpose was immaterial, it was how he might confront the problems offered him now that mattered.

So far he had, by trial and error and the use of what he considered good sense, solved two problems. He had found the first door and he had supplied himself with food and drink. Both of those answers had merely required persistence and patience. Now he was faced with that one that demanded more in the way of experimentation.

The walls were sealed, and he believed any attempt to scale them would be useless. So—what did that leave? The floor!

Again he thought that he could be better served by his sense of touch than his sight. Sander slipped from the stool to his hands and knees, and selecting the nearest corner, he searched that carefully before he started out, sweeping inch by inch across the pavement which, though not quite as smooth as the walls, was uniformly level. First he made a circuit around the base of the four walls, hoping to find at one of them the release he was convinced lay somewhere.

Failing any such discovery, he launched farther into the middle of the room. It was only when he realized that he had entirely swept the whole of that surface that he sat down, with his back to that impenetrable wall, to again consider what he termed the facts of his case.

He had entered through that wall, the one now directly opposite to him. But the hidden latch there was plainly unresponsive to any return. He had searched the three other barriers, and the floor. Nothing.

Dully he leaned his head back against the wall at his back and forced himself once more to consider that room. There were four walls, a floor, high above his head a ceiling that the walls did not reach. There was the table, the box that had fed him, two stools that could not be moved far enough to aid in any climbing.

Table—stools—box— He had explored everything else. Did the secret lie in the center of the chamber after all? Excited by hope, he got up. Neither stool could be shifted any more than his first try had proven. And the knobs—surely they were meant for food delivery, not, as he first conceived, for operating some device of the walls. Now—the table.

For all his exertion of strength, he could not shift it even a fraction of an inch. The metal legs, though they appeared to rest on the surface of the floor, might well be embedded in it for all the good his pushing and pulling did.

Table, stools, box—

Once more Sander subsided on the stool to think. The patterned colors of the knobs were before him—red, green, yellow, brown—Red since the beginning of time had registered with his species as a signal of power—of danger. It was the red of a fire that destroyed if it could not be curbed, of the flush that anger brought to a man's face.

Green soothed the eyes. That was the color of growing things—of life. Yellow—yellow was gold, treasure, sunshine, also a kind of power, but less destructive than red. Brown—brown was earth—a thing to be worked with, not that would work of itself.

Why was he wasting his time considering the meaning of colors? He had to find the way out—he had to!

Still, he could not break his intent stare at the rows—red, green, yellow, brown. They provided food; they were useless for his other need.

Brown—yellow of the gold hidden in the earth—green of the things that grew on it—red—of fire that could lick earth bare of life. Somehow a pattern began to weave in his mind, though he tried to drive such foolishness out, to think constructively of what he must do. But were such thoughts foolish? Fanyi would say no, he supposed, her belief in her Shaman powers being such she was able to accept without doubt strange vagaries of the mind. Sander had never believed—really believed—in anything he could not see, touch, taste, hear for himself.

Still, on this journey he had already met with that which could not be so measured. As a smith he labored with his hands, but what he so wrought was first a picture in his mind, so that he followed a pattern no other man might see. Thus he, too, in a way dealt with the intangible.

Should he after all his experiences of these past hours now refuse to use imagination when that might be the one key to defeat the walls? That voice from the air that had addressed him earlier had used a smith's words. True, they had been intermingled with others Sander could not understand, but he was certain of those few. He must take that as an omen of sorts and now trust his guesses, no matter how wild they might seem.

"Brown," he spoke aloud, and thumbed the darkest of the buttons on that row. "Gold." He sought out the brightest there, one that reminded him most of molten metal as it ran, fiery swift, into a mold. "Green." Not the dark top one there, but one halfway down the row, which was most akin to the fresh growth of early spring. "Red." And this one was that shade a dancing flame might own.

A grating noise sounded. One wall broke apart as a panel pulled upward, leaving a narrow space open. Somehow Sander was not even surprised. He had had the feeling as he pressed the buttons in his chosen order that he had indeed solved another small segment of a mystery.

Now he walked forward with some confidence, passing through the opening to face once more the unknown.

This was not another room as he had expected, rather a narrow corridor boxed in by blank walls. Sander strode along with that new confidence his solving of the door code had given him. Nor was he surprised when, as he approached the far end of the way, a section of the blank expanse facing him rolled aside without any effort on his part.

Sound filtered from beyond. There was a hum, a clicking, other noises. Once more he slowed, trying to judge what he might have to face. Sander had an idea that whoever used this strange maze was not one to be easily met in any confrontation or even menaced by either weapon he carried. The dart thrower, his long knife were as far removed from the things he had seen as those weapons were in turn from some unworked stone that might be snatched up by a primitive being to do battle.

Making his decision, he fitted the thrower back into its shoulder case to step through that second portal empty-handed. An increased glare of light made him blink. Nor could he begin to understand what he saw—webbings of metal, of glass, squat bases from which grew those webs, flashing of small lights.

Among all this there was one familiar sight. Rhin bounded toward him, giving voice to yelps that meant welcome in such a crescendo of sudden sound it was as if the koyot found in Sander's arrival vast relief.

The animal's rough tongue rasped across Sander's cheek. He himself clutched the loose hide across Rhin's shoulders. In all this strangeness the koyot was a tie with a world Sander knew well.

At that moment, once more he heard the voice out of the air. This time he could not understand even a few words of its gabble. The machines, if these rods sprouting webbing were machines, stood about the walls, leaving the center of the area free. Sander advanced into that, one hand still resting on Rhin's back. There was nothing in this place that was in the least familiar though he was forced to marvel at the workmanship of the installations.

What were their purpose? Now that he could see those lines in their entirety, he was also aware that not all of them glowed. In fact, lying in broken fragments upon the heavy bases of a few, were the remains of webbing, while there was a pitch of sound issuing from others that made him flinch and the koyot yelp protestingly as they passed them.

But of any living creature there was no sign. Sander raised his voice to call Fanyi's name. There was no answer, save the clatter and drone of the machines.

"Who are you?" For the first time then he dared the Voice to answer. It did not reply.

With Rhin beside him, glancing quickly from right to left, half expecting a challenger to arise from behind an installation, Sander traversed the room. There was a second archway, beyond which he found quite a different scene.

Here, the center of a large chamber was occupied by an oval space around which were two lines, also curved to the oval, of cushioned chairs. The oval itself was sunk below the surface of the floor and filled with what Sander, at first glance, thought was a remarkably still pool of water. Then he realized that this was also glass or some equally transparent material.

Leaving Rhin, the smith pushed between two of the chairs (a nudge informed him these were fastened in position and could not be moved) and stood gazing down at that glassy surface, a dull dark blue in color. That, like the food box, it had some highly significant use, Sander was sure. The whole arrangement of this room suggested that people had once gathered here to sit in these chairs, to look down onto that surface.

It was not a mirror, for, though he stood at its very edge, it did not reflect his image. Nor were there any of those knobs along it, which the food box had displayed. Slowly, he went from chair to chair, until he reached the one at the left-hand curve of the oval. There, for the first time, he noted a difference. This chair had very broad arms studded with buttons, each bearing some of those symbols Fanyi had called letters.

Slowly, Sander lowered himself into that seat. It was very comfortable, almost as if the chair instantly adjusted itself to his form. He studied the knobs. They had something to do with the glass surface just beyond the toes of his worn boots, he was sure. But what?

There were two rows of them on each of the wide arms, arranged for the ease of anyone resting his elbows on those supports and stretching out his hands naturally. There was only one way to learn—and that was by action. He brought the forefinger of his right hand down on the nearest button.

There came no response, to his disappointment. But only one button—much had perhaps ceased to function over the long years. He could hope that enough remained active to give him some idea of why men had gathered here to watch a dull-surfaced and non-reflective mirror.

Methodically, he pressed the next button in line with no better response. But a third gave him an amazing answer. Points of light appeared on the mirror, lines glowing like quickly running fire came to life, outlining large patches, irregular in size and shape. Sander leaned forward eagerly, tried to make some meaning of that display.

177

There were four—no five—large outlined shapes there. Two were united by a narrow, curved string, the other two larger shapes had a firmer junction. There were also smaller ones here and there, some near to the larger, others scattered farther away. The brilliant points of light were, in turn, strewn by no orderly method over the outlined patches.

Regretfully, though he studied it hungrily, Sander could deduce no possible meaning. He pressed the next button and the pattern flashed off. New lines moved, assembled in another quite different form. Only the bright points of light now totally vanished, and many of the outlines of the patches were blurred and weak.

"Our world—"

Sander swung around, his hand already reaching for the hilt of his long knife. He did not need Rhin's growl, though for a moment he wondered why the koyot had not given earlier warning, for this voice had not come, disembodied, out of the air. Those two words had been spoken by a man, a man who hobbled forward, watching Sander as warily as the smith eyed him.

The stranger was not an attractive sight. Once tall, he was now stoop-shouldered and bow-backed. His overthin arms and legs were emphasized, as was his swollen belly, by the fact that he wore a garment of gray made to cling tightly. His head was covered with stiff, whitish bristle, as if the dome of his skull had been first shaven and then allowed to sprout hair again for an inch or so. A long upper lip carried a thin thatch of the same wiry growth, but his seamed face was otherwise free of beard. What skin showed, which was only that of his face and knobby-fingered hands, was of so pale a color as to resemble that of the White Ones, yet it had a gray cast also.

In one hand he held, pointed at Sander with care, in spite of the trembling of his hands so that he had at times to strengthen his grip by the aid of the other, a tube that Sander believed a weapon. And for any armament that might match the surroundings of this place, the smith already had a hearty respect.

178

"Our world," the apparition in gray said for the second time, and then coughed rackingly.

Sander heard a whine from Rhin and glanced in the direction of the koyot. The animal, whom he had seen charge even a herd bull and keep that formidable beast busy until the riders of the Mob could rope it, was crouching to the floor as if he had been beaten. And at the sight of that Sander's temper flared.

"What have you done to Rhin!"

The stranger grinned. "The animal has learned a lesson. I am Maxim—no beast shall show teeth to me. Be warned, boy, be warned! I have"—he made a gesture to embrace perhaps more than the room they were now in— "such powers at my command as you poor barbarians outside cannot even dream of! I am Maxim, of the Chosen Ones. There were those who foresaw, who prepared— We, we alone saved all that was known to man! We alone!" His voice scaled up thinly with a note in it that brought another whine out of Rhin and disturbed Sander. The smith thought that the line between sanity and madness already had been crossed by this twisted man.

"Yes, yes!" the other continued. "We preserved, we endured, we are the only intelligence, the only civilization left. Barbarian—look well at me—I am Maxim! There is here"—with one knotty finger he tapped the front of his head—"more knowledge than you could hope to gain in two of your limited life times. You think to steal that now? There is no way—it is locked here." Again finger thumped forehead. "You cannot even understand what you lack—so reduced is your species. You are not human as were the Before Men—!"

His babble grew more and more strident. Sander had only to look at Rhin to realize that this madman had formidable weapons, and he did not doubt that the other was equally ready to turn them on anyone or thing he might encounter. What had happened to Fanyi and the fishers? This must be the storage place she had sought, of that Sander was sure. But had she met this Maxim and paid for it? As his anger had been aroused by the sight of Rhin cowed by this mockery of a true man, so it was heightened by a mental picture of Fanyi perhaps meeting death at his hands.

"What want you?" Maxim demanded now. "What have you come to ask of Maxim? Ways of killing? I can show you such as will melt your mind with horror. We knew them, yes, we knew them all! There are diseases one can sow among the unknowing, so that they die like poisoned insects. We can keep alive a man's body to serve us, but destroy his will, even his thinking mind. We can blast a city from the earth by pressing a single button. We are masters. This place, it is of our planning, for we knew that some must be saved, that our civilization must live. And it was preserved, and we did live—"

His voice trailed into silence, the animation faded from his unhealthy face. For a moment he looked lost and empty as if he himself had been the victim of one of the mind-destroying weapons he had enumerated.

"We live," he repeated. "We live longer than any man has done before. And after us our children live— How old do you think I am, barbarian?" he demanded.

Sander refused to make a guess that might be wrong, one that would arouse the ill will of this mad creature.

"Each people," he chose his words cautiously, "has its own norm of life span. I cannot tell yours."

"Of course not!" The man's head wobbled in a nod. "I am one of the Children. I have lived near two hundred of the years by which men used to reckon."

Which might even be true, Sander decided. How many more of these inheritors of what (if he had heard the listing correctly) seemed the worst of the Before Men's knowledge still existed?

"Near two hundred years," Maxim repeated. "I was wise, you see. I knew better than to risk my life going out into the dead world, mixing with the barbarians. I told them they were doing wrong. Lang, I told Lang what would happen." He laughed. "And I was right. Barbarian, do you know how Lang died? Of a pain in his belly—of something that a minor operation would have cured. She told me that—she who said she was Lang's daughter. Of course she lied. No one of us would mate with a barbarian.

She lied, but I could not deal with her for her lies because she had Lang's own transmitter.

"We were programmed from the first so there would be no quarrels among us. We were such a small number then—and it might be that we would be sealed here in this complex for generations. So there must be no quarrels, no misunderstandings. All of us had the transmitters for our own protection. You see, barbarian, how everything was arranged? How there could be no trouble we were not equipped to handle?

"And the children. Like Lang, they had their transmitters from birth. It was all so carefully thought out. The Big Brain in the sealed chamber—it knew everything. It knows everything. It has not made any contact for a time now. There is no need, of course. I, Maxim, I know all that is necessary."

"This girl who told you of Lang's death"—Sander had no doubt there was a reference to Fanyi—"where is she now?"

Maxim laughed. "She lied to me, you know. No one must lie to Maxim. I can see a man's thoughts if I wish. I can see your thoughts, barbarian! When she came, I knew there would be others. I used the—" He stopped again and eyed Sander warily. "I brought you here, barbarian. It was amusing, very amusing. There were the old testing rooms, and it was of interest to see you working your way through. She did not have to do that—not with Lang's transmitter. But you showed a certain cunning, not human, but amusing, you know. I had to have you here. The rest of your kind—they want my treasures—but they can be stopped. Since you came through my barriers, I knew I must get you all the way to be safe."

"I'm here," Sander pointed out. "But the girl—what did you do with her?"

"Do with her?" The laugh degenerated into a giggle. "Why, I did nothing, nothing at all. There was no need to. The Big Brain has its own defenses. I listened to her, pointed her in the right direction, and let her go. There was no need at all for me to concern myself farther. She was even grateful to me. I—" That same tinge of bewilderment crossed his pouched and flabby face. "There was something about her. But, no, no barbarian can have any trait that Maxim cannot master! To control beasts— that I can do too. See how this mangy creature of yours fears me. Now the problem is—how to make you useful. You have no transmitter, so, of course, you can be mastered."

"But I have!" Whether he spoke the truth or not, Sander did not know. But that he must make some move on his own part to face up to this caricature of a man, of that he was certain.

"You cannot!" The man's tone was petulant as that of a stubborn child. "Lang was the last to go forth. He left me, in spite of what I told him over and over, he left me! He was stupid, really. Being the youngest of the children, the breeding must have worn thin in his genera- tion. And Lang had only one transmitter. They do not last long—not more than fifty years or so. Then they have to be recharged. So yours, if you do have one, is inoperable. It would be that of Robar perhaps. And he went longer ago than Lang. Do not try to trick me, bar- barian! Remember, I am Maxim and the knowledge of the Before Time is all mine!"

"I will show you." Carefully Sander reached for the front of his outer coat. He saw that tube in the other's hand center on him, but he had to take this chance. He brought out the band of woven wire.

Maxim cackled. "That is no transmitter, barbarian! You are indeed no more intelligent than this beast. A trans- mitter! You do not even know what the word means. *She* did not know. She thought it magic—magic such as the superstitious savage plays with! And now you show me a mass of wire and call it a transmitter!"

Daring to provoke some action from Maxim, Sander again fitted the band around his head. Perhaps it would serve his purpose now if this survivor of the Before Men judged him, too, childlike and superstitious.

"It is cold iron," he said solemnly. "And I am one of those who fashion iron, so that it obeys me." He began the smith's chant.

A flicker of faint interest answered him. "That—that is a formula," Maxim observed. "But it is not right, you know. This is the way it should be." His voice took on something of a Rememberer's twang as he recited words. "Now that is the right of it. So you hoard scraps of the old learning after all, do you, barbarian? But what is cold iron? That expression has no meaning whatsoever! And— I have wasted enough time. Come, you!"

He pressed one of the spots along the side of his tube. Instantly Sander swung partly forward, pulled by the same compulsion that had brought him here. But his hands tightened on the arms of the chair.

Iron—cold iron. His smith's belief in the Old Knowledge—belittled as it had been by Maxim—that was the only weapon he had left.

He concentrated on holding to the chair, setting his teeth against the pain of the iron heating about his forehead. No—no—and NO!

Maxim's face contracted, flushed. His mouth fell open, showing his pale tongue and teeth that were worn and yellow-seeming.

"You *will* come!" he screeched.

Sander clung to the chair arms. The misery of that struggle within him was fast approaching a level where he could no longer bear it, he would have to surrender. And if he did, then he would be lost. He did not know why he was sure of that, only that he was.

The air between him and Maxim was aglow. Sander held on to the chair with such a grip as deadened all feeling in his fingers. His head was afire. He must—

A tawny shape arched through the air, paws thudding home on Maxim's hunched shoulders. The thin man was slammed down and back against the pavement to lie still, Rhin's forepaws planted on him, the koyot's muzzle aiming for the old man's throat.

As the tube spiraled out of Maxim's grip, the intolerable pressure on Sander winked out. He managed to croak out an order to Rhin not to kill. He could not allow the koyot to savage the other in cold blood. After all the man was mad, he was old. And what was most

183

important now was to find Fanyi and warn her. Into what kind of trap Maxim had sent the girl, Sander could not guess. But he suspected that the end of it was death in one form or other.

He used part of his rope to bind Maxim. Then he raised the skinny body to put it into one of the chairs, again making fast more binding.

Finished, Sander turned to Rhin:

"Find Fanyi!" he ordered.

The koyot still faced the unconscious Maxim, growls rippling from his throat as if he had no other wish than to make an end to him. Sander came over, slapped the animal's shoulder, reached up to tug at an ear.

"Fanyi!" he repeated.

Even in this place the girl's scent must lie somewhere, and Rhin was the best tracker he had ever known. With a last threatening growl, the koyot looked from Maxim to Sander. He whined and nudged at the smith's shoulder. The animal's puzzlement was clear to read. Rhin saw no reason to leave Maxim alive; his reasoning was sensible. But at the same time Sander could not bring himself to kill the now helpless man or to let Rhin do it for him.

One might kill in defense of his own life or to protect those he had some kinship with. He would front the amphibians, as he had, or the White Ones and feel no qualms as he watched his darts go home. That abomination they had confronted in the forest glade, or the monster on the once-island—those were such horrors as aroused Sander's deepest fear. But it was not in him to put an end to this flaccid being roped into the chair, head hanging, held in place only by the bonds Sander himself had set.

Sander stooped and picked up the rod Maxim had dropped. There were five dots along its side. But he had no idea what forces it controlled nor any desire to experiment with it. What was important now was time, to find Fanyi before she blundered into full disaster.

"Fanyi!" For the third time Sander repeated her name, waving Rhin away from their captive.

The koyot barked once and came. He rounded the oval of seats and kept straight ahead, Sander trotting at a brisk pace to match his guide's. Rhin moved with such purpose Sander believed the koyot knew exactly which way they must go. Perhaps the animal had even witnessed the girl being set on her way by the malicious, ancient guardian of this place.

Sander could not accept that Maxim was the only inhabitant of this hideaway. Though the other had mentioned only two names, both of the men now dead, that did not mean that all the colony meant to outlast the Dark Times had entirely vanished. Nor was the smith sure, after witnessing the confrontation between Rhin and Maxim at their first meeting, that the koyot would give him any alarm. It was only because Maxim had been so intent on taking Sander that Rhin had had a chance to rebel.

They threaded a way through rooms and halls opening one into another. Some were filled with installations, some were plainly meant for living, with divans and various pieces of oddly shaped and massive furniture.

Sander paused once when he came to another chamber where a food machine sat. This was larger than the one that had occupied the room to the forepart of this maze, with more numerous rows of buttons. Sander used his fingertips confidently and produced more rounds and wafers, cups of water, not only to feed Rhin and himself, but to carry as extra rations, which he tumbled into the food bag and poured into his water bottle. How a machine could produce food apparently from nothing was a mystery, but the results were tasty, not only for man but for koyot also. And Sander was more satisfied in results and less interest in means at the moment.

Rhin pattered on until they passed out of a last grouping of rooms into another long hall, one with the same smooth walling and bars of dim light, though here all those were lit. The air remained fresh, with a faint current now and then. Sander continued to marvel at all the knowledge that must have lain behind the building and equipping of this refuge.

Sometime he would like to return once more to that room with the pool of glass and see the strange outlines that could be summoned to appear there. If Maxim had been right that the second series of pictures showed their world as it now was, then the earlier series must have been the world of the Before Days.

Sander carried with him a memory of the vast changes in those lines. But if the alteration had been so great, then how had this particular series of burrows managed to survive practically intact. He could understand that the inhabitants, once they had survived the worst of the world-wide changes, had their own methods of protecting themselves against the looting of any wandering band that approached their outer gate. But he could not conceive of a protection strong enough to stand against the fury of earthquakes, volcanoes, and disrupted seas.

This hall seemed to continue forever. Now and again Rhin dropped nose to the floor, then always gave one of his small yelps. They were on their way, the right way—to where?

At the end of the passage, a ramp led downward again. The bars of light were fewer here; thick patches of shadow lay between each. At first the slope was gradual and then it grew steeper. It would seem that whatever the Before Men wished to hide here they had burrowed deeply to insure that it would not be disturbed by any upheaval of the earth.

Nor was the air as good. This supply had an acrid smell leading Sander to cough now and then. He remembered Maxim's threat—that what Fanyi had come this way to seek had its own defenses, an idea that made him proceed with added caution. What had Maxim called it—the Great Brain? Could a machine *think?* Sander wished he had paid stricter attention to the Rememberers. Had any of their tales ever hinted at such?

Just as Sander thought that they would continue to descend forever, deeper and deeper into the heart of the world, the ramp straightened out. Here the glow of the wall lights was dimmed by films of long-deposited dust. Underfoot, he shuffled over a velvety carpet of the same.

However, it was disturbed by prints. Even in this subdued light Sander caught sight of the fishers' claw-tipped tracks and boot impressions only Fanyi could have left.

It was colder here. He drew up his hood, tightened its string. He could see his breath in small frosty puffs on that too-still air. Rhin fell back, his muzzle on a line now with Sander's shoulder, no longer ranging ahead. Now and then the koyot uttered faint whines of uneasiness.

There was movement in the shadows ahead. Sander came to a halt, freeing his dart thrower, having thrust the weapon he took from Maxim into his belt. Rhin growled, then gave an excited warning yelp. The answer was a clanging sound that had no kinship to anything Sander had ever heard, unless it was the ring of a light hammer against metal.

The thing that trundled forward was not, he saw, as it wove in and out of those patches of wall light, any living creature. It could not be. Instead, it mainly resembled a round kettle such as the Mob used for a fall feasting. That moved on rollers, set beneath its surface, at a steady, if slow, pace. But it was what erupted from the kettle that made Sander wary. For it sprouted a series of weaving, jointed arms, all of seemingly different lengths, and they ended in huge claws with formidable teeth. These arms were in constant motion, sweeping the floor, or scraping along the walls, while the claws clashed open and shut. The thing provided such an opponent as no dart could bring down, no matter how skillful the aim might be.

Rhin uttered a series of heavy growls, pushed past Sander to snap at the trundling metal thing. But the koyot kept well beyond the reach of the arms that now swung toward him, the clatter of the claws growing louder as they opened and shut faster and faster.

The koyot danced just beyond the extreme limit of the arms, snapping in return, but always retreating. Sander reached for the rod he had taken from Maxim. If this weapon had any power, it could be their only chance against a moving machine.

Still holding the more familiar dart thrower in his left hand, the smith sighted along the tube, which he now cradled in his right, then he brought his thumb hard against the side. But not before he whistled Rhin back out of range, for he could not be sure what was going to happen in that attack.

A beam of light shot out past the koyot, to catch the kettle shape dead center. For a moment there seemed to be no effect. Sander began to stumble backwards, Rhin once more beside him, for those flailing arms with their trap claws clattered in a snapping whirlwind toward them.

Then, where the beam was touching that swell of metal, there appeared a spot that grew deeper and deeper red. The ray appeared to be burning into the thing's body. But the moving machine showed no discomfort; if anything, its rush toward them speeded up. One of those clutching set of claws caught on a dusty light pillar, tightened, and crushed it with the ease of a knife slicing through a meal cake.

Sander whistled again to the koyot, signaling retreat. He wanted to turn and run, but if this Before Weapon was to be stopped, he must go slowly and keep the rod steady, eating in upon the same glowing spot.

A darker heart grew in that circle now. The force of the focused light must have eaten through the outer casing of the creature. Sander held the beam steady, backing away, trying to match his retreat to the pace of the thing's forward roll.

Then—there came a flash of light so intense and searing that he was blinded. Crying out, he grasped for Rhin. He could see nothing, but his hold upon the koyot pulled him back until his heels hit the end of the ramp that had brought them here. Only then was he aware that the rumble, the clashing sound, which the thing had made, was stilled. It must at least have been stopped by the ray.

Still Sander retreated farther, partway up the ramp, blinking his eyes, striving to regain his sight. The fear that the explosion of light might have indeed blinded him was a near terror that he flinched from facing.

Rhin pulled free from the smith's hold, padded away in spite of Sander's voice commands. He heard a clatter and the growling of the koyot. Then Rhin bounded back, nudged Sander with his shoulder.

Warm metal brushed the smith's hand. He put his weapon away, groped outward until his hands closed upon a jointed rod. He felt it with his fingers and found on the end of it a claw frozen well apart.

He *had* put the thing out of action! But his elation at that fact was tempered by his blindness. What if—if he was never to see again!

Sander put the thought firmly out of his mind. The crawling thing had been stopped. And there was no need to retreat again. He had Rhin—the koyot would give him warning if any more such disputed their road. Better go forward than skulk back into the intricate complex where he had left Maxim. Let the madman discover that Sander was in any way helpless and he would have no defenses.

Taking a tight grip on the lashings of Rhin's harness, he moved forward. His confidence was heightened as he began to capture, if dimly, a small suggestion of light to one side. He must be sighting one of the wall lamps.

Rhin paced slowly, then stopped with a whine. Sander, still keeping his grasp on the koyot's lashings, used the detached arm Rhin had brought him to sweep the floor before him. Metal rang against metal with a clatter. They must have reached the destroyed thing.

Sander knelt and felt about with both hands. Broken metal, hot to the touch, lay in a mass. Slowly and carefully he pushed and piled the pieces to one side. His eyes were watering now, moisture trailing down his dust-powered cheeks. He could see a little, enough to clear their way.

Then, once more with Rhin for his guide, he started on, tapping before him with the iron claw to be sure nothing lay there to stumble over. His eyes smarted, but he was careful not to rub them with his dusty hands. Was the machine just destroyed the only one roaming these ways? At least, unless the weapon had exhausted itself in that attack, he had a counter for such. But he remembered what Fanyi had warned about her light: that these tools and weapons of the Before People had limited lives, and he might have expended the full force of Maxim's tube in that single action.

Sander sneezed and coughed. Fumes, which must have come from the destruction of the clawed sentinel, made his throat hurt, attacked his nose. Rhin wheezed in answer. But at least the smith could pick out of the general fog ahead new gleams of wall lights. And the sight of those heartened him. Maxim had said that whatever Fanyi sought was well protected. Could this machine have been one of those protections?

The smith fingered the arm, touched gingerly the teeth in the claw. It was a vicious thing, like enough to those weapons Maxim had boasted were controlled by those who had built this place—disease—all the rest. What kind of people had they been? The White Ones, the Sea Sharks killed. But not at a distance, and not without risking their own lives in return. There had been that female thing that the forest men had given them to, the monster on the island. Again, those were flesh and blood. And so, in a manner, to be understood. But this metal crawler, those other weapons Maxim had listed with such mad satisfaction—

More than the dust and the fumes struck at Sander. His own revulsion against those who had fashioned this lair made him sick. Had they all been mad from the beginning? Was Maxim merely tainted with the legacy that was his from birth?

The corridor took an abrupt turn. Herein the air was slightly better, though the lights were still befogged when Sander looked at them. He swept the arm back and forth, stirring the dust, his hearing alert to any sound that might come from their own passing. It was thus that he became conscious of a kind of beat or vibration that might have been carried by the stale air itself. Where had he felt this before? The sensation was dimly familiar. In the forest! When they had been snared by the tree men!

But there were no trees here, nothing overhead except the walled roof of the corridor.

"Rhin?" He spoke the koyot's name aloud because that

191

familiar syllable somehow linked him with another living thing.

The koyot was silent, save that his nose touched Sander's cheek for an instant. There was the feeling of awareness, of danger to come, flowing from Rhin to him more strongly than the man had ever felt such a warning before. Still the koyot was quiet. Not even the near soundless growl he sometimes used could be felt through Sander's hold on him. The smith searched within his jacket, brought out the thong with its knot of wire, and put it once again about Rhin's throat.

They moved on, aware of what was akin to the beating of a giant heart not quite in rhythm with the pump of Sander's own blood, but near enough to it. The smith blinked his dust-assaulted eyes. Finally he stopped, freed the water bottle from its lashing, wet part of a spare undershirt, and held the damp, cool compress on his closed lids. Three such applications and his sight cleared, showing him details of the dusty hall.

With the disappearance of the haze, he could also see a door ahead. It was shut fast, and there was no sign of a latch or knob or of any way of opening it. All that was visible on the smooth surface fronting them was a hollow at about eye level. Reaching the barrier, Sander strove to insert his finger into that hollow, to so exert pressure that the surface would either slide to one side or lift up. But it remained stubbornly immovable.

Would the cutting power of Maxim's rod clear a path for them here?

Sander fingered the Before Weapon. There was a risk in what it might do. Use of the beam might trigger some retaliation. Yet he could not just give up and walk away.

Fanyi must have gone through here—what method had she used? Was it that gift from her father that had perhaps brought her safely past the guardian he had beamed down? He ran his fingers about the depression in the door. Though he was only guessing, Sander believed it was just of a size that Fanyi's pendant might fit into.

Being not so equipped with any answer to the barrier, he held the rod closer to one of the two wall lamps that flanked the sealed door and studied it. This was the spot he had pressed on the rod to bring about the destruction of the sentry. But there were four other such markings on the part of the rod that formed the hand grip.

There was only one way to make sure—that was to try. Waving Rhin back so that the koyot might not be engulfed in any sudden disaster born from the smith's recklessness, Sander set the firing end of the tube directly into the edge of the door's depression.

He pressed the first button.

There was nothing at all! Nothing until Rhin gave a howl and lowered his head to the floor and pawed at his ears. Quickly Sander released that button. Was this what Maxim had used to bring the animal to submission?

Rhin shook his head vigorously; his growls were deep-chested. Now he looked at Sander, baring his teeth.

The smith was almost argued out of trying the next of the marks. He had no wish to unleash upon himself Rhin's full anger. And he did not see how he could make the koyot understand that he had applied such torment, not by wish but through ignorance alone.

To go at once to the full power of the rod—yes. But first make sure he was not temporarily blinded a second time. Sander draped his head in the dampened shirt, tucking its folds into the edge of his hood. He sent Rhin back down the corridor, then set the rod firmly into the depression again. Bearing down hard, he applied the full force of whatever power it held.

Even through the improvised shield across his eyes, he caught a flash of white fire. There was a clank of tortured metal. Then carrying acrid fumes, a blast of damp heated air hit him full in the face.

He also heard something else. There was no mistaking that savage hissing. The fishers! And by the sharpness of the sounds they now faced him.

Sander pawed the shirt away from his face. The door had split into two, providing a space wide enough perhaps for both him and Rhin to squeeze through, but still not clearing the whole of the archway. Light, stronger than that of the corridor, streamed out, showing very clearly both Kai and Kayi, one on either side, humped and ready to spring into battle. Beyond them was a confusion of objects, brilliantly lighted, that he could distinguish clearly.

To harm the fishers, that he did not want to do. He raised his voice and called, over the dryness of his throat: "Fanyi!"

The vibration grew stronger, beat with greater power, while the battle sounds made by the fishers became louder. Only the girl did not answer.

Had she been injured—trapped by one of the protective devices Maxim had hinted at—thus arousing her companions to battle anger? Or had she purposefully set them here on guard to ward off any interference with what she would do? Either answer could serve, but it would not remove Kai and Kayi.

They must know his scent and that he had been accepted by Fanyi and had traveled with her. Would that small familiarity aid him now? Behind him he heard the pad of Rhin's feet. There must be no provoking attack between the animals.

Sander retreated a few steps, eyeing the fishers narrowly. They made no move to advance from the other side of the door he had forced open. He searched in his food bag, brought out some of those small cakes that tasted so much like fresh meat, the ones Rhin had gobbled with a visible relish. To each of the fishers he tossed three of these.

Kayi sniffed first at her offering. She tongued one of the biscuits and then gulped it whole. A second one was crunched between her jaws before her mate consented to try his share. They still watched Sander as they ate, and their hissing continued. But they licked up each crumb avidly as if they had been long hungry.

Sander could not touch them as the girl did, that he was wise enough to know. But he squatted down, bringing out two more cakes, tossing one to each. As they snapped them up, he spoke in a voice he made purposefully level.

"Fanyi?"

Perhaps he was as stupid as Maxim thought him to be, to try to communicate with the fishers by voice. How

194

could his repeating a name mean anything to the animals still watching him so intently that their stare was daunting? But patiently he repeated that name the second time.

"Fanyi?"

Kai reared on his haunches, his head now well above that of the squatting smith. From this position the fisher need only make one pounce to carry Sander down under rending jaws and claws. Kayi stared, but she did not assume the same upright position.

"Fanyi—Kai—Kayi—" This time Sander tried the three names in linkage. What might be passing through the fishers' alien thinking processes he could not even guess.

Kayi stopped hissing. She bent her head to lick her right paw. But the bigger male had not changed what seemed to Sander his challenging position.

"Fanyi—Kai—" Now the smith only used two of the names, aiming his voice at the big male, with a slight turn of his head that cost a special effort of will, because to let Kayi out of his full sight was a risk.

Kai dropped to four feet. Though Sander could not read any expression on the fisher's face, somehow he sensed that the beast was puzzled. And beneath that puzzlement was something else. Fear? The man could not be sure.

Taking a last risk, Sander got slowly to his feet and made a movement forward. "Fanyi!" he repeated for the fourth time with a firmness he was not sure he could continue.

Kayi backed away. Her eyes swung to the looming back of her mate and returned to the man. She uttered a sound that was not that of warning. Kai hissed, showed his fangs. But Sander, taking heart from the attitude of the female, moved a step closer.

The male fisher subsided to four feet, backing away, still hissing, but yet retreating. Kayi had turned around and was padding off. Finally the big male surrendered, though he still eyed Sander suspiciously.

Rhin followed at the smith's shoulder, crouching a little and making a struggle to win through that door slit.

195

But the fishers did not threaten now. Together they had turned their backs on Sander, seemingly satisfied, and were on their way, threading among incomprehensible masses of glass and metal that seemed to fill this chamber.

Here the lighting was brilliant, a glare enough to cause Sander trouble with his already impaired sight. And the room was alive. Not alive as he knew life, but with a different form of energy, one that caused colors, some strident, some richly vivid, to flow along through tubes and otherwise bathe some of the installations. The warm and humid heat of the place made him unlace his hood, unfasten his jacket.

He had no desire to pause to look about him. The play of the colors, the wholly alien atmosphere of this place, repelled him. Once he found Fanyi they must get out of here! His flesh tingled and crawled as if some invisible power streamed over him.

Sparks shot from the band of metal he wore. It was warming up. Still, he would not take it off. Cold iron had saved him twice, and he clung to what he had learned might work for him, the more so when he now was surrounded by what he could not understand, dare not even examine too closely.

The fishers guided him directly to a very small room on the other side of the place. It was hardly larger than a good-sized cabinet. Its walls were clear, so that one could look through them. Seated within, her hands clenched about the pendant still lying on her breast, was Fanyi.

Though her eyes were wide open, seemingly staring straight at him, Sander realized she did not see him. What did she see? He grew chill for a moment in spite of the heat of the outer room. Expressions passed fleetingly one after the other across her face. There was fear, a kind of horror, revulsion—

Her bush of hair stood erect, as if each strand were charged with energy from root to tip. Small beads of sweat gathered on her upper lip and forehead and rolled down her cheeks as if she wept without ending. There was a terrible stiffness about her whole body, which betrayed some tension beyond the ordinary.

Kayi pawed at the front of the cabinet, but there was no shadow of recognition on Fanyi's distorted face. She was like one sealed into a nightmare with no means of escape.

Now her body began to jerk spasmodically. Sander saw her mouth open as if she were screaming. But he could hear nothing. He ran forward and caught at the bar at waist level on the door, hoping it was the latch. Against it he exerted all his strength. It did not budge.

It was as if she were locked in past any hope of escape. He could see her eyes rolling from side to side, her head moving back and forth. He grabbed one of the darts from his case, inserted it between the bar and the door and tried to pry it up.

Now Fanyi's whole body was jerking steadily as if she had no control over her own muscles. There was no longer any sign of intelligence in her face, her mouth fell slackly open, while from her lower lip drooled a thread of spittle.

Sander fought the door. The dart snapped in his hands, but not before he had forced a small amount of movement. He snatched a second shaft and this time dug with all his might at the line of cleavage just beyond the bar. The dart point caught and held; he pounded it deeper.

There was a splitting crack as he gave a mighty heave upon the bar, stumbling back nearly off balance as the whole front of the cabinet yielded at last. Fanyi slumped with it. Sander was just in time to catch her totally inert body and lower her gently to the floor.

For one moment of such fear as he had never before known, he thought her dead. Then he felt the pulse in one thin brown wrist, saw the rise and fall of her breasts in fast, shallow breathing. Her eyes were rolled up, so he could see little but white between the half-closed lids.

Not even getting to his feet, he crawled and dragged her with him, away from the prison in which he had found her, seeking temporary shelter in a corner of the room as far from that cabinet and the rest of these devilish installations as he could get her. There he settled her head on his folded coat. Her hands were still so fixed about the pendant that he had to work slowly and with all the gentle force he could exert to loosen them finger by finger. He was sure that the pendant itself was part of the danger that had struck at her.

She still breathed with those quick and shallow breaths, as if she had been running, while her skin felt cold and damp in spite of the heat that filled the room. The fishers came to her, Kayi crowding in on the far side, stretching her length beside that of the girl as if, with the additional warmth of her fur-clad body, she could give some comfort.

Fanyi muttered and began to turn her head back and forth on the pillow Sander had provided. Clearly, un-slurred, she began to speak, but he could not understand the words that came out, save that now and again he thought he caught an echo of the voice that had addressed him out of the air.

He drew off his second jerkin and put it over her, then caught her head in a sure grip while he dribbled a little water between her lips. She choked, coughed, and suddenly opened her eyes.

D ead—!" her voice shrilled. "Dead!"

Though she gazed straight at him, Sander realized that Fanyi saw something else—not his face, perhaps not even this room.

"I—will—not!" The girl took a long breath between each word as she spoke. There was determination in her voice. "I—will—*not!*"

Fanyi struggled to sit up until Sander caught her shoulders, pushed her gently down again. He was afraid. The eyes the girl turned upon him held no recognition. Had her experience in that prison box made her as mad as Maxim?

"You do not need to do anything"—he strove to keep his voice under even control—"which you do not want to—"

Her mouth worked as if it were nearly past her power to get out word sounds.

"I—will—not—" and then she added, "Who are *you?* One of the machines—the machines—?" Again her tension was rising, her body grew rigid under his touch. "I

199

will *not!* You cannot force me—you cannot!"

"Fanyi—" As he had when greeting the fishers, Sander repeated her name with authority, with the need to win awareness from her. "I am Sander, you are Fanyi—Fanyi!"

"Fanyi?" She made a question of that. And the import of such an inquiry chilled Sander even more. If she could not remember her own name—! What had this devilish place done to her? He was filled with a rage so powerful that he wanted to flail out about him, smash into bits everything in this chamber.

"You are Fanyi." He spoke as if to a small child, schooling the anger out of his voice. "I am Sander."

She lay still, looking up at him. Then, to his relief, a measure of focus came back to her eyes. She might have been peering through a curtain to seek him out. Her tongue tip moved across her lips.

"I—am—Fanyi—" She said slowly, and gave a great sigh. He watched her relax, her head turn on the pillow he had improvised, her eyes close. She was asleep.

But they must get out of here! Perhaps if he could lift her up on Rhin—That tingling, skin-crawling sensation he had felt ever since he had entered this place was growing worse. There was something else—a kind of—nibbling was the only word Sander could find to describe the feeling—a nibbling at his mind! He brought both hands up to the wire circlet. It was warm—hot—he should take it off —much better—better.

The smith snatched his fingers away. Take that off! That was what this—this presence here wanted! He looked over his shoulder quickly. So sure was he at that moment that there was another personality here that he expected to see Maxim, or one like him, coming down the aisle between the installations.

Cold iron—

Swiftly Sander beckoned to Rhin, and when the koyot crowded beside him, he lifted Fanyi and fastened her on the animal's back. Kayi snarled at his first move to disturb the girl, then apparently saw that Sander meant her no harm. The smith made her slumped body fast, so she lay with arms dangling on either side of Rhin's neck.

When he was sure she was secure, Sander started back through this nightmare chamber that was haunted by the will plucking strongly at him. Could the unknown take over the animals, turn Rhin and the fishers against him?

That a sensation which they disliked and feared reached the animals he knew because of their incessant snarling, the way the fishers swung their heads back and forth as if seeking an enemy they could identify. Rhin growled, but he did not hang back as Sander urged him forward.

They passed the broken-open block in which he had found the girl. With that behind them, Sander drew a breath of relief. He did not know what he had expected might reach out of it—he had begun to believe that he could not really trust his own senses or impulses here.

The outer door was before them, and the fishers flashed through the crack. However, the opening was too narrow for Rhin carrying Fanyi. Sander unstrapped his tool bag and, as he had done in the tunnel out of the city, took up the largest of his hammers.

With all his might he swung it first against one side of that slit and then the other, dividing his energy, until, at last, the leaves of the opening yielded with a harsh grating and Rhin could wedge through successfully. Sander did not return the hammer to his bag, rather carried it in one hand as they went. Like the iron band he wore, the feel of its familiar heft in his hand gave him more confidence than he gained in handling either the dart thrower or the rod weapon from Before. This was part of his own particular calling, and as a smith he was secure. At this moment he needed such assurance.

The fishers did not range well ahead as they were wont to do outside. Rather they paced along, one on either side of Sander and Rhin. Now and again they uttered soft hisses, not those of anger and warning, but rather communicating with each other.

There had been no sign of consciousness from Fanyi since she had said her name, claiming her own identity. That she now lay in an unnatural sleep Sander was certain.

He wanted to get her as far away from the place he had found her as he could.

They passed the scrap heap of the machine sentry. At another time Sander would have liked to study the remains of the thing, perhaps appropriate other bits of its arms. Now he had a feeling that the less he allied himself with anything belonging to this maze, the more sensible he would be.

Rhin climbed the ramp, Sander steadying Fanyi with one hand and carrying the hammer in the other. That climb seemed twice as long as the descent had been. But it was good to emerge into fresher air, fill his lungs again with that which was not tainted with the acrid odors so strong below.

In the upper hall Sander decided to head back to the room where he had found the larger food machine. Though the fishers had wolfed down all the biscuits he had fed them, he guessed that they were not yet satisfied. Also perhaps he could coax from that strange supplier of nourishment something to revive Fanyi.

Rhin went forward confidently and Sander did not doubt that the koyot was retracing their journey. The feeling of pressure, of nibbling, was growing less, the further he withdrew from the chamber below. If the seat of that disturbance lay there, perhaps there was a limit to its influence, though it had reached out before to draw him here. He had no intention of taking off his iron protection to test its strength.

They reached the room he sought. There he loosed Fanyi and lowered her from the riding pad, once more stretching her on the floor with his coat under her head, his second coat over her body. Her skin was still chill, and though she did not open her eyes or seem conscious, she shivered.

Recklessly, he thumbed the buttons on the machine, tossing to the three animals the meat-tasting biscuits that they snapped up eagerly. But at length, one lucky choice provided him with a capped container that was nearly filled with a hot liquid having the smell and consistency of a thick soup.

Cradling Fanyi's head against his shoulder, Sander called her name, roused her so she murmured fretfully and feebly tried to escape his hold. But he got the container to her lips, and finally she sipped.

As she drank at his soft-voiced urging, she appeared to welcome the liquid and finally opened her eyes as if to look for more. He speedily got a second helping from the machine and supported her until she finished that also to the last drop.

"Good—" she whispered. "So good. I—am—cold."

Fanyi still shook, visible shudders running through her whole body. Sander managed to get his coat on her, rather than merely laid over her. Then he turned to Rhin, stripping the koyot of all their gear and pulling over the girl the thick riding pad, strong-smelling though it was.

Having covered her as best he could, he called the fishers and they obediently settled down on either side of her, lending their body heat. Only then did he go to the machine and feed himself.

He was tired; he could hardly remember now when he had slept last. And that ordeal in the lower ways had sapped his strength. Dared they remain here for a space? If Rhin and Fanyi's fishers would play guard—

In all his journeying through the rooms of the complex, Sander had come across signs of no other inhabitants. The rooms that he guessed had been intended for living quarters seemed empty of any presence save their own as they passed through. Still Sander could hardly believe that Maxim was the sole remaining inhabitant of the place. And any such would have weapons and resources past his own knowledge. The sooner they themselves were out of this underworld, the better. But even as Sander thought that, his head slumped forward on his chest and he had to fight to keep his eyes open. There were too many chances of facing disaster still to come, and he could not meet them worn as he was now. Rest was essential.

He made a further effort and gave hand signals to Rhin. The koyot trotted to the far door and lay down across the entrance, head on paws. He would doze, Sander knew, but he would also rouse at the first stir beyond.

Sander stretched out, the haft of his hammer lying under his hand, on the other side of Kayi. The strong smell of the fishers was somehow comforting and normal, part of the world he knew and trusted, not of these burrows.

"Sander—"

He turned his head. There was an urgency in the call that woke him out of a dream he could not remember even as he opened his eyes. Fanyi was sitting up, his coat slipping from her shoulders, her face drawn and worn as if she had not yet thrown off the effects of some daunting and debilitating illness.

"Sander!" Now she stretched forth a hand to shake his shoulder, for Kayi no longer lay between them.

He sat up groggily and shook his head.

"What—" he began.

"We must get out!" There was a wild look in her eyes. "We must warn them—"

"Them?" Sander repeated. But her excitement reached him, and he got to his feet.

"The Traders—the rest—all the rest, Sander. Your people—everyone!" Her words came with such a rush that he had trouble understanding them. Now it was his turn to lay hands upon her, steady her so he could look straight into her wide eyes.

"Fanyi—warn them against what?"

"The—thinker!" she burst out. "I was wrong—oh, how wrong!" Her hands clutched his wrists with a grip tight enough to be painful. "The Thinker—he—it—will take over the world—make it what it wants. We shall all be *things*, just things to do *its* bidding. It has summoned the White Ones—is pulling them here to learn—learn monstrous things. How to kill, destroy—"

Once more she was shaking. "It was made by the Before Men, set to store up all their learning because they foresaw the end of their world. And it did—by the Power, it did! Then, when it was ready, something twisted it— maybe the Dark Times altered what the Before Men set it to do. They—they could not have all been so evil! They could not! If I thought so—" She shook her head. "Sander, if I thought that in my mind lay such inheritance from them, then I would put a knife to my own throat and willingly. That—that *thing,* it remembers the worst. It wanted me to serve it. And it was taking me—making me into something like it when you came. We must get out of here! I know that it controls this place and—"

She paused, looked to Sander. "But it did not hold you. Was that because you did not have one like this?" She pointed to the pendant Sander had not taken from her, not knowing whether if he did he would remove some protection she needed, as Maxim had suggested.

"It can take over one's mind, one's will. It—it promised me"—her lips quivered—"all I wanted, all I sought. I was only to go into its direct communication chamber, open my mind. But what it poured into me—hate—Sander, I thought that I hated the Sea Sharks, but I did not know the depths, the black foulness of true hate, until that taught me. And it wants everything, all of us, to serve it. Some people it can rule quickly. The Shamans of the White Ones, it has already made its own servants. Do you understand, it summons them now—to learn.

"There are things stored here, other things that can be made, easily made with *that* to teach. And it shall then loose death. Because in the end it wants no life left—none at all!"

"You say 'it' and 'that,' " Sander said. "What is 'it' in truth?"

"I think"—she answered slowly, again shivering, her hands loosing their hold on him to half cover her mouth as if she hardly dared speak her belief aloud—"that part of it was once a man—or men. It has a kind of half-life. And through the years it has grown more and more alien to man, more and more monstrous. Those who stayed here—while they tended it, it kept to a little of the purpose for which it was made. But as those grew fewer, feebler, it grew stronger and finally cut all ties with those who were left. Some—like my father—went out to see what had happened to the world because they were not influenced by *that* so much.

"But the ones who stayed— Have you seen the one who calls himself Maxim?"

205

Sander nodded.

"He is a thing, though he knows it not. For a while yet he will serve as eyes and ears for *that*. It still needs humans if it would contact the uncorrupted outside, bring in fresh minds— Sander, it feeds upon men's minds! It strips from them all their knowledge, all their spirit; then it fills them with what it wants—hate and the need for dealing death!"

"As it tried to do to you. And how were you saved?" Sander demanded.

"I am Shaman born, Shaman trained. Not as the Shamans of the White Ones, who use men's blood and terror to summon up their power, but working with life and not against it. It could not reach that part of me it wanted most, the source of my Power. Though it might have blasted through, had you not come. And you, Sander, why did it not seek you?"

"Cold iron—it is smith's power." He was not sure that the band about his forehead had saved him, but he thought that it had.

"Cold iron?" she repeated wonderingly. "I do not understand—" Then once more her fear flared. "Out— Sander—we must get out! It will not let us go willingly, and I do not know what Power it can command."

He had summoned Rhin with a snap of his fingers and was repacking the burdens. Then he lifted Fanyi once more to the riding pad.

"Can this thing of yours control the animals?" He wondered if their companions might now prove to be the weak lines in their small company.

"No." She shook her head. "Their minds are too alien, lie beneath the range of *it*. Kai, Kayi tried to stop me from going. I—I used my power to hold them off." Her face was stricken as she glanced at the fishers.

"Maxim used this on Rhin." Sander held out the rod. "Press this and Rhin is in agony." He indicated the stud on the side.

"How did you get it?"

"From Maxim," Sander said with satisfaction. "I left him tied up. He gave me all his attention, so Rhin brought him down." The smith paid credit where it was due. "And it was Rhin who traced you."

"Let us get out—quickly!"

Sander agreed with her urging. He did not know how much to accept of the crazy story she had gabbled. This business of draining a man's mind and refilling it— But the suspicion, which had long been his, that the Before Men had far more than the Rememberers knew, was enough to make him agree they would be much better out of this place. He had no longer any desire to learn anything connected with this complex. Fanyi's descent into hysteria, her fear, brought grim warning that there might be far too high a price to pay for learning what lay on the other side of the Dark Time. He was willing enough to head out and away with all the speed they could muster.

The smith was not sure of the way they had come, but he depended on the koyot to nose out the back trail for them. As they went, Fanyi appeared to regain her control somewhat. Sander caught glimpses of things in the rooms through which they passed that intrigued him a little, that under other circumstances he would have paused to examine more closely.

But Fanyi looked neither right nor left. She stared straight ahead as if the very fervor of her desire to be free was forceful enough to speed their retreat.

"How many people still live here?" Sander asked, after they had gone some way in silence, during which he had found himself listening for some hint that they were not going to escape so easily, that there would be someone or something in ambush.

"I do not know. Certainly very few. It needs more to serve it. I think there is some service it cannot itself perform that keeps it alive. Therefore, it wants more empty minds to control. For the rest—it will kill. It hates—" Tears spilled from her eyes and she did not try to wipe them away. "It is sick with hate, swelled with it as a corrupted wound swells with evil matter. It is foul beyond belief!"

Sander had kept a careful lookout as they traversed the rooms. Again he was sure he saw nothing to suggest that any had been recently occupied. Was Maxim perhaps the last remaining servant the thing had? But Maxim had not considered himself so—he had spoken of a "Great Brain" that had withdrawn from communication with man.

Now the smith had a new cause for worry—this departure was far too easy. He had expected to meet some opposition before now. Fanyi claimed vast power for the thing she had met; surely if it controlled the installations here, it must be working to capture them again.

When nothing moved, illogically his wariness increased. Fanyi still rode, looking only ahead. Sander stole glances at the koyot, the fishers. They padded along at what had increased to a trot, though Sander had not urged that. The animals were alert; he saw as well as sensed that they were using their own methods of testing what lay about them. But they gave no warning of any ambush or attack.

Their party came at last to the chamber where the chairs were lined around the oval, which was not a pool. Sander pushed ahead here, ready to handle Maxim. But the chair in which he had tied the madman was now empty; not even cut or broken bonds remained. Sander swung his hammer, weighing its strength in his hand.

"He's gone. I left him here."

For the first time since they had started, Fanyi turned her head a little, her gaze shifting to Sander.

"We must find the way out," she told him, and there was a new note in her voice, as if some of the hysteria was again rising in her. "The way—it can be hidden."

Her hand moved toward the pendant and then away. "This thing—I can use it perhaps. But also—it is of this place. Through it one can be controlled."

"Then do not try it!" he answered her. "Leave our passage to Rhin, to Kai and Kayi. I will depend upon their senses before I will on mine."

The animals pattered on out of the room of the chairs into that which held the webs. Those that were intact blazed high with light. Rhin threw up his head to howl with a note Sander had heard out of him only once before —that time he had touched the wrong button on the shaft of the rod. To his outburst were added cries from the fishers. The animals pawed at their ears, slobbered, and foamed. Sander felt a strange pain in his own head. Fanyi held both ears, her face twisted in agony.

To this, Sander could see only one answer. Though his body was suddenly awkward and his coordination faulty, he tottered to the nearest of those flaming filaments. Raising the hammer in spite of an involuntary twitching of muscles he had to fight to control, he brought it down to smash the webbing.

Sparks burst; there was a throat- and nose-rasping odor in the air, but Sander staggered on to the next web and demolished it with a blow, then the next and the next.

He moved through a world that had narrowed to hold just those alien creations, his only thought that they must be destroyed. Sometimes his aim was faulty, and he did not bring the object he fronted into fragments with one blow or two, but had to stand wavering and pounding for three or four misdirected and weakened swings until he achieved its shattering. He had cleared one row; he was aiming now for the first installation of the second. Around his head the band was a searing brand of fire that dimmed his thoughts. Only instinct kept him going. Three— another—

Then, as it had come, so was the outside pressure gone. Sander sank to his knees, panting heavily. His head felt light; he was dazed. But the light that had hurt his eyes had ebbed.

"Sander!"

That shriek aroused his half-conscious mind, jerked him around.

Maxim was there, raising a rod. His face was contracted; there was nothing human remaining in his bulging eyes. He was going to—

Sander made the greatest effort of his life, lifting the hammer—Maxim was too far away to pound. There was no time to try for a dart or even the rod tucked in the smith's belt. He whirled the hammer once around his head and threw it, despairingly, sure that he was already Maxim's victim.

A furred fury burst past Sander, Kai's shoulder striking

209

his as the animal leaped. That touch, light as it was, knocked the smith off balance. He fell against the base of one of the machines, but not before he saw the hammer strike, not with the head but with the edge of the shaft against Maxim's chest.

The man staggered. Sander felt a searing heat lick his own upper arm. Then Kai made a final leap, carrying Maxim down, the rod whirling out of his grasp. Maxim screamed, a sound that was cut off with shocking suddenness as Sander clawed his way once more erect, drawing himself up by pulling on the base of the shattered installation against which he had fallen.

There was a wave of (Sander groped for words to make clear to himself the nature of what it was that filled the air, weighed upon him so he could hardly move) rage—hate—as if the very walls about were animated, living tissue of some vast creature. The fisher drew back, his muzzle foully stained. He reared, snarling, hissing, striking out in the air with extended claws, though there was nothing visible to threaten him.

Sander swayed back and forth. Only his grip upon the base of the shattered installation kept him upright, for that mighty rage sent impulses of force through the chamber to beat at him like physical blows. The wire about his head was hot agony, but Sander fought back. His teeth were bared as were those of the animals. He voiced, hoarsely and defiantly, the smith's chant.

He was not a *thing*, he was a man! And a man he would remain. Step by wavering step, he clawed his way along the base that was his support. His attention was fixed on the hammer, which lay a little distance from the body he willed himself not to face directly. Kai might have brought Maxim down, but it was his own blow that had opened the way for the fisher.

Sander stooped, his hand closed upon the haft of the heavy tool. And once his fingers were around that familiar grip, he felt a small sense of victory.

He was a *man!*

With care he faced around, Rhin, the fishers, had drawn together. Their fangs were visible. The koyot snapped at the air, white bits of froth gathering at the corners of his lips. The fishers were battle-ready with no foe upon which they could turn.

Fanyi sat erect on the riding pad. Her face was drawn, haggard with strain and pain. With head thrown back, she too mouthed words, words he could not understand. As he tottered to them, seeming to breast some hostile current as he moved, she met his gaze.

"*It* will not let us go," she said simply.

"I know the doors—"

"There will be no doors now, not unless it wishes."

He did not want to accept her certainty. But before he could speak again, she was holding the pendant.

"*It* will let me come to it—with this I can reach *it*—"

It seemed that when she spoke there was a lessening of the pressure about them, that the rage, which was almost a tangible cloud to wall them in, ebbed a fraction.

"No!" Sander raised the hammer.

"If I go, I can perhaps make terms—"

He could read the truth in her eyes. She knew that if she went she would be lost—as lost as that husk of a man Kai had killed to save them all.

"I am half of the blood of those who have always been its servants. It will listen—"

"To no one," Sander returned. "The thing is mad, you have read that for yourself in its thoughts. You will save nothing, you will accomplish nothing."

"To get me it will bargain." She refused to accept his refusal. "I can get it to let you go forth, you and these—" With a gesture she indicated the animals. "If you are free, you can carry a warning. The White Ones must not be allowed to reach here, the Traders must be prepared."

"If this thing is all-seeing, all-knowing," Sander replied stubbornly, "then it will never let anyone free to carry such a warning. Why should it?"

"There is a difference," Fanyi said slowly. "If I go to it willingly and without any barriers raised, it will gain more of what it wishes than if it must wrest my strength from me. It wants me whole, not maimed. To it you are of no value, save that you have disturbed it by violence. It would be willing to let you go—thinking that would be only for a short space of time until it can muster into its forces those others whom it has summoned. Do you not see—I can buy you time!"

Sander shook his head. "There is no way you can trust any bargain. Listen—" His mind was working faster now, like a runner who has gained his second wind. "Can you find where this thing is?"

She must have had an instant flash of his intentions. "You cannot! Its defenses are complete, there is no way to reach it save by its will."

"But you can go—"

"Yes, if I surrender my will. It will have gained a victory—and you can profit by that."

"Yes, in my way." Sander swung the hammer a fraction. "Can it overhear us?" He glanced from one line of the shattered machines to the other.

"I do not think so. It can strive to control us through its own will, and it deems itself invulnerable." A little color had returned to her wan cheeks.

Sander once more swung the hammer. With it in hand he felt himself, somehow apart from the fear of things he could not touch. This "thing" thought itself invulnerable, yet it had not been able to defend the outer part of its own domain without Maxim. And Maxim had died as perhaps none of his kind had done for generations, by the fighting rage of an animal.

The smith had no plans, only a determination. Fanyi's offer to surrender to the thing—that could even be dictated by a residue of its attack upon her when she was imprisoned in the box. Sander was sure of one thing—no trust could be put in any bargain with this enemy. To even try to bargain was a defeat, for the Presence that ruled this complex would consider any such to be an admission of weakness. It could promise anything and break the oath as it pleased.

But he did believe that Fanyi might be the key to reach it. He raised a hand, ran a thumb along the band on his forehead. There was no "reason" in the working of the old superstition, yet work it did. If he could take the force of the pain that had struck at him before, they would have a bare chance—a small one, but still it was there.

"You have a plan." Fanyi did not ask a question, she made a statement. Leaning forward on the riding pad, she gazed at him intently.

"No plan," Sander shook his head. "We do not know enough to plan. We can only go—and hope to find a chance—"

"We? But you cannot! It will not let you!"

Once more Sander touched that band. "We cannot be sure of that until we try. You say it cannot deal with the animals?"

"It could not with the fishers. They would have kept me from it before. Though what it can send against us when aroused—that I do not know."

He remembered the many-armed metal creature. Only he now knew how to handle one of them. And he would have two rods, the first one that he had taken earlier from Maxim, the new one the man had produced here. Sander went to the crumpled body to reclaim it.

When he returned, he pushed the first of his trophies into Fanyi's hands. With a few words he made plain how it was used.

"You will do this, you are determined?" the girl asked, when he had done.

"Is there any other way? A man holds to life while he can. I believe that we are dead unless we can best this Power."

"I tell you—I think it would let you go if I went to it willingly."

"You will go to it willing, if you agree," he told her. "But I shall go with you. Perhaps it will know that I am

214

with you—but this we shall do—if you go ahead it may believe that you have eluded me, that I once more am hunting. Not too far apart—we must be close enough so that it cannot take you and perhaps shut me out."

Fanyi sat silent for a moment. Then she slipped from Rhin's back.

"This is an action that will bring you to your death, smith. But be sure of one thing. Though I seem willing, it shall not use me for its purposes. I have this." She weighed the rod in her hand. "It can be turned one way as well as the other. And *that* cannot use a body blasted beyond repair. What of our companions?"

"They, too," Sander said. He pulled the gear from Rhin's back. "This we shall leave." He did not add that it might well be they would never need any of those supplies again. Also he placed on top of the pile his dart thrower, though he kept the long knife, principally because he had worn it so long he was hardly aware that it still hung at his belt.

The smith's hammer that was his heritage, from which he now drew inner strength—that stood for all that was normal and right in the world he knew, and the rod that was a part of this—those were his weapons. No, rather his tools, for he did not altogether look upon what faced them as a battle, but rather a need to deal with something that was badly flawed.

"This is your free will?" Fanyi looked now as might a chief about to bind someone by blood oath.

"My will," Sander agreed.

She turned from him to the animals. The fishers came to her, and she rested a hand on each head. They stood so for a moment, and then they arose to lick at her cheeks. Rhin had watched them. Now the koyot also moved, but he came to Sander, nudging the smith's shoulder with his nose—their old signal that it was well they move on.

"Their will also," Fanyi said.

As Sander had suggested, she took the lead. He allowed her and the fishers perhaps the length of an aisle, then he and Rhin followed. Fanyi once more clasped her pendant in her hands. She had not retraced her path to the doorway through which they had come. She went to the right, down another short way between the stumps of the installations Sander had smashed.

Within moments she fronted what looked like a blank stone wall. But, reaching up, she held the pendant between her flattened palm and one block of that barrier. A section pivoted to give them a door.

The way was narrow. Rhin could barely scrape through. And there were no lights. The door shut with an intimidating snap when they were all inside. Sander could only trace those ahead by the faint sounds of their passing.

There were curves and corners, against some of which he struck with bruising force as he moved blindly. But there was only one passage and no choice of side ways, so he advanced with what confidence he could maintain, sure that Fanyi was ahead.

Finally, there came a burst of light, and he believed she had opened a second door. He hurried forward, lest that close and leave him and Rhin caught in the dark. The room they came into was unlike any he had seen elsewhere.

Fronting him was a wall with a glassy surface, much like that on which he had seen the lines form, those that Maxim said were the outlines of the world—the Before World and this. But here was only one chair and that was placed with its back directly to the slick surface. Fanyi sat in that chair, the fishers crouched before her, growling.

Her hands rested on the arms of the chair, but there were no buttons to be touched. As Sander came to face her, she raised one of her hands and pulled the loop of chain supporting the pendant from about her neck, throwing it from her as if she so removed all that might keep her from the domination of the thing holding rule here.

Sander caught it out of the air by the chain. He could not wear the device himself, but there was a hope that it somehow might still provide a weapon. Now the girl drew the rod from her belt, tossed that also from her. In that chair she sat defenseless and alone. And then—it was not Fanyi who sat there.

Her features seemed to writhe, to grimace, twist, to be-

216

come partly the countenance of someone else.

"Come to me!"

There was nothing enticing in that command, for it was a command, baldly uttered, with the arrogance of one who expected no denial of any authority. And such was the power of that order that Sander took one stride toward Fanyi-who-was-no-longer-Fanyi.

Rhin was beside him in an instant, the koyot's mouth closed upon the man's shoulder with force enough to awaken pain. In turn that pain broke the spell.

Fanyi smiled, and the smile was none that Sander had ever seen on any human face.

"Barbarian—" Now she laughed. "Your straggle of people—you—" Now her tone changed, became cold and remote. "You pollute the earth. You are nothing, not fit to walk where true men once walked."

Sander heard the words, let the thing that had possessed Fanyi talk without dispute. The clue to its hiding place must be here somewhere—he needed that. But would he be able to gain it in time?

"Give me your weapons, barbarian," Fanyi said with icy contempt. "Do you think any such can be used against *me?* Fool, I have that which could blast you into nothingness a thousand times over. I let you live only because you can be of some small service to me—for a while. Even as this female serves me—"

Rhin swung a little before Sander, edging him away from Fanyi. But the koyot's head was pointed toward the wall behind the chair. The smith saw that slight prick of ear. Though Rhin appeared to be facing Fanyi, herding Sander away from the girl, the animal's attention was rather for the wall behind the chair.

Sander gripped the haft of the hammer more tightly.

"You are mine, barbarian—"

There was a timbre in that voice which rang in Sander's ears. Was a mist curling up about the chair on which Fanyi was seated, or were his own eyes in some manner failing him? The metal on his forehead was heating, too. He found it hard to breathe.

He was no one's! He was himself. By cold iron, which

217

only a smith could fashion—he was himself!

"Barbarian, I can suck the life from you by will alone. Thus—"

Sander fought for breath. This was the time he must move—he had no longer any choice.

Cold iron. He fought against the pressure the other had set upon him, seeking to batter him to the ground, to make him crawl as no man should ever humble himself.

"Cold iron," he cried aloud.

There was a slight change in the pressure, as if the thing he confronted was surprised.

Sander moved—not toward Fanyi, where the thing that ruled here had meant him to grovel, but rather to the wall. Exerting all his strength, with an effort even mightier than that which he had used (and which he had then thought the ultimate) when he fronted Maxim, he brought the hammer crashing against the smooth surface.

There was a splintering, a radiation of cracks running out from where the hammer head had met the wall.

In his mind, gathering about him—such a force, a pressure meant to crush him.

No! He denied that will bent now to stop him. His body swayed. Rhin, the fishers, he could feel them close, supporting him. For the second time he struck, and the blow fell true on the same spot.

There was a crackling, a tinkling as of falling glass. A hole slightly smaller than his fist opened. In return Sander was slammed nearly to his knees by a wave of force that he could never afterwards describe.

But he crawled closer, fighting that pressure with all his will, with his belief that if he surrendered, all that made him what he was would be lost, he reached the wall.

He inched his hand up and up, having dropped the hammer. Now he hooked fingers into the hole, though the jagged edges cut into his flesh. When he was sure his hold was complete, he swung the weight of his whole body on that hand.

For a moment of pain and fear, he was afraid his effort was not enough. Then the glass, or what was like glass, broke, to shower his head and shoulders with splinters. A gust of air blew over him that had the same taint as had been in the lower reaches when he had shattered the cabinet holding Fanyi.

Sander groped for the hammer. His right hand was slippery with with his own blood. He was afraid that he could not keep his grip upon the tool. But with his left hand—yes!

He brought up his hand, holding the hammer awkwardly and ill-balanced. Even so a blow fell again, to break the edge farther. This was the door to the thing, even though he could pass through it only on his hands and knees, near crushed with the pressure.

Sander pulled himself over the high threshold formed by the frame. He fell forward into another chamber. There was no one here. He blinked in dull surprise. Though Fanyi had ever alluded to the ruler of these ways as "it" or "the thing" or "that," he had somehow pictured it with at least some kind of a body—maybe like the metal traveler with the claws. But what he saw were only tall cases, rows of them. On the faces of some, lights flashed or rippled.

There was one relief. As he had fallen through the aperture beyond the feeling of pressure had vanished. If this was the lair of Fanyi's enemy, then here its defenses were singularly lacking—maybe it never expected to be found.

"Unregistered and unlawful entrance—"

That was not the voice that had issued from Fanyi's lips. It sounded more like the one that had gabbled at him earlier during his journey through these burrows. Where *was* what he sought? Hidden in one of these case—?

"Mark one protection—"

He did not know the meaning of all those words. It was enough that they must be a threat. Not attempting to get to his feet, Sander took from the front of his belt the rod that had armed Maxim. He thumbed the highest button on its length and aimed it at the tall box that showed the most lights. The beam struck full, ate into the metal. At the same time Sander was aware of a trundling noise. Coming toward him out of the shadow was a mobile metal thing.

"Seize for interrogation—" yammered the voice, as the metal creature scuttled toward Sander.

He was backed tight to the broken wall. Dare he turn the rod on that thing moving toward him? If it were controlled elsewhere, what—

There was a flare of light. The box he had attacked spurted small tongues of flame. He did not wait, but swung the beam to the next one that showed activity. Something closed about his ankle. A line had snaked forth from the running machine, had locked about his flesh. Another was whipping toward his body. Then a furred form flashed between. There was a growl as the line wrapped around Kai, imprisoning the fisher.

Sander continued to play the beam on target. The second panel blew. Kayi had joined her mate, only to be caught, yet keeping the lines spun by the sentry away from Sander.

The smith pulled to the full length allowed by the one caught about his ankle to spray the beam down the line. Four, five, six—suddenly the line that held him uncurled, fell limp to the floor. Sander scrambled up, moved to destroy more of the panels. When he reached them, the beam no longer responded. But then neither did any more lights show. The burnt odor was stifling. He attempted to close his cut hand. If that would serve him, he would try to finish off the rest by hammer. Was this the lair of the Presence? If it was not—

Sander choked and coughed, his eyes smarted, his throat was painfully dry. The air here hurt deep into his nose and throat as he breathed. He must get back—out, even if he had not completed the job—

Through a haze, Sander pulled his way back, holding onto one half-melted panel and then the next, seeking the entrance hole. When he pulled through, he saw Fanyi—not sitting now, but lying in a small heap on the floor, as if she had slid helplessly from the chair. He lurched to her, but the fishers were ahead of him, Kayi licking the girl's face, pawing at her body, uttering small whimpers.

Sander went cold. Had—had he killed Fanyi! Was she— He stumbled to her. Kayi growled warningly, but let him lay hands on the girl, his cut one leaving blood prints on her shoulders and her arms.

Her eyes were closed, her face empty of expression— but she was alive!

He subsided there, her head resting in his lap, his wounded hand stretched along the seat of the chair. It was then that he saw the pendant he had tucked into the front of his belt. One-handedly he drew it forth, laid it on her breast where she had always worn it.

Fanyi's eyelids moved. She gazed up at him in an unfocused way that again awoke his fears. Then her gaze cleared. It was plain she knew him.

"*It* is—crippled!" she said.

He gave a sigh. So he had not won completely after all.

"How badly?" he asked.

There was a long moment before she replied. "It—it is part gone—those who know how might still use some of it."

"No!" He remembered what had brought him here. The thing he had destroyed might make any man master of this riven world. But there was no man strong enough, wise enough, no man left to use such knowledge.

"No," she echoed him.

"Your weapons to save your people—" he said.

"Your smith's knowledge—" Hers matched with his.

"*It* is of another world," she said slowly. "Even though that which made *it* our enemy has gone out of it, let it be. It is not ours."

He thought of the Traders, of the White Ones whom this thing had summoned.

"It must be no one's."

She nodded, pulling herself up. Then with a cry of concern she caught his hand.

Later they sat on the floor by their worn trail gear. He had dragged Maxim's body out of sight. Fanyi treated his hand with her salves, but it would be days before he could use his hammer again.

There was a coldness in this place, a sense of life gone, that was akin to the terror of those storm-battered heights.

221

The girl fingered Maxim's first rod, which she had thrown away in the chamber of the Presence.

"*It* cannot repair itself. And I do not think it has anyone to serve it here now. Maxim must have been the last, but there might be those who would try."

"There is still some power in that," Sander nodded at the rod. "Perhaps enough to seal the outer entrance."

Fanyi touched the pendant that still hung around her neck. "I do not think there is another one of these. If we can do that—seal the entrance—no one will find it. The White Ones, they do not know exactly what they seek. Their Shamans are dreamers—of dreams sent by that thing."

"Machine—or man?" Sander wondered.

Fanyi shivered. "Both. But how the Before Men could do that—! It may still live, though you have destroyed that which gave it power. If so—what a horror faces it— life locked into a prison without end."

"What of your people?" he asked.

"What of yours?" she countered.

Sander answered first. "Mine do well enough. They have a smith, not as good as my father, but one they trust. I—they are kin. Still I find it hard now to remember any face among them that I long greatly to see again."

"I am yet bound." Fanyi held the pendant. "We may be able to seal one danger in the earth. There are others without. What I can do to aid my clan, that I shall, though I bring no greater strength with me. I failed Padford, therefore the debt is mine."

"And how will you repay?"

"There are ways to travel south. If any of my people live captive there, then they still have claim on me."

Sander stirred, his hand hurt when he moved it, in spite of the dressing she had put on the cuts. Traveling one-handed for a while would be awkward.

"South it is then. Once we have made secure what lies here."

She frowned. "This is no duty of yours, smith!"

He smiled. "Perhaps so. But I have chosen the out trail. Does it matter where one wanders when one is kinless by will? There is this thought in mind, Shaman. We came here seeking knowledge. We have found it, though not as we expected."

"Your meaning, smith?"

"Just this: we have tried long to live upon the remnants of the Before Time, ever looking backward. But why should we? There is no night without a star, so the blackness of our night can be lighted by our own efforts. We are ourselves, not the Before Ones. Therefore, we must learn for ourselves, not try to revive what was known by those we might not even want to call kin were we to meet them. I am no kin of Maxim!"

"No kin—" she repeated. "Yes, that rings true, smith! Neither am I kin to those who stored such knowledge as that thing strove to make me use. We begin again, light our night stars, and hope to do better."

"We begin again." Sander agreed and then added, "to the south, Fanyi, since you are duty-bound. Let us see if the Sea Sharks can be defied by our own means. After all, have we not bested here something far worse than any peril we knew?"

"Smith, you are a man who believes in his own worth."

Sander, nursing his torn hand, rose to his feet. He put out his sound one to rest on Rhin's shoulder.

"It never harms a man to value himself," he returned mildly. "And if he has good companions and a trade, what more does he want?"

Fanyi laughed now. "Well, perhaps one or two things more, Sander. But those shall doubtless also come in their own season. No night lasts forever."

FREE
Fawcett Books Listing

There is Romance, Mystery, Suspense, and Adventure waiting for you inside the Fawcett Books Order Form. And it's yours to browse through and use to get all the books you've been wanting . . . but possibly couldn't find in your bookstore.

This easy-to-use order form is divided into categories and contains over 1500 titles by your favorite authors.

So don't delay—take advantage of this special opportunity to increase your reading pleasure.

Just send us your name and address and 35¢ (to help defray postage and handling costs).

FAWCETT BOOKS GROUP
P.O. Box C730, 524 Myrtle Ave., Pratt Station, Brooklyn, N.Y. 11205

Name_____
(please print)

Address_____
City_____ State_____ Zip_____
Do you know someone who enjoys books? Just give us their names and addresses and we'll send them an order form too!

_____
Name_____
Address_____
City_____ State_____ Zip_____

_____
Name_____
Address_____
City_____ State_____ Zip_____